# THE DAUGHTER IN LAW

## NINA MANNING

Boldwood

First published in Great Britain in 2019 by Boldwood Books Ltd.

Copyright © Nina Manning, 2019

Cover Design: Nick Castle Design

Cover Photography: Shutterstock

A CIP catalogue record for this book is available from the British Library.

Paperback ISBN 978-1-83889-216-6

Ebook ISBN 9978-1-83889-218-0

Kindle ISBN 978-1-83889-217-3

Audio CD ISBN 978-1-83889-254-8

MP3 CD ISBN 978-1-83889-352-1

Digital audio download ISBN 978-1-83889-215-9

Boldwood Books Ltd
23 Bowerdean Street
London SW6 3TN
www.boldwoodbooks.com

*For my dad, Bob, who would have loved this cunning plan.*

'Happy is the man whose faith in his mother remains unchallenged'

— LOUISA MAY ALCOTT

# PROLOGUE

I sat very still and felt the fear wash through me as the reality of the situation became clear. Little shots of pain pulsated around my body; my abdomen contracted. I felt dizzy and realised that at any point I could lose consciousness. I never thought it would be so easy to surrender myself but teetering on the edge here, I was faced with a choice: carry on or give up.

I tried to cast my mind back to a time when everything made sense, but I couldn't remember when that was. He was supposed to save me. Now I was lost and another part of me was missing. What was the point in fighting any more? Where could I go from here? I knew I deserved this. It had been inevitable. I had got away with it for too many years already. This was my comeuppance.

Yet somewhere deep within me, a spark was still ignited. If I concentrated hard enough, I could feel it whirring quietly, like a small vibration. An instinct was pushing me forward, forcing me to fight and recover what was mine. It was a desire that was becoming more urgent. I knew what I needed to do and somehow, I would try to push past the weight of despair to find my way to the light again. To find my way to my love. And to the beautiful gift that was stolen from me.

# 1

ANNIE

My favourite room is the spare bedroom at the front of the house. It gets all the light in the morning and looks so inviting. I've done it up like a picture I saw in a lifestyle magazine: a checked throw across the end of the bed, floral sheets and hooked back curtains, a little wicker chair in the corner with a few well-read paperbacks stacked on top of it, and a white vase on the bedside table. It really is the most comforting place to be. Of course, no one ever uses it. I like to keep the house looking nice. But it was only ever going to be me and my son.

Getting out of bed was particularly hard this morning. It has been every morning since Ben left. I keep thinking, what is the point? I've been feeling that empty hopelessness for several months now. Since Ben deserted me.

For her.

I'd heard all about empty nest syndrome but I never imagined for a moment it would happen to me. I never actually thought he would leave. I thought we would just keep existing together. Forever.

He kept so much of his stuff here initially, that I felt sure he would return – but just last month, he came and took the lot.

It's so quiet here now. It was quiet anyway, that's why I took the house. It's the house I grew up alone in with my father, but fled from as soon as I was able to support myself.

How do you define an unhappy childhood? In those days it was unheard of to make an allegation about your relative. I accepted the violence – it was, after all, part of him and all I had ever known. Throughout my motherless upbringing, the beach house provided a sanctuary for me with plenty of places to hide. I got stealthier as I grew and with my legs pulled up tightly into my chest and my head pressed to my knees, I would squeeze myself into an alcove, the airing cupboard or the shed with the ringing sound of my father's threats in my ear. Later on, I would sneak out and find my way back to my bedroom past my father's drunken snores. The next day he wouldn't remember a thing. Had I not been able to escape down to the shore to skim pebbles or poke about in rock pools, then I would have run away sooner. The sea kept me safe. But as soon as I turned sixteen I took myself hundreds of miles away. I never heard a whisper from my father, who had told me daily I reminded him too much of my brazen excuse of a mother. Then he was dead and the beach house was mine. I left it sitting empty for a while, too scared to return, too busy trying to salvage my own marriage. Then Ben arrived and I knew it was time.

When I returned here all those years later with my son, it was fairly run down and rotting in places I couldn't get to, much like my father for all those years. The brown weather-worn cladding needed a sand down and varnish and the white framed windows were peeling, but overall the exterior wasn't so bad. I did the best I could with it and I could over-look most of the natural decay when I scanned the vast horizon and breathed in the fresh sea air.

It's a remote spot, perched right on the edge of the penin-sular before it slopes round into the sea. Standing in the garden or looking out of the window, you would be forgiven for thinking there were no houses for miles, but there is one around along the shore and to the left and then they begin to scatter more frequently as they feed towards the village. People rarely walk this far down as the shore is a little more rustic with huge pieces of driftwood and great mounds of seaweed washing up daily. Besides, the stretch of beach at the end of the garden and over the low battered wall essentially belongs to me. We are protected a little from the wind by a few surrounding trees, but it does get a little breezy here at times. But when it's still and the sea looks like a flat piece of mirror you could walk across, that's when I love it the most. Of course, I love the waves too, especially the ferocious ones that thrust themselves towards the wall. I like to watch those waves and feel my own fury in them.

A house on the seafront, much like a savannah plain, is the perfect spot to see when enemies are approaching. And anyone who tries to come between me and my son, I consider an enemy.

But despite the weather and the waves, I know the house is empty. And although I try to fill my days with mundane daily tasks, I too feel empty. I need to feel fulfilled again. I need my son back. Back where he belongs.

There's no one downstairs humming a tuneless song whilst they make their breakfast. There are no dirty trainers in the hallway, or piles of washing in the laundry basket. There are no toast crumbs on the kitchen side, or butter streaks in the marmite. The house is so eerily quiet. I have never experienced this. Not since having Ben. I forced all the bad memories away from the time I lived here as a child and made it all about me and Ben. It's our sanctuary; our hub. Our place away from the world.

Now he's gone. He hardly texts or rings. She has him wrapped around her little finger. Calling all the shots no doubt.

It was a real shock when Ben told me he had met some-one. It was more of a shock when he told me he had gone and got himself married. He had been spending a lot of time at her house, that I knew. But I had no idea things had evolved so quickly. And to have done it without telling me, his own mother, first. We used to be so close. I am not coping so well.

I did the right thing, of course. I invited them over for something to eat – mostly because I needed to get a good look at the woman who thinks she has replaced me.

But I know it's only temporary. I can't be replaced. My son can't live without me.

The thought of her coming into my house tomorrow, the woman who I have never met who has taken my son away from me, was almost too much to bear. But I caught the despair before it developed into something more distressing and just felt thankful that Ben was coming home to see his mum.

I stood in the front spare room, letting the light from the morning sun heal me all over. The faint salty smell from the shore just a few feet away creeps through the open window. I could hear the gentle lap of the waves and I like the way a little of nature sneaks inside. Even on a bitter winter's day like today this room brings with it a feeling of hope. A promise that today will be the day. It's encouraging me to feel something. And I can. Just about. The sun edges around the house to my bedroom later in the day – at different hours depending on the season – and occasionally I take my time to lie down and bask in its glorious rays. I almost go into a state of meditation. I'm not a meditator. I wouldn't even know if I was doing it right. But something about it feels so relaxing that it must be doing something to my soul.

I looked out of the window at the ocean at the way the morning light glitters across the tips of the waves. It still fills me with awe and a profound sense of invigorating peace. I couldn't possibly be anywhere else but here. I chose well when I decided to raise a family here.

Ben and I made some glorious memories.

I like to get out at least two or three times a week. Since retiring from the pharmaceutical business a few years ago, I have endless units of the day to fill. Of course, when Ben was here I filled it with tending to his needs. Now it's just me and the sudden spate of time before me every day.

I drove my little blue Fiat car into the village, found a space in one of the bays and took my basket into the small greengrocer's. It's so nice that certain things just stay the same. I've been going there for over twenty years and it is still owned by the same lady that owned it back then.

I walked into the grocer's and heard the sound of the bell above the door let out its familiar ping. June looked up from behind the counter and beamed one of her smiles.

'Hello, Annie.'

'Hello, June.' I walked over to the vegetables and started placing items into my basket all the while thinking about what I would cook tonight.

I have been so used to whipping up meals for the two of us that now I find cooking for one difficult. Ben has such an appetite that it was like cooking for a family of four. He would always go in for second and third helpings and finished up the leftovers without hesitation.

So I started to freeze meals, my intention being that every time Ben visits I can send him off with a batch of homemade food. But he hasn't visited. Not for over a month. And I cannot conceal the contempt I feel, the anger that begins in the pit of my stomach and then consumes me so I feel the need to run out to the wall at the bottom of the garden and scream into the vast ocean.

I can't imagine for a moment that Ben's new wife has time to stand and cook a meal at the stove like I do. Of course, I couldn't always cook. There was a time when cooking terrified me. But I had to do it. It was expected of me and once I began, I enjoyed it. Being able to create something from raw ingredients and watch it develop into something wholesome and magnificent is truly a satisfying experience.

'Any tomatoes today?' June hollered, wrenching me from my thoughts. 'Got some lovely ones over here.' She pointed to a large box of ripe red tomatoes next to her.

'Oh yes, go on then.' I walked over to the counter. 'I'll take six.' I thought about Ben as I watched June choosing the tomatoes and how he loved one grilled for his breakfast.

'How's things today, Annie?' June took a brown paper bag and started dropping the shiny red fruit into it.

'Oh, you know. Same as,' I said as I looked away from her and out of the window.

'How's that boy of yours getting on then?'

I began imagining Ben as a small boy when he would run around this very grocery store and help me count out the vegetables.

'Yes, you know, same as usual.' I felt a pang in my stomach, a gut tightening feeling and I was overcome for a moment with sadness that Ben wasn't that little boy any more, that June couldn't comment on his floppy dark locks and tell me he was the apple of my eye, and I would nod and say yes, he was my everything.

'They are so busy at this age, aren't they? Flitting about. No time to think of anyone but themselves.'

I nodded. 'Yes, but he loves his mum.' I didn't even consider that I should share the news about his marriage. Or the other news.

June smiled at me and handed me the brown paper bag.

I left the grocer's with the dinging of the bell in my ears. As I stepped out of the shop I turned right to go to the butcher's. Between the grocer's and the butcher's was a small electrical store selling LED TVs and docking stations and all the modern appliances young people couldn't live without these days. As far as I was concerned the shop was an eye sore. And as for that colossal TV screen in the window, I mean, who needs a sixty-inch television in their lounge? But today as I passed, I couldn't help but turn my head to look at the image showing on the TV that towered above me and suddenly something was so very familiar. I tripped slightly and the basket slipped from my fingers. I didn't look down at the tomatoes that had fallen out, but I knew the ripe fruit would now be a red smashed mess around my feet. I couldn't take my eyes off the screen. I could feel bile rising in the back of my throat and I thought I could very well be sick. The size and imposition of the TV was instrumental in showing in full HD colour, a news report with the headlines underneath.

And above that, the face of the person I'd hoped I would never see again.

# 2

---

DAISY

'Hi Mum,' Ben sang and fell into his mother's arms as she patted his back as though she were winding a baby.

It was early December and I was practically shivering by the time we had reached the front door where Annie was already poised ready to greet us. I stood and patiently waited, I watched with intrigue as Annie took her son in her arms and ignored all presence of me over his shoulder.

I could hear a different voice coming from him, one he obviously only reserved for her and I tensed at the sound of it. Something about it unnerved me; it was a new tone to me, a part of Ben I had never seen or heard before. I had tried so desperately to uncover every piece of my husband so there were no surprises after rushing to get to know him. Perhaps in my haste there were things I had missed.

Finally, she released her son and I took my cue. I walked into the tiny porch, the sea breeze whipped my hair across my face and I pulled the stray stands behind my ear. The sun, which had been eking its way through a cluster of clouds when we arrived, was gone, casting everything in a gloomy grey light.

Behind me a lone seagull let out a desolate cry.

It was clear the saltwater-worn porch could not comfortably accommodate all three bodies but there we huddled regardless. My arms were pressed firmly to my side and I listened as Ben rambled a ridiculously extravagant introduction, something about me being the second most important woman in his life. I watched as Annie, with her lips tightly sealed, flicked her eyes up and down me in one swift movement – it was as though she barely looked at me at all. She then rested her gaze upon my face and her tight pout dissolved into a broad smile.

'Hello Daisy, it's nice to meet you.' Annie spoke politely and confidently as she held her hand out towards me. Without hesitation, I grabbed it and shook it, only realising afterwards how quickly I had responded. I stepped back, slightly flabbergasted at my own speed to appease her. My palm buzzed from the pressure of Annie's firm handshake.

Based on the photograph I had seen of her, I'd expected to be warmly embraced by the woman who was now my mother-in-law. Ben talked about his home life, I knew how he was raised, but he rarely spoke of his mother, he merely showed me a photo. She looked fluffy – as though she had a wholesome chuckle. Maybe someone who would wrap you in her arms with real affection. But it was apparent that looks could be deceiving.

I knew more than anyone that trying to paint on a smile everyday was a tiresome task and some days you just couldn't succeed. Annie presented an air of glamour with her sleek brown bobbed hair with only a smattering of very light grey that resembled highlights from a distance. She was dressed younger than her sixty years in a perfectly pressed white shirt and blue jeans.

But her smile was merely her face scrunched up so her eyes became little slits through which she could safely view me.

It was a forty minute drive from our flat in town to Annie's beach house, almost entirely in silence. I had allowed Ben to drive my car, a silver Renault Clio. I loved my little car and when he moved in I was worried he might insist we switch it for something more manly, but he seemed content driving it. He was a careful driver, meticulous and completely focused, never wavering to look at anything other than what was in front of him.

We were minutes away from arriving when Ben turned into a dusty track which would lead down to the house on the beach and quietly announced we would arrive in less than one mile. Panic pulsed through my body. For it was now, only five months since Ben and I had met, that we were on our way to meet the woman I would come to know as my mother-in-law. We had been so wrapped up in our bubble that it didn't occur to me to wonder why Ben had waited so long to introduce us. It hadn't fazed me, we didn't need anyone else intruding into our perfect world; we were happy as just us. Families made everything complicated.

Now as I stood here seeing her in the flesh I could tell there was a coarseness to Annie; her face was a myriad of untold stories and emotions, something which that momentary captured image neglected to show. I looked at Annie's starched white shirt and then looked down at my faded grey T-shirt with The Rolling Stones 'tongue and lip' logo and the baggy green combat trousers with the top button that I could no longer do up. I took comfort in my sacred red heels I religiously wore, knowing I would only be able to wear them for a few more weeks before they became uncomfortable. Today, as I met my mother-in-law for the first time, I hoped they were the little sparkle of distraction I needed, for I was conscious that my bulging abdomen was an awkward representation of exactly how long Ben and I had been together; a life that was created the night we met almost five months ago.

That extra hour I had convinced Ben to spend in bed with me had taken its toll. I looked down at my own unplanned outfit that I had grappled around for at the last minute. I hadn't expected her to have this sort of impact on me. Was Annie looking past the veneer? If she was, then she didn't need to look very hard. I could feel my guard had not only slipped but was disintegrating with every second that she looked at me. I had a feeling I was getting sussed out and I didn't like the way I suddenly felt so exposed.

I watched as Annie's gaze was drawn down to my abdomen. The baby bump was apparent and taut skin was slightly exposed under my T-shirt that had edged its way upwards.

I could feel her look of disdain but Annie didn't say a word about the human life that was growing within me, her own flesh and blood.

'You're late, son. That's unusual of you.' Annie flashed a look my way.

'Sorry, Mum, traffic.' Ben said.

I watched Annie's contorted smile as Ben hopped from one leg to another like a restless child.

'Oh, for goodness' sake, Ben, get through into that lounge.' Annie gave an elaborate shooing motion with both hands before turning to me. Her fake smile faded and it seemed she could do nothing to stop it. I saw the realisation spread across her face, manifested as a sort of flickering of her head and then watched as she desperately tried to drag that smile back. There was a searching in her eyes, I could see her mind mulling something over very quickly, and then she looked at me with intent, as though she knew me. Panic surged through my veins. It wasn't possible, I reassured myself.

Annie spoke, but it was too loud for the situation.

'Come, come on through then.' She held one hand out to guide me into the house. I followed Ben as Annie closed the heavy wooden door behind me.

I found myself in a large stark hallway on wooden floorboards with doors leading off in several directions. I stood looking along the walls for pictures or photographs, but there was nothing that stood out, no statement pieces that suggested a mother and her son had lived here all their lives. I usually relished arriving at a new house and looking around, trying to piece together a story about the person, but this house was not giving away any clues.

'There's no room to swing a cat in that porch. Come through, get settled and I'll get you a cup of tea.' Annie wittered away as she walked in behind us.

Following Ben, I found myself in a large lounge with huge windows that showed a shingle beach just beyond a wall at the end of a garden. Ben took a seat on one of two small distressed sofas that were facing each other. Annie waited for us both to be seated and then walked out of another door opposite me into what I presumed was the kitchen. I busied myself getting comfy on the sofa opposite Ben. Neither of us removed our jackets, the chill from outside lingered in my bones. I looked at Ben, he gave a small wink and I smiled back. I found myself relaxing a little as I sat back and took in my surroundings. It was the epitome of a classic beach house. Spacious, brilliant views of the sea. The décor was a little dated; the faded floral design on the sofas was evidence that Annie had not updated her interiors for a good few years, if ever. The house seemed far too large for just one woman to live in all alone, but then of course, up until a few months ago, Ben had been here too.

There was a fireplace to my left, central to the two sofas and above it a long wooden mantelpiece. On one of the large windowsills was a green vase with some fake flowers. Scattered around were plaques which read statements such as 'Home is where the heart is'. My eyes were drawn to a smaller plaque perched upon the mantelpiece above the fireplace. I focused hard on the writing which was just within reading distance.

> The bond between mother and son is a special one
> It remains unchanged by time or distance
> It is the purest love – unconditional and true
> It is understanding of any situation
> And forgiving of any mistake.

It was the sort of thing that would be a gift and I wondered if Ben had bought it for Annie.

I sat back and took in more of the room. I looked out through the window, my eyes drawn to the sight of the ocean. I realised I didn't take advantage of living so close to the sea, or perhaps I had never seen it looking so vivid and inviting as it did from Annie's window.

I noted there was no television in the lounge. No hi-fi system or radio either. Just an old solitary turn table in the corner of the room. It was deafeningly quiet.

Annie arrived back into the room and punctuated the silence. She was struggling with a tray laden with tea, a selection of foil-wrapped biscuits, and a fresh-looking Victoria sponge cake. Annie placed the tray onto the coffee table in the middle of the two sofas and positioned herself carefully next to me. She let out a loud sigh accompanied by a small smile.

I looked at the tray, keen to be of assistance and show willing, I leant in towards the teapot.

'I'll be mum then,' I said jovially, but before I could reach the pot, Annie intercepted. Suddenly I found that my hand was pressed against the scalding pot. I immediately felt the searing heat penetrate through my fingers before I had time to retract. I sucked my breath in through my teeth as the sting from the heat resonated through my fingers. I looked anxiously at Annie who now had both hands on the pot, ready to pour, seemingly oblivious.

'Don't you worry yourself, dear. You just sit back and relax,' Annie said softly without taking her eyes off the tea pot and cups. 'This is some of my best crockery you know, Daisy.' Annie poured out and handed me a small white china teacup and saucer. She turned back and poured another cup.

I slowly sat back and cradled my tea, gently stroking my index and middle fingers where the fuzzy feeling still remained. Something was preventing the words that were appropriate to the situation from forming in my mouth. I could feel agitation rising through my chest. I looked up at Ben who had his eyes firmly locked on the screen of his new Blackberry phone, a device he was clearly quite taken with. He had apparently missed the whole incident.

'Help yourself to milk and sugar, dear. Oh, and I made

this cake. Ben's favourite. Did you know?' Annie's eyes were wide open and reminded me of the saucer I held in my hand.

'No, I didn't.' I looked into my teacup.

'Oh yes, been making Victoria sponge cake for years, haven't I, son? It is a special occasion after all, isn't it?' she said, her face remained fixed upon the coffee table.

I took a sip of tea and found that my hand shook and caused a ripple of clinking china which attracted a brief look from Annie. I was now completely on edge and shot a glance over towards Ben, urging him to look up and rescue me but he was too absorbed in his phone. The new millennium had brought with it a necessity for technology. Somewhere tangible to store more things that people didn't want others to see, a concept I wasn't yet wholly comfortable with.

'You're starting to show, I see. Was it planned?' Annie's tone reeked of distaste.

Annie's facetious comment hung in the air. I hadn't expected to get pregnant during the first week of knowing Ben. I don't think Ben had quite realised the enormity of it yet. He was going through the motions, asking the right questions. At a time when I was struggling to feel anything for the baby, I was glad Ben had yet to make any emotional connection either.

Annie continued, 'I didn't realise first-time mums showed so much at this stage. And you realise babies are expensive, don't you Daisy? How are you going to manage on Ben's wage as a musician? He only works the odd weekend.' I could hear the authority in Annie's tone, as though she was the only woman who had ever raised a child.

I said nothing but flashed a small smile. What was there to say? We hadn't really discussed the ins and outs. We just knew it felt right and it would all work itself out. If I ever raised money issues with Ben, I was pretty sure his response would be to tell me that love would find a way.

But I didn't care to say those words out loud to Annie.

I sipped my tea and clinked the cup back into the saucer taking care to do so as quietly as I could. There was a small gold antique clock on the mantelpiece which seemed to tick louder than before. I could hear clicking as Ben pressed the buttons on his Blackberry. I blew a piece of hair away from my face as I felt a hot flush rising through my body. I brushed the thin fabric of the sofa with my hand.

'Lovely sofas' I lied, so I could break the silence.

'Yes, these old things. Charity shop finds. I bought them when—'

'Mum.' Ben was up on his feet alarmingly fast, he shoved his phone into the back pocket of his jeans. 'How about some of that cake?' Ben rubbed his hands together.

Annie regarded him for a second and I sensed his agitation. Annie picked up the knife and held it in front of her as she looked at Ben 'Well, let's just hope he's grown up enough to be functioning out there alone without his mum!' Annie hooted then she sliced through the cake 'He needs looking after from time to time, don't you Ben? But that's what us women are good at. I suppose you may find that now, what with you being older?'

I glanced up at Ben who rolled his eyes surreptitiously.

The age gap had yet to make any impact on us. My twenty-eight years to his twenty-four years hadn't created any problems. But apparently Annie was already searching for flaws in the relationship.

Ben bent down, picked up a slice of Victoria sponge, and began chewing with intent, a frown firmly fixed on his face. I watched Annie frantically trying to cobble together a small white porcelain plate and tiny dessert fork.

'I think what I want to know from you both is why you decided to do it all behind my back?' Annie held out the plate and fork to Ben who had already finished his cake. She lay the redundant crockery back on the tray and patted her hair.

'And so soon after meeting. What about your mother, Daisy? Have you told her you're married?'

Ben sat back down again and tried to flash me an encouraging smile but he seemed distracted.

I paused and took a moment to breathe in so the rehearsed words would flow freely. 'She and my dad are probably over it by now. They're likely glad to have avoided the expense of a wedding.' I laughed with too much enthusiasm and looked up at Annie's expressionless face. 'Plus they live in Australia.'

Annie turned her body to face mine. 'They went without you?' She screwed her face up in disgust

I cleared my throat and nodded. The faces of my parents flashed before my eyes then disintegrated as quickly. I knew I didn't need or want to think about them, but I always did.

She turned away from me, her attention on the tea tray again 'Well, Ben is one of one. My only child. So being involved was important to me. Being told your son has got married three weeks after it happened is not what any mother wants to hear.' Annie poured another cup of tea and held it out towards Ben. 'Son, your tea,' she said flatly.

Ben leant forward and took the tea and placed it in front of him on the table. He ran his large soft hands through his thick dark hair. 'Look Mum, we've been through this already. If you want to blame anyone, blame me. I'm sorry. We're sorry. It was a mad...' Ben paused. 'A mad spur of the moment thing.' The last few words fell out of his mouth. He looked at me firmly and spoke with intent. 'But we love each other and that's that.'

I couldn't stop the smile that spread across my face and the tension was already leaving my body.

Words of apology were just forming in my mouth when Annie said: 'What's done is done. I can't do anything about it now, can I, son? I need to get the chicken in the oven.' Ben raised his eyebrows at me and I stifled a laugh. It was brought on by a bout of nervousness – the nervousness that was now leaving my body as Annie stood and walked out of the room. The atmosphere physically lifted.

I looked at Ben, blew out the breath I had been holding and raised my eyebrows in relief.

\* \* \*

At the kitchen table, Annie pushed the food around her plate and took tiny bites.

'This is delicious, Annie. The chicken is so moist.' I prodded a slab of meat and watched the juice ooze out 'How do you cook it?'

'I do it in a brick. Always have done since Ben was a little boy.' Annie placed her knife and fork together on the plate indicating she had finished, yet her plate still remained full of chicken breast and vegetables.

Then Annie was on her feet. I noted how sixty years had treated her well, she had a very youthful face with very few wrinkles, and that hair cut made her appear at least five years younger. It was only because she displayed some stiffness when she walked that you might think this woman was nearing retirement age.

Annie retrieved something from the dresser then walked back over to the table and placed a small package in front of me. I glanced down and saw a delightful neat square box, wrapped in silver paper with a thin pink bow on the top. I looked at Ben. He shook his head, just as surprised.

'What's this?' I placed my knife and fork together on my plate and gently dabbed my mouth with the paper napkin. My heart started to quicken. I hadn't always feared present opening. I do remember a time as a little girl when tearing open the wrapping paper was done without inhibition. But then there was one time, when I was in a room, tentatively opening presents on a day that should have been filled with such happiness – yet I had never felt more alone. And I guess that memory stuck harder.

'Well, open it and see, dear.' Annie busied herself with clearing the plates.

I carefully peeled away the paper as though there could be something inside that might bite me. I stole intermittent glances at Ben, who shrugged his shoulders, indicating his ignorance. Inside the paper was a small grey box. I let out a gasp. I imagined inside there'd be an antique ring or brooch handed down from generations and now it was being given to me. The thought of owning something so precious and possibly expensive suddenly filled me with excitement. Maybe this was why Annie was so put out at not being involved with the wedding, she obviously had kept this for Ben's big day. The thought of receiving such a grand present when we had not involved Ben's mother or anyone else in our wedding made me wonder if we did the right thing by marrying so quickly. It had never crossed my mind before. I hadn't even invited my best friend, Eve, and Ben never mentioned any regret. But the feeling reared itself and so I prepared myself to shower Annie with gracious thank yous. I removed the lid and there before me were words, bold in black, surrounded by a trail of flowers, painted on a small ceramic plaque.

Daughter-in-law
   A child that destiny forgot to give you.

My first instinct was to stifle the involuntary laugh that nearly came out so when I did speak my voice was high and strained.

'Oh, thank you, Annie. That's so lovely. Thoughtful. Isn't it? Look, Ben.' I took the plaque out of its box and displayed it in front of Ben's face, to take some of the pressure off my own poor performance of gratitude. Only then did I see the back and realise the plaque was a fridge magnet, and probably the sort of thing you would pick up from a pound shop.

'Wow, that's gorgeous Mum. So thoughtful. Well done,' Ben looked at me and gave me a sympathetic smile. I realised it was not novel to him, this was possibly the sort of thing he received regularly.

Annie eyed the pair of us up without smiling. She continued to remove the plates and walked towards the sink.

'That's okay, son. I just wanted to get something nice that Daisy could keep, a little welcome into the family.' There was a vagueness to her voice as she walked away.

'That was nice of your mum,' I said quickly in a hushed tone but I knew my expression did not match my words. Ben didn't have time to respond as Annie was back at the table. I forced my face into a smile.

'I'll stick it on the fridge at home.' I said loudly and stuffed the box with the wrapping paper into my handbag, knowing it would stay there for many weeks along with screwed up receipts and packets of chewing gum. I turned to Ben. 'Fancy showing me your room, handsome?'

\* \* \*

I stood in Ben's old bedroom looking at the neatly arranged paraphernalia along the tops of the drawers and the endless framed photographs of Ben and Annie together. I noted that there was never anyone else posed with them.

My mind flooded with a hundred thoughts, all with one binding theme, how much did I really know about Ben? Here I was in his childhood home, having tea with his mum and yet I could sense an absence. Annie's obvious dislike towards me was palpable and the beach house bore a sadness, a feeling of loss; the missing parent in the photographs illustrated that clearly. I wondered if perhaps the lack of a father figure in Ben's life played a stronger role than he or Annie would ever admit.

Ben had dived onto the double bed and was lying on his side, supporting his head with his hand. His dark hair, although persistently tousled, bore a slight shine from his shower that morning and I was tempted, as I always was, to run my hands through its silkiness. He usually had some stubble but today he had shaved for the occasion, highlighting his strong jaw and full lips. He blinked slowly, and gave me the softest of smiles.

It was hard for me to believe he had only begun moving out of this house three months ago, in September. We'd only been together for two months, but by then we knew about the baby. Ben was overjoyed and so began bringing more of his things from home to the apartment I shared with Eve.

Now looking around Ben's old room, I could see how Annie had converted it into a museum, a shrine to her only son. It made me think about the rest of the house that I had seen so far, that bore no memories or photographs. It was as though Annie had wanted to cram it all into one room, away from prying eyes.

I carried on looking around the room and made a show of pointing at various school certificates in neat wooden frames.

'What?' Ben said in a high-pitched voice. 'What can I tell you Daisy, I'm a much-loved boy. My mother is very proud of me,' he said with definite sarcasm and lay back on the bed placing both hands under his head.

I cocked my head and screwed my face into a frown. 'What is it? You're golden balls in her eyes? Why is that so terrible?'

'Come here,' he commanded, therefore side-lining my question. I joined him on the bed where we entwined ourselves around one another, each limb clambering for space. Ben kissed my neck which made me squirm around; the sensation was just too much for me, so I began laughing hysterically.

With the noise of my laughter, neither of us would have heard the floorboard outside let out a soft creak as it was relieved of the weight of a stationary body.

# 3

ANNIE

I knew there was something about my new daughter-in-law that was so familiar. She was striking in her overall appearance. Tall, long golden hair, rosy cheeks – she was a handsome woman, there was no denying it. I could see what Ben saw in her.

But there had been something else that played on my mind after they left. I had seen her somewhere before. I knew something about her.

All I needed to do was cast my memory back a few years, when the face from the sixty-inch TV screen had haunted my every waking hour, when I read newspapers back to back to follow the reports. That was when I had seen Daisy before, her face had come to me unexpectedly amongst the chaos of those years, the article on her tangled in with the trail of words I read daily, checking, always checking. I remember her story leapt out at me and for a time, distracted me from the face I didn't want to see. Initially I felt sorry for her, looking at the photo of her in her school uniform, just a girl, but as I read on, I discovered there was more to a photograph than meets the eye.

I had never forgotten that news story, and I had read a fair few. I read the papers for years, never wanting to miss anything. Then one day I finally felt safe and stopped. But not before I had seen Daisy's story.

So when she arrived at my house I knew straight away I had seen her before. I could tell by the way she presented herself that she was holding tightly onto her past and that she was trouble. To arrive wearing red heels when pregnant? What does that say about her? That girl was danger. I was adept at knowing when danger was approaching and I knew exactly what I needed to do.

I needed to protect my son.

After Ben and Daisy left, I sat alone in the front room staring out through the window where the darkness had enveloped the view of the sea. Having returned from the shops and seen the face on the TV screen just the day before, I was still in shock and now I was on extra high alert. I thought about the vast expanse of water just a few feet away and hoped it would protect me.

Even through the darkness and the closed windows, I could feel its energy and its intensity. It soothed me – that feeling, brooding and melancholic as it was, was better than the nothingness I felt without Ben. His presence had been fleeting but I could still hear the echoes of our conversations; I could see the empty tray from our tea and the dishes were stacked in the kitchen from our lunch. But he was gone again now.

He had slipped away too easily and all I could think about was how was I going to bring him back.

I blamed his father. He wasn't the man he should have

been for that boy. I thought about contacting Rory on a few occasions as Ben grew older. But I was scared. Scared of how he would react. Scared of the man he had become in the time we had been apart. But mostly I knew I was scared of who I had become since we parted.

I was a mother. My pure raw love was for that boy of mine and no one else would ever feel from me the sort of emotions I felt for Ben.

It was always going to be me and Ben. And no one else.

Until he met her.

# 4

## GRACE

It was a mild spring afternoon when I saw the advert in the local magazine. A lady who had a large kitchen was running cookery classes from her home and so I signed up, eager to improve before any children came along. I had an idea in my mind that when I became a mother, I would also become an earth goddess capable of whipping up any meal for any occasion to appease my husband and satisfy my children's hunger.

I arrived at Emily's house one warm mid-March morning and signed myself up for several weeks of cookery classes.

Emily with her large waist and ample bosom, looked at my name on the paper and said:

'Grace – that was my mother's name.'

I took my place behind the large circular counter and nervously eyed up the other women. Then my eyes fell upon the lady next to me before my focus was moved to the little boy playing next to her feet. He was a bonny lad, only about two or three years old. I watched as he opened the door of the train carefully and shut it again without any force. Feelings came rushing back to me. Feelings of loss. A longing for all the dead babies. I was supposed to be a mother so why wasn't it happening? Why was I being punished? I just needed my body to hold on to the next baby, that was all. I was determined to make it right. I thought that if I became the housewife I was meant to be then the babies would come. And so the cooking was going to help. I needed my husband to look at me again with those eyes, just like he used to.

He had been so distant recently. After the last baby. What was it? The sixth? Or was it the seventh? By this point I had lost count. I didn't mean to. The last three came and went so quickly I had simply lost track. I named them in the beginning. But he said I was ridiculous. If the babies were being stubborn, though it pained me too much to even admit it, at least I would be able to offer my husband something else in the way of homely wife skills until we were blessed with the gift.

I thought we would be able to have dinner parties; I would cook for all his work colleagues and people would say, 'Oh yes, that wife of yours, she sure can cook. You've got a good one there.' Then eventually the gaping hole in our marriage that should by now have been filled with the joyous manic messiness that children bring, wouldn't seem so empty and obvious.

He came from a large Irish family. His parents were waiting to be grandparents again. I knew that I alone would never be enough for him. He needed me to have a child. I would start with the cooking. Show how I could be a good wife.

Then keep trying for the babies.

A miracle was sure to happen.

# 5

DAISY

People think we married too soon. Maybe we did. But when we found out I was pregnant, it felt like the right thing to do. Only time would tell. Maybe we should have done it the other way around and found out more about the other person before we committed our lives to one another.

I will always remember the night I first laid my eyes on Ben, in the club on the quay in town. I had seen him arrive while I was dancing wildly, then suddenly I was enjoying the sensation that he was watching me too. I couldn't stop looking at him as he made his way to the bar. Our eyes locked for a moment, and he smiled a bashful smile right at me before lowering his head. But after I went to get more drinks, the place where he had been standing had become a gap slowly filling up with more sweaty bodies.

It became an urgency, the desire to find him. How was it possible to have such a connection with someone from so far away, with no words?

I was so hot I felt I needed some air. But then suddenly he was behind me.

'Are you leaving?' I heard the voice as I headed towards the main exit. The bass from the club was a dull thud from behind the double doors as we stood, just the two of us in the foyer. I stopped, turned and smoothed a stray piece of hair against my head and raised my eyebrows. There he stood, tall, thick dark hair that hung around his ears, a hint of a stubble. He was still wearing his black leather jacket. It was old and battered but it suited him, like it was made for him.

'Well, I'm not sure now,' I laughed.

'You look, um, great.' He pushed his hair away from his face and looked sheepish. His eyes darted between me and our surroundings.

'Thank you,' I said with a small self-conscious smile. I felt the energy build between us in the small space.

I went on to tell him that I was a fitness instructor and after a few minutes he found the confidence to invite me back to the bar. We found seats amongst the chaos and ordered margaritas with salty rims.

'I hope I didn't appear creepy. Following you outside like that.' He was possibly feigning coyness as he tucked his long thick dark hair behind his ear. I couldn't help but be reminded of Michael Hutchence, with his battered black leather jacket and sultry look.

I looked down at his hands which were large and looked incredibly clean and soft; they were hands that hadn't grafted.

'Is this your bag? Clubs like this?' he asked

'Sometimes, I'm with my flatmate Eve; we like to dance. Let off a bit of steam. You?'

'Not really. I was persuaded by a mate to come in for a quick drink. We've just finished a gig next door.'

'You're in a band?' So he really was a rock star.

'Many. I go where the work is, take whatever I can.'

'So you're like a prostitute, of the musical world?'

He stared at me blankly for a second. My heart raced as I anticipated a negative response to my throwaway comment. Then his mouth grew into a huge smile.

'Yes, that is exactly what I am.' His whole face visibly lit up.

I threw my head back and laughed loudly. I loved his subtlety; he had no ego, everything about him was enchanting and magnetising me more towards him.

I knew then, that moment, I had to have him.

We talked and drank and laughed and I slipped in closer to him on a stool so our bodies were touching. My hand kept finding its way to his leg. At one point he turned and looked at me and neither of us spoke for a second – we just took one another in. I felt a rush of emotion that I had never felt for anyone before and all I could think was how I didn't want the night to end. My mind had already wandered to the following day and if I would see him again.

When my friend and flatmate, Eve, made an appearance next to us, I raised my eyes at her indicating I was fine. She walked away backwards making an over the top thumbs-up sign behind Ben's back, but he caught her out of the corner of his eye. I began laughing hysterically and when he looked around properly, Eve had transformed the action seamlessly into a ridiculous dance move. He seemed casually amused.

We ordered beers and drank them in near silence. Occasionally sniggering at some of the more inebriated clubbers. I felt warm and fuzzy with alcohol and I supposed he did too.

Then he asked me, 'Are you ready to leave now?'

I looked at the face of the stranger just inches from mine, his eyes twinkled from the alcohol. I knew I was ready.

I collected my coat from the cloakroom on the way past and we headed outside. The quay was alive with people bustling to and from pubs.

I felt his hand slip into mine and the intimacy from a stranger's touch was addictive. I didn't want to let go. We walked over to the quay wall.

A boat was arriving back in from a cruise party, a string of fairy lights hung across the deck and on board it was brimming with drunken laughing guests. Two young girls in high heels and tiny short skirts walked past howling and jeering. Ben lit a cigarette and offered me one. I shook my head. He sat and smoked it whilst I leant into him and I could smell the citrus scent of his aftershave and the leather of his jacket that had been lingering next to me all night. I inhaled him like he was a drug. He finished the cigarette and threw it on the floor, half stamped on it and we both watched as the bright ember faded and struggled to remain alight.

He put his arm over my shoulder and pulled me closer to him. I looked up; I could feel the buzz of the alcohol but above and beyond that, an aching intensity that started in the pit of my stomach and soared through my legs and arms, into my neck, across my face and then finally ended where my lips met Bens.

It had been a long time coming, this feeling of completeness.

I had succeeded.

He was all mine.

\* \* \*

I had expected to wake up in horror, as I had done countless times, to realise that the shadows of the past few hours had concealed an ugliness of the stranger in my bed, but this time, something was different.

The hazy morning light of my bedroom set a perfect scene as we slowly woke next to one another. Something within me had shifted. I didn't feel all those feelings of hatred and despair that were the typical by-product of a one-night stand with a stranger. Despite feeling slightly on edge, trying to come to terms with this unfamiliar sensation of wanting to lie next to a man in the morning, it felt almost normal.

Until then, I had forgotten I was capable of feeling normal.

We dressed and went into the lounge where I brought him coffee and toast. I had to press my heels into the floor to stop myself from launching across the table and into his lap.

He slurped his coffee, an action I added to the long list of endearing qualities I was racking up: from the way he rubbed his stubble so it made a scratching noise to the way he double blinked when he was listening intently to me, showing his concentration.

I asked him what he did again. He wrote songs and depped for bands, he reminded me.

He tapped his teaspoon on the side of the table in a drumbeat.

'Ah yes, musician, that was it. I wondered why alarm bells were ringing. My mother warned me away from musicians,' I told him jovially, vaguely able to recollect a lucid one-sided conversation with my mum that consisted of her listing unsuitable men.

'What's wrong with musicians?' A smile crept out of the corner of his mouth as he leant back in his chair. He stretched his arms up. His grey T-shirt was crumpled after a night on the floor next to my bed and I felt my cheeks flush at the memory of him removing it.

'You are all so melancholy and a little bit flaky.' I looked into my coffee. 'Creativity comes before anything else, and well, basically you're all a bit hard up.'

Ben nodded. 'Yep, sounds about right. I'm a skint melancholic flaky musician.' There was an air of sarcasm to his tone.

I quickly added. 'It's just one of those little bits of advice that mums give to their daughters, you know? Did your parents not give you any advice growing up?'

Ben gave a sniff and turned his head away from me. 'I don't have a dad. It's just me and my mum. We live in a beach house up the coast about thirty miles away.' He breathed in and let out a loud sigh. He suddenly seemed agitated and pulled out a packet of cigarettes from his jeans pocket and lit one. He inhaled, pushed his hair back with one hand and then opened his mouth in an exaggerated 'O' as he exhaled. 'I was only here last night for a gig, I rarely come out. I'm a bit of a hermit normally.' His voice was raspy, from the night before when we had shouted to one another over the music.

I was fully aware that he had glided over the subject of an absent father and it made me think about something that Eve had told me about absent fathers, and what to look out for, specifically in boys: depression, self-criticism, low self-esteem.

Cheaters.

I looked at Ben again, at his stubble, at his large soft tender-looking hands that had clearly never done a day's real labour. At his dark eyes, that were like pools waiting for me to dive into, so I could swim into his soul. He dropped his cigarette into his empty coffee cup.

All the while I watched him and drank him in, I was acutely aware of what he could be thinking about me. How I presented myself? What did he see? Would he ever be able to know the real me?

I asked him what tune he was tapping out with his active teaspoon that had found its way to the edge of the cup, saucer and sugar bowl.

He told me the song questioningly as though I wouldn't have heard of it. 'We played it last night at the gig. The crowd love the old sixties classics.'

'It's such an awesome tune,' I said, looking down at my coffee. 'My dad played it all the time when I was a kid.' As I hummed along in my head, nostalgia flooded my body and became overwhelming. I bit the inside of my cheek. 'It's one of my favourites.' I gulped down the tears that were constricting my throat.

I let out a long sigh. I locked eyes with Ben and smiled again, conscious he might be able to see the glint of tears welling in them. Who would pull away first? It was Ben. Shy, mysterious Ben, who allowed these fleeting moments of self-consciousness to seep through.

We sat for a few moments, perhaps even minutes. I was surprised at how easy the silences hung between us.

'You know' Ben began, as he picked up a piece of toast 'You've met me at a junction in my life. I'm just trying to figure a few things out at the moment.' He looked thoughtful as he took a bite.

'Aren't we all?' I said as a thousand images of my past life flashed before my eyes.

The memories didn't fully surface though. I had stored them safely where at times even I failed to reach them. There was plenty of time for us to find the skeletons in each other's closets. I asked him, 'So what instruments can you play?'

'Pretty much anything I can get my hands on.' He instantly seemed brighter when talking about music. I needed to see that side of him right now, not the despondency. 'But mostly, bass guitar and drums. I gig with whatever bands I can. To be honest, I need to put myself out there more. I'm hoping next year will be a better year. But I've got a few things going on at the moment. Just trying to work some stuff out.' He was rushing his words and rubbing his stubble as he spoke. Maybe telling me things he was anxious to get out; perhaps conscious he was sharing a lot of information at once. And yet again, I ignored my cue. I wasn't ready to share any more of myself than I absolutely needed to.

'Hopefully I can get some serious work soon. I've probably held myself back more than I should have done. More for my mum's sake. My teens just kind of rolled into my twenties without me noticing. I feel I need to start doing something more with my life now, before it's too late.'

'Life is pretty fluid, not static, it's just one big journey,' I said, then realised the seriousness to my tone too late. Ben looked at me and I could feel my face flush. I knew if we kept going, that the questions would soon be turned on me. 'I mean I love my job though, if I couldn't get up and jump around every day I'd die!' I said, probably with too much enthusiasm. Ben eyed me with a knowing look. Then he stood up and stretched, and I caught a glimpse of his midriff, the very skin I had touched last night. Ben looked down at me just as I was looking at him and his noisy stretch morphed into a laugh. I laughed back and relaxed again.

'Well, don't. Die that is. That wouldn't be good.' Ben took my hand. I felt a rush of lust and I had to quickly look away and feign interest in the window. Images of the two of us together from last night flashed into my mind, and I could barely concentrate any more. I let a few moments pass then I stood up and flopped onto the sofa. Ben took the hint and followed me. I leant back into the soft fabric and with Ben next to me I thought about the last few hours in the company of this complete stranger; how could I feel and act this way with him? Completely at ease and throwing myself at him as though I had known him for years.

We had lain for hours that morning just staring at one another's faces, examining the lines that were waiting to tell the stories of our lives. I was overwhelmed with a yearning to know the intricacies of him and to avoid the subtle embarrassments of a new relationship; yet I also wanted to bottle this addictive feeling of anticipation that came with being with someone who knew nothing about me; knowing that every moment spent together was a discovery. And that my past was safely in the past and that was where it could stay – if that was what I wanted.

'You're different, Daisy. I've never met anyone like you,' Ben whispered and I could hear the desperation in his voice. Every word he spoke was like being spoon-fed honey and I closed my eyes for a second to absorb it all. I wanted to be able to say all the words that were forming in my head, words like 'you're the one, I think I'm in love with you, you're making every fibre of my body shudder'.

I settled for the safety of, 'I've never met anyone like you either.'

Ben squeezed my hand. He squeezed it hard with both of his and I felt an urgency in that squeeze. Something that suggested he was lost, lonely and in need of something that perhaps even he didn't know. And I knew we were destined to be together.

Two lost souls found.

We sat there on the sofa and stared at one another. Every now and again, we allowed a small smile to creep across our lips.

At some point Eve appeared and attempted to ask us if we wanted more coffees. Eventually she gave up and walked away leaving us with our fingers entwined and our eyes locked upon each other.

Oblivious to everyone and everything around us.

# 6

ANNIE

It was Ben's birthday today, the first birthday I wouldn't spend with my son.

He was born so close to Christmas that I feel me and Ben and Christmas all belong together. It was the 17<sup>th</sup> of December 1982 and he was due Christmas Day but popped out a week early.

The roads were so icy that night and luckily the midwife was on duty in the area, so Ben was a home birth. She arrived just as his little head was appearing. I remember the story as though it happened yesterday. It's always there in my mind ready to tell anyone, but of course no one asks, because it's always just been me and Ben.

Now as I stood in the kitchen, stirring my tea, with no one to cook for, my son miles away with his new wife, I should have felt joy. I should have been planning a celebration, the way we always did with his favourite meal and a bottle of beer. Instead I felt a tiny seed of something within me. It was going to grow. It had spawned from betrayal, and it would develop into something bigger still.

And there was nothing I could do to stop it.

# 7

## DAISY

'Happy birthday handsome,' I said and bent down to kiss Ben on the head while he was sitting on the floor. He and Eve had been up for hours and they were now sorting through the Christmas decorations. I hadn't slept well. I felt nauseous all night and the baby bump was already causing me discomfort in bed.

'Thank you.' Ben reached for my hand and held on to it as I shuffled to the chair still in my pyjamas and slipper socks and sat down.

'What's occurring? This looks busy.' I surveyed the sea of greens, golds and reds on the space on the floor between Eve and Ben.

'Just helping Eve get these ready.' Ben held up a scary-looking knitted Santa. I motioned with my head towards Eve, so Ben could grasp this was not one of my purchases. Each year she would arrive home with an eccentric tree decoration and that particular one had been part of the family for four years.

'Yes, he's been super. Actually, we were just saying what a

bummer it is having a birthday so close to Christmas. Ben was saying how much he dislikes Christmas – imagine that!' Eve was, even on a non-work day, dressed immaculately. Today she was in her knee length A-line black skirt, a burgundy turtleneck, black tights and burgundy patent Mary Jane shoes. You'd never catch Eve in sports casuals. Even on DVD nights in she wore satin pyjamas and a silk Japanese robe.

'Yes that's right, he's a bit of scrooge, aren't you babe?' I said with a laugh but Ben's sullen expression told me he hadn't found it funny. I was aware by now that Christmas was not his favourite time of year but I'd just put it down to the fact his birthday was so close to it. I was beginning to think there was more to it, something that he wasn't telling me.

'Well done.' I yawned as I got comfy. 'I'll project manage. From the sidelines.' I curled my feet under my legs.

'So, babe,' Ben began and, even though we had only been together just over five months, I recognised the tone. He was about to hit me with something.

'How do you feel about me popping to the Outer Hebrides?' My stomach lurched and my mouth went dry.

'Oh yeah, that.' Eve winced at her own words.

'What? You knew already?' I said to Eve

'I could hardly not, sleeping beauty. He just took the phone call an hour ago, here under my nose'

Ben scooted closer to my chair and rested his hand on my leg. 'It's not a holiday Daisy. It's working with this band, recording. I'm getting paid. It's an actual job.'

'But Ben? The baby? You'll be in... where is the Outer Hebrides anyway?' I could feel my jaw tensing; my stomach was making some sort of butterfly sensation but not the sort I liked.

'Scotland.' Ben touched my hand and looked into my eyes, his head slightly tilted, his mouth stretched into a strained smile. The look he gave me was one he always wore when he really wanted me to understand something. 'It's supposed to be beautiful, quiet, a very inspiring place to record music. I know, Daze, it's not perfect timing, but what is?' He motioned to my ever-growing stomach.

'But... I thought... the bloody Outer Hebrides. You may as well be in outer space!' I knew I sounded childlike. I looked over at Eve who was far too engrossed in the fairy lights. I looked back at Ben. 'For how long again, did you say?' I said in a small voice.

Ben swallowed hard. 'About three months, give or take. Obviously they are flexible, and they know our circumstances.'

'Three. Months.' I could feel actual panic setting in. He was leaving me, he was deserting me. How would I cope with the baby? I could be giving birth. Alone.

Ben shrugged his shoulders 'They really like me, Daze.'

'Well, that's not hard.' I paid the compliment glumly.

'And hey, first babies come late, right?' Ben looked over at Eve for confirmation and I felt my stomach lurch again. Yes, first babies often did.

'How should I know?' Eve flashed a look our way, then continued to tug furiously at the lights.

There were too many feelings racing around my body. This moment with Ben, this felt out of my control.

'Daisy, I'll make sure I'm back for the birth.'

I looked at Eve sitting opposite. Cool Eve who let her boyfriend, Patrick, go and do whatever he wanted yet he still came running back like a lovesick puppy every time. That's the attitude I knew I needed to adopt. But I was fearful of being rejected. I was scared of being pushed away again, of losing someone precious.

'Maybe your folks will come back for the birth? It would be nice to meet them?' Ben looked up at me.

Sweat prickled in my arm pits, and my mouth went dry as my body prepared itself for fight or flight mode.

'It's a long journey to make,' I said quietly.

'Sure.' Ben nodded. He had asked as much about my parents as I had asked about his absent dad since our first night together. He always seemed to accept my one-dimensional answers.

I knew what I needed to say to Ben to make it right, to show him I was strong. He didn't need to know I was weak and broken.

I took a deep breath. 'But there is absolutely no doubt in my mind. You should do it. You've worked hard all your life and someone is offering you a wonderful opportunity. It would be completely selfish of me to hold you back. Just get back in time for the baby.' I delivered the lines I knew he wanted to hear perfectly whilst my body contorted inside.

Ben stood up then sat down on the edge of the chair and stroked my head. 'We both knew when we got married that this wasn't going to be easy. I've got stuff I need to do, and so have you. It was you who pushed me to do it, remember? You told me to take the gig with Griff and he was the one who introduced me to the band. You've opened something up inside of me that I could never quite get to before. You've given me the strength and courage to start living a life.'

I listened intently. Was it possible that I could have influenced something good?

'For God's sake. This is impossible,' came Eve's voice as she threw down the fairy lights and stood up. 'Hey, you two, there's a lot to be said about getting married so soon after meeting. You're both still so polite and giving. Not wanting to upset the other one. All supportive and nice. You make me sick.' Eve gave a theatrical smile.

'Not the psychobabble stuff again, Eve,' Ben said in a mock whine.

'Hey listen, pumpkin.' Eve flicked her vibrant, red, bobbed hair. She stood over Ben and pointed a long mani-cured red nail at him. 'If I was going to psychobabble you, as you so articulately put it, then you would know about it. I was merely making a simple observation. We're all psychologists anyway, Ben. We constantly assess and analyse situations and people. It's natural.' She turned on her heel and walked out of the door. 'It's called being human.'

'Anyway.' He rubbed his hand over his face. It looked like I wasn't the only one who didn't sleep well. Last night his mumbling in his sleep had become irritating. I was struggling to sleep as it was, but Ben's restlessness probably kept me awake for longer than necessary. He took my hands in his; they felt cool and soft. 'I won't leave until after Christmas. I need to do a short stint in London and then I'll come back. I will miss your birthday but we can celebrate when I get back, and then I will have to go – and that reminds me...' Ben took out his Blackberry and added another note to his calendar. It was still so strange to me to see him suddenly using a device so often these last few weeks, and one that did so much admin for him, when he was such an old soul, always writing lyrics in a notebook.

He tapped away in the notes. 'Need to go to the music shop and get one of these mini disc players, have you heard of them? I can record all the songs onto it and it will help me learn them.' Ben spoke slowly as he typed, then he shoved the phone back into his pocket and put his arm around me.

'You'll be glad to have me out of your hair while you do all your nesting and stuff,' he said.

'But I like you hanging around and annoying me.' I touched his arm.

'You know this means we will have money. Money for the baby, money for a proper wedding party knees up,' Ben said and grinned.

'Our first dance!' I said with wide eyes.

And Ben started humming the song he'd tapped on his coffee cup the morning after our first night together. It had unconsciously become 'our song'.

'I love being married to you.' Ben kissed me.

'Happy birthday, handsome,' I said again. Ben's face fell and he looked away to the window, his go-to place for thought or avoidance.

'What? What is it?'

'Just birthdays, Daze. It's not really a thing I ever did. Mum made a bit of an effort...' His voice trailed off.

'Listen, if anyone knows how to do birthdays in this house, it's Eve. Just you wait and see.'

\* \* \*

At 7 p.m. we were dressed for dinner. I got Ben settled in the lounge and went to the kitchen to prepare drinks. 'Beer for me,' Ben called after me. I followed the sound of pumping music to the kitchen where I found Eve miming into a wooden spoon, her eyes squeezed shut. She opened them as she sensed me arrive, grinned at me, and returned to stirring the pot of beef bourguignon on the stove.

'Beef is ready to rock and roll, mash is warm in the oven. Where the hell is Patrick?' Eve said with agitation. On cue, the buzzer went. I noted how Eve pulled off her apron in one swift movement. She had changed into a bright green vintage wraparound dress. She smoothed herself down and pushed her bosom high into her chest with both hands. She gave me an exaggerated smile as she eagerly sashayed her way past me.

'Finally,' I could hear her saying as she reached the door. I heard Patrick's deep booming voice and I imagined his large body filling the hallway and bending down to embrace his girlfriend. I grabbed two beers from the fridge and arrived in the lounge at the same time as Patrick was shaking Ben's hand and wishing him a happy birthday. Ben had hauled himself off the sofa and had managed a charming expression, as though his mood was lifted at the sight of another male in the vicinity.

Patrick turned to greet me.

'Hey, Daisy. You're positively radiant. Pregnancy suits you.' He took my whole body in his arms and held me tightly. I ignored his comments about my ever-expanding stomach. Instead I inhaled the earthy woodiness of his aftershave, a complete contrast to the citrus scents that Ben wore, and melted into his embrace for a second. Patrick was a few years older than me and Eve, and he seemed wiser in his ways; more like a father figure to me than just a friend.

His strawberry blonde hair was damp with perspiration around his forehead from his walk. This evening he had attempted to cover up his protruding waistline with an Aran jumper that was a size too small and made him look even more like the schoolteacher that he so desperately wished he wasn't.

'The table looks good, darling.' Patrick spoke with the public-school accent he had inherited from his years at Harrow. All that private education and training to become one of the country's greatest sportsmen, then suddenly one fall and his rugby career was over.

'Here's a beer, Patrick.' I handed him the cold bottle and gave the other to Ben. Patrick took a long gulp, swallowed half of the fizzy liquid and turned to Ben.

'So how's work, Ben, have you secured any gigs lately?'

Ben's head was tilted downwards as if apologising for his height next to Patrick who was a few inches shorter.

'Well, funny you should ask, mate.' He gave his neck a self-conscious stroke.

I left the room. I couldn't bear to hear Ben talk of leaving. I knew he had to do it. To stop him would stunt our future – now was when we needed to make the sacrifices. So I folded away the fear and insecurity I felt and pushed it back amongst all the other memories and feelings I wanted to forget.

I took my place back in the kitchen as chief overseer.

I loved watching Eve in action. She was no gourmet chef by any standards, nor was she a great sewer or runner or monopoly player, but what was great about Eve, was that whatever she did she made it her own. And cooking was one of those things you had to be there to witness because it was like watching the cirque du soleil, there was always a certain amount of theatrics involved. But it always came out tasting amazing in the end. I leant against the kitchen counter to get a front-row seat.

Eve and I had made a great team ever since our uni days. We weren't a classic best friend duo, who mirrored one another's style and looks. Eve was five foot four with

delightful curves, vibrant hair and a raucous laugh that
would turn heads in the university library. I was five foot ten
and slim with long blonde hair. I turned heads with my looks.
I wanted – needed – people to see beyond the exterior and it
had only happened with three people. One of whom was in
the lounge, while another was here with me in the kitchen.

Eve worked herself around the compact and bijou
kitchen, and her ample hips lifted and swayed to shift past
every corner and surface as though they were an entity separate from the rest of her body. There was something special
about Eve that I couldn't even put into words. I just loved her
so much and wouldn't want to be without her. After a few
minutes of working the room with pots, pans and wooden
spoons raised above her head, she softly said, 'love ya, babe'
as though she knew what I was thinking while I watched her.
She wasn't just a psychologist, she was a bloody mind reader.
It was just what I needed to hear. She would always be there
to deliver the right lines at the right time; unprompted. It was
the most uplifting feeling of joy and I would never falter in
telling her how I felt back.

'Love ya too, babe'

Three delicious courses later, the four of us were sitting with
full bellies and, as usual after an evening spent with Eve and
alcohol, my sides were aching from laughter. Eve had lit a
cigarette. After a couple of drinks she would always treat
herself to a one-off cheeky fag. She had been telling another
anecdote about one of the inmates at the prison where she
worked, which was highly inappropriate and would

undoubtedly have broken every code of conduct regarding patient confidentiality.

I let out a long sigh and leant over to touch Ben's arm. I could see he was inebriated from the red wine and now the Cognac, which was in an oversized brandy glass that he held loosely in his hand. Occasionally he lifted it to his mouth and took a sip.

Eve took a last drag of her cigarette and dropped it into her coffee cup.

'Well, I've had a fab birthday, thanks, guys. A wonderful way to turn twenty-five on planet Earth,' Ben said as he picked up Eve's packet of cigarettes and motioned to her with his eyes. Eve waved her hand for him to help himself.

Eve launched herself onto Patrick's lap and kissed him hard on the lips. Patrick's flushed cheeks were the only visible sign of intoxication, despite consuming nearly one of the two bottles of wine we had shared between us. He was now making his way happily through the Cognac. I smiled and looked at Ben.

'Thank you,' he mouthed before he lit his cigarette. I looked around at the three people at the table. I reflected on the simple meal, the mismatched crockery. I looked at the faces of pure contentment and felt a glimmer of gratification at what I had been given.

'And here's to my wonderful wife and mother-to-be.' Ben blew out a plume of smoke, raised his glass and the others followed in unison. 'You're going to make a wonderful mum.' Ben looked at me, the light from the candles reflected in his eyes. I found a smile and plastered it across my face.

'Thanks,' I mumbled. But I knew his words were wasted on me, for I already felt like the worst mother on earth.

# 8

ANNIE

It was Christmas Eve and the day had begun much as every day did, with the whisper of a promise. By lunchtime I was already feeling the weight of its lie.

I had spent the morning, like I did most mornings, moving from one room to another, making sure everything looked pristine. As the hour edged nearer to midday, I tried to ignore the perpetual push of anxiety that manifested itself in the manner in which I yanked the sheets to perfection. The anxiety had made its way round my body and was becoming apparent in my breathing which was no longer natural and rhythmic. It was laboured and I felt an over-whelming urge to keep taking deep breaths, not always succeeding. When I could catch one, it brought momentary release that was addictive and caused me to continue striving for that deeper relief.

It had been almost a month since I last saw Ben and the first time I met Daisy. Her face had plagued me ever since. But now I knew who she was.

I was still being tortured daily by the face from the TV

screen in the village as well. I didn't need to be reminded of that face that I had been trying to forget for decades so I forced it out of my mind, the way I had before. It was why I chose not to have a television or a radio in the house. I couldn't stand the things anyway, so much noise and invasion.

I was so pleased when Ben said he would come for Christmas Day. Christmas Day is my favourite day of the year. I always make it so special for him. Of course, she will be here too, but to have Ben near me again is worth the stress of having her in the house.

I carried on with my chores for the morning. I folded some towels and took them to the airing cupboard on the landing. As I laid them on the shelf, my eyes were drawn to the floor at the back. I stretched my neck to get a better look and there was a pale blue piece of material. I leant in at an angle and felt around until I grasped a softness between my thumb and forefinger. I pulled it out and immediately recognised it as Ben's old comfort blanket. I was surprised to see it after so long and the memories of seeing him holding it as a small boy came flooding back. I longed for those days again.

It had been washed so many times and was frayed around the edges. One corner still bore the effects of Ben's consistent rubbing and the crochet pattern had expanded apart and created a larger gap with two thick edges on either side. After the rubbing created the hole, Ben sought comfort in those thick sturdy edges.

I headed downstairs, clutching Ben's blanket, and poured myself a large brandy. Brandy always relaxed me.

Then, once it had done its job, I began to look around at my achievements. The lounge looked glamorous, the food I had stored in the larder would be delectable and moreish, the lights would sparkle with fairy tale magic and the house would be filled with Christmas carols. There was just no other time of year like it.

I had no idea what sort of Christmas Daisy expected, but I did things my way in this house. My Ben and I had always had the most perfect time. I may not have been able to give him the nuclear family, but one thing I did do was make Christmas special.

I had always struggled. And as a single mother, it was harder still. Things took longer as a result. I was sure that was why it took Ben forever to smile at me, but when he finally did I was moved to tears. All that effort and hard work had finally paid off. I can't say it was easy. There were times when I just wanted to give up completely. But I knew I couldn't. He was my son. So I made it work. I came through the bleak period. I suppose every first-time mum experiences the blues in the beginning. I just wasn't prepared for it though. When you want something so badly, you don't expect it to bring a feeling of panic and despair. However, once we were out of that dark phase, Ben began to thrive.

This time of year brought with it memories so palpable, I could almost taste the nostalgia.

I sat down at the table in the kitchen and held Ben's comfort blanket. I stroked the edge he had created over the years. Christmas carols were playing on the record player very low; the familiar notes flowed through into the kitchen. I clutched the blanket closer to me and remembered how he was nearly twelve years old by the time he gave it up. I remember because he was due to start high school. The day I told him it was time for him to give up the blanket I heard him weeping into his pillow. I took it, washed it and hid it from him in the highest shelf in my wardrobe. I forgot about it until I was having one of my massive clear outs a few months later. I found it in Ben's room folded up inside his bed side table drawer under a pile of magazines. It smelled of him so I knew he had been using it each night. I left it there and said nothing more about it. The attachment to it was so fierce; if it kept him happy, what harm could it do? He only kept it with him in his bedroom, so no one would ever know about it.

When he left to live with her, he left it behind. He must have tossed it into the airing cupboard when he was packing. It was no longer needed. That item that bore so much significance in his life for so long was now cast aside just the way I had been. I wondered how it was he could have had such an attachment to something and then simply pretend it never existed. He had been brainwashed by her, that's what had happened and I needed to make him see that.

I knew it wouldn't be long before he would be sitting back where he should be, leaving his coat on the back of the kitchen chair and spilling coffee granules all over the kitchen surface. I could live with that, as I always had done. What I couldn't live with was the fact that he had left me for her. A blatant liar.

And I knew by whatever means I had to get him back in my life.

With every ticking moment, Christmas Eve was coming to an end and Christmas Day was almost here. And then I would see Ben. And her. Such a manic contrast between anxiety and excitement were my feelings that I had to pour myself another brandy. It was doing its job nicely, taking the edge off.

By five o'clock the brandy had well and truly relaxed me. I went into the lounge and turned off the record player. I poked the fire as the last embers burned out and turned off the Christmas lights. I was tired and would head up for a bath and get to bed early, ready for their arrival tomorrow.

I sat down in my chair that faced out towards the window.

Somewhere out there behind a blanket of darkness, was the same view of the ocean I had witnessed thousands of times, but I sat in the warmth and kept looking, kept staring, always with that perpetual notion that something would change and alter. But here I was after all this time. Even with Ben, whom I lived and breathed for, I was still staring into the darkness.

# 9

DAISY

'Are you coming or what?' I hollered through the hallway of the flat, knowing that my loud booming voice that I reserved for my fitness classes would reach Ben's ears in the bathroom where he had been hiding away for the last twenty minutes. I was waiting at the front door wearing earmuffs and a brown sheepskin jacket. Waves of nausea swept through my body. I thought I was done with the last of the morning sickness sensation but it had reared its ugly head again. I took deep breaths and stroked the fabric of the coat to distract myself.

I had no desire to spend Christmas Day with Annie. I'm not sure Ben did either. But she had asked and he accepted for both of us. The way I was feeling I needed to crawl into bed and stay there for a few months.

It would only be my second time meeting Annie and I still felt a bit weird about the teapot incident and, of course, her impertinence at mine and Ben's decision to marry one another and getting pregnant so soon. But I was trying to put it down to her pure frustration. Without Ben around any more, she was probably quite lonely.

I was desperately trying to see it from her perspective, to analyse her behaviour, from the scolding my finger on the teapot, to the way she scanned my face for too long.

As I waited for Ben, I looked through the glass pane of the front door. Outside, it was bitter. No snow, just a frost that covered everything but it was the perfect back drop to Christmas Day. Our first Christmas Day together as husband and wife. A time of year I knew Ben was not wholly keen on but had yet to tell me exactly why. So did I know my husband yet? Can you truly ever know anyone? We all have secrets. Secrets we must hold on to. Our past has a funny way of showing up and ruining everything and with the pregnancy feeling more real to me every day, I was being drawn back to a time in my life I wasn't ready to confront. So I decided, not today. Today was Christmas. And Christmas was for unwrapping presents – not the past.

Eve arrived in the hallway just then, wearing just a skimpy leopard-print silk dressing gown that barely grazed her backside, accompanied by her fluffy tiger slippers and an amused expression. She stopped next to me and leant her voluptuous hips against the wall.

She looked at me for a few seconds and for a moment I knew she was analysing me, the way she liked to sometimes. 'You okay? How you feeling?'

'Tired. Fat.'

I looked down at my feet. I shifted my weight onto my left leg and then back again.

'Come on, Daze, you're still beautiful, even more so because you're going to be a mummy!' Eve looked at me like a wide-eyed child.

Why was Ben taking so long? Then he was there.

'Ahh my husband!' I said with too much emphasis as Ben

wandered down the hallway towards me, his head down and his shoulders hunched.

I looked at Eve, she shrugged her shoulders.

'You okay, babe?' My hand found its way to Ben's shoulder.

'Me, yeah, I'm fine.'

I knew he wasn't. On top of his apparent aversion towards 'the most wonderful time of the year', Ben was also going to break the news to Annie that he had a proper job. His first proper job by all accounts, and that he would be leaving to work away to record an album with an up-and-coming band. It was the sort of news a parent should have been thrilled about, but he was dreading having to deliver it to Annie. I guess Ben felt he had surprised his mum so much already what with moving out, marrying me and now the baby, that one more blow like moving away for months might actually tip her over the edge.

Eve pushed herself away from the wall, her hands cupped around her tea. She kissed me on the cheek and added one of her 'I know you' looks for extra value. I opened the door and the cold air hit my face.

'Just call me. Anytime, you want to talk about... you know, anything.' Eve put her hand on my back and kept it there for a few seconds. I blinked back the tears that must have been brought on by the icy breeze.

'Have a wonderful Christmas Day, you two. Can't wait to see you tomorrow.' Eve stood, waving enthusiastically.

I picked up the Christmas-themed paper bag that was leant against the wall and we both headed outside. I looked back at Eve who winked at me and I blew her a kiss with my gloved hand.

'Patrick round later?' I said.

'Oh yeah, baby, you bet ya!' Eve said, laughing as she flashed me her red lacy negligee which matched her vibrant, neatly bobbed hair, before she closed the door.

We stepped into my Renault Clio, looked at the frost-infested windscreen and then at one another. We let out synchronised sighs and, armed with ice scrapers, we got out and set about clearing the windscreen. We each stood on our side of the car and began removing the ice. I looked at Ben who looked back and each time the smile grew larger across his lips, until eventually we were laughing and flicking bits of ice at each other. I hoped that any passers-by or neighbours who might haven stolen a look out of their window, would see a cute goofy couple and perhaps they would feel a pang of jealousy at the young man and woman who were hope-lessly and madly in love on Christmas morning.

The journey to Annie's would take less than half an hour but it was enough time for me to probe Ben.

'So how are you feeling about spending Christmas Day with your wife and mother,' I said light-heartedly before looking away out of the window. Ben's non-response was all I needed to know that he was not all right with it. The silence hung for a few minutes before he spoke.

'I wanted to spend it with you. Just us, you know? But Mum's asked... I'd feel a bit wrong not seeing her at Christ-mas.' I squeezed Ben's knee. 'It's a strange relationship, I know, but it was always just us. No one else, she never let anyone else in. She has a hard time trusting people.'

'Well what about your mates, you must have had mates at school?' I asked

'Mmm, not really. I remember this one kid, Joe.' Ben spoke with fondness. 'One day I went round to Joe's house after school. Mum had to go into hospital, she had a dodgy leg or something and needed an operation. I remember because she was beside herself. She didn't want to leave me. Joe's mum had made fish pie with fresh green cabbage and homemade brown bread to mop up all the white sauce afterwards. I had a huge glass of homemade lemonade and two helpings of homemade fruit trifle. I even got given a portion to take home with me in a little silver foil tray with a lid. I remember that meal so vividly; Mum's food was good, but this was like, different good.' Ben released the wheel with one hand to give my hand a quick squeeze. 'That day I remember, I had fallen over at school and torn my trousers, so when me and Joe were tucking in, Joe's mum sat and sewed up my trousers, whilst I sat in a pair of Joe's old trackie-bottoms. It was nice. She sat and listened to us boys chatting, you can imagine it, can't you? Two young lads, manic from a day at school, so much to say. Anyway, she was awesome, Joe's mum, because she joined in our conversations every now and again and the rest of the time I felt, well, just really comfortable in her silence.

'I got home that night and told Mum all about it. I told Mum about the food, I gave her the trifle portion and said it was for her and then showed her the place where the hole had been in my trousers. I remember her face, all screwed up, looking at the trousers and examining the perfectly neat sewing and then she just turned her nose up. I remember it. I remember that look, Daisy.

'I wanted to say to my mum, is that what a mum should be like, is that how I should normally feel? Because it felt so good. Because usually, Daze, it feels, I don't know how to explain it, awkward, I guess. I know she's my mum, but sometimes she can be hard work, you know?'

I knew.

I waited a beat before I asked, 'What do you suppose it is, Ben?' This was the most he had ever opened up and right then it felt right, like I wanted to know. Then maybe at some point I could tell Ben everything.

'I dunno, I'm sure it's to do with my dad. Like with him not being around and her never telling me anything about him.'

I looked at Ben whilst he continued.

'That night I found the silver container of trifle in the bin, uneaten, and I was never allowed to go to Joe's house after that. In fact, I was never allowed to go to anyone's house. And no one ever came to my house to play. That huge house by the sea. What a waste, hey?'

I felt my heart ache a familiar ache.

'So, you see, Daisy. You're the first. You are the first person I have ever taken back to my house. Ever.'

'Families…' I paused. 'Families are tricky. Why do you suppose your mum refuses to tell you who your dad is? I mean we have a right to know now we have a baby coming surely?'

Ben stayed focused on the road. 'Sometimes I don't know if I want to know.'

I left Ben's words hanging and turned my thoughts to my own complex life. Was it my turn? Did I now need to offer a confession in return? Is that how a marriage worked? I figured it was about love. Trust. But everyone has a past, we all make mistakes, did things we cannot correct. But then we move on and beautiful new things happen. Like Ben.

He had barely questioned my past, except for a few one-sided conversations about my parents and when would we get to meet them. I batted his queries away as quickly as I could, reminding him the cost of travelling to and from

Australia was too great for either party. He seemed to accept this for now. What I didn't reveal was that the relationship between me and my family was like an ancient lost relic, buried deep in in my subconscious, never to be unearthed again.

Suddenly Ben was speaking again. 'My relationship with my mother is and always will be a strange one. I mean, what kind of mother doesn't let their kid play with another kid? I have vague memories of children. Children I played with whilst my mum was working maybe?' Ben continued to monologue while he drove.

'I remember their faces. They must have been the only children I played with as a kid. Apart from them, there was no one. We never had any parties, no after school play dates. Nothing.'

Ben stopped the car as the traffic lights turned to red. He looked hard into the distance.

'Except I do remember something. A vague memory, a cake... singing. Everyone clapping and smiling. Lots of people. Can't think what that would have been. It could have been someone else's party, I suppose; I'm sure Mum must have let me go to one of their parties. Do you think that's odd, Daisy?' He turned to face me and gave me one of his double blinks.

My face was screwed up with sadness for him and also for me. 'I think it's incredibly sad Ben.' The traffic lights changed and Ben's forlorn expression turned back to face the road again.

'And then there was Mrs Keeley when mum had to go back to work, I spent a lot of time with her. I can see her face still. She was such a beautiful woman, such a kind face. I think she had a couple of kids. It was such a long time ago. But I still remember that face. But when I met you I knew I wanted to be with you. It was a bit like sitting with Joe and his mum. It felt so right. I've met people along the way with my job and I've met girls obviously, but when I saw you that night in the club, dancing and laughing, it was... well, I was magnetised, I had to be with you.'

I placed my hand on his leg and rubbed it.

'You're all I need,' Ben said with a laugh, but I could see the tears twinkling in his eyes. I leant over and planted a kiss on his cheek and pushed my hands through his long hair. Ben responded and relaxed his head against my touch.

'And me too. You complete me. You're all I need, Ben. Do you understand? Nothing else matters.'

The radio was on and I could just about decipher the odd chord so I turned it up and was pleased to hear it was my favourite seasonal song by Chris Rea, 'Driving Home for Christmas'. I turned to Ben and smiled, then sang along, accentuating words to make them count for his sake. Ben pulled his mouth into a semi-smile.

* * *

Annie was standing at the door when we pulled up. She was wearing a tinsel crown, and a green knitted jumper with a Christmas pudding on it. She must have been looking out for us. I thought how cold she must be standing at the door without a coat on and for a moment I felt something, a sort of pity for her as she stood alone waiting for her son to arrive on Christmas morning.

Ben helped me out of the car and went to the boot to collect our overnight bags and the presents we had brought for Annie.

'Daisy, you look nice,' Annie said absently, looking like she'd had a fit in a Christmas pound shop. I noticed her Christmas tree earrings that were flashing an offensive red light. 'I always go a bit kitsch for Christmas, don't I, Ben? As it's always been just us two you see, I like to go a bit overboard. Had this jumper, what, five years now, Ben? You bought it for me, do you remember? Gosh, that was a lovely Christmas.' Ben nodded and mumbled something I couldn't quite catch. 'Right who's for a drink? I have eggnog.' Annie attempted an American accent as we followed her into the house. Ben dumped the bags and closed the heavy front door. The sound loudly echoed through the bare hallway. I swung around, startled by the noise and noted how Ben had finally cracked a smile at his mother's absurdity. I had to admit that Annie's seasonal mood was quite infectious and the smell from the roasting turkey and the prospect of a Christmas alcoholic beverage, albeit a small one, made me feel cosy and warm inside.

'Eggnog sounds fantastic, Annie,' I said, realising I would need to show extra enthusiasm for both of us to get us through the day.

'Should you be drinking in your condition, Daisy?' Annie said and looked directly at me with those accusing eyes. I wondered when she might begin to think of the baby as her grandchild and not a condition.

'Well, surely one drink can't hurt anyone can it, Annie?' I said. Her eyes remained fixed on me for a few seconds whilst Ben busied himself removing his boots. Both of us held the stare without wavering, then suddenly she spun around and headed for the lounge. She walked straight over to the tree and began fiddling with an ornament.

I pulled Ben towards the lounge but stopped in the
doorway and gasped, astounded by the décor.

There was no suggestion from the outside of Annie's
beach house that it was Christmas. There were no lights or
decorations anywhere outside the front door to hint that it
was one of the most special times of the year, yet when we
entered the lounge area it was like Annie was the Grinch and
she had stolen Christmas and stuffed it in its entirety into her
front room. My eyes prickled with tears. There was a huge,
albeit fake, Christmas tree, decorated with gold and red bows
and twinkling fairy lights and hand-painted ornaments. A
gold star was planted on the top. All around the tree were
presents wrapped in an array of seasonal coloured wrapping
paper; golds, reds and silvers sprouted from beneath the
branches. Next to the fireplace was an ornamental nativity
scene and on the coffee table was a large bowl full of nuts and
oranges with cloves in them. The smell hit my nostrils and I
could feel my heart quicken. This was Christmas. I realised
that what I was feeling was an overwhelming sense of nostalgia. Annie was by my side looking at me.

'Do you like it, Daisy?'

'This room... it's... amazing.' I gave my eyes a surreptitious
wipe. Ben was smiling, but only at me. 'I can't believe my
eyes!' I looked at Annie who stood behind us looking like a
pleased twit in all her Christmas getup.

'Well, yes, I like to make an effort at Christmas.' She
walked over to the mantelpiece. 'I have kept all the decorations from when Ben was a little boy and each year I buy a
new ornament for the tree, don't I, Ben? Except that year
when I had to buy all new ornaments.'

'Mum, please.' Ben looked visibly stressed. He pulled his

hand through his hair and squeezed it hard at the nape of his neck.

'What's all this about?' I asked, looking back and forth between them both.

'Well, it's just Ben has a little fascination with Christmas trees, don't you son? He almost burnt the house down one year. Couldn't have been more than six or seven...'

'I was five, Mum,' Ben said firmly.

'Oh yes that's right, you remember it better than me, my brain isn't as young as yours. You'd better tell the rest.'

I looked at Ben with a frown etched across my face. 'Ben?'

Ben let out a loud sigh and rubbed his forehead. 'I have vague memories of sneaking down the stairs that Christmas and switching the lights back on. I was obsessed with them. Next thing, I remember hearing the alarms and seeing the smoke. It's pretty hazy, I was very young, but I remember Mum was livid.'

'Oh, son, I'm over it now, I'm just glad you were okay. We only lost a few things.' Annie waved her hand as if to dismiss his dismay. But Ben looked sad. This was why he hated Christmas so much. The magic of this time of year was tainted by the irresponsible actions of a tiny boy. I found my way over to Ben and placed a hand on his arm and rubbed it. 'You were just a kid, Ben,' I said softly. Ben pulled his lips into a tight smile.

I looked over at Annie who was watching us.

'Well, that's our little story anyway,' she said as she finished rearranging the ornaments. Then she walked back over to me and escorted me to the sofa. I began to remove my coat. 'Oh, very nice jacket, Daisy.'

I smiled, glad I had pleased Annie. 'Right, I'll get that

eggnog then.' Annie marched from the room taking my new coat with her.

'I love you,' I whispered in Ben's ear and pulled him onto the sofa. He nuzzled his face against mine and I breathed in his sweet citrus scent.

'And I love you and the baby,' he said as he rubbed the bump. I squirmed a little. 'When do we get the first scan picture, shouldn't it be about now? I wanted to show Mum.'

'Yeah, we get it soon.' I took his hand from the bump and squeezed it in mine. What I hadn't told Ben was the appointment for the first scan photo had lapsed. It had even passed the time when we would be able to book in for the second scan photo, the time when we could find out the sex, something I was sure Ben would want to know in advance. But there was very little I wanted to know about this pregnancy, let alone if it was a girl or a boy.

'Here we are!' Annie made her announced entrance carrying a tray full of eggnog. 'Come and get it whilst it's... eggnoggy!' I looked at Ben and we both smiled at Annie's efforts.

'Thanks Mum.' Ben stood up and took the tray from Annie. I watched curiously as Ben, who towered over her, put the tray down on a high side table next to the Christmas tree. Annie placed a hand on his arm and gave it a half pat, half rub.

'You're welcome, son. It's good to have you here.' Annie turned to face me; aware that their awkward intimate moment was being observed.

'I wouldn't be without him,' Annie said with a matter-of-fact tone to her voice.

'I know, I know,' I said.

Ben put an arm around his mum, but as I watched, I saw

it was forced and uncomfortable; they didn't seem to have an easy mother and son way about them. For two people who had spent their lives together, living in close proximity and with such intimacy, I couldn't work out why they touched one another as though each of them were covered in prickles.

* * *

That night, as Christmas Day edged its way into Boxing day, I struggled to sleep in the unfamiliar room that Ben had slept in all his life. I thought back over the day. Annie had made a real effort. The food was good, but I wished I was able to drink more, then maybe I wouldn't have struggled when I had to open the presents she gave me. I had to force my face into a smile when I saw that she had given me floral embroidered handkerchiefs and a coarse-looking lavender soap. Annie accepted our Yankee Candle and chocolate fondue set with grace, but there was an edge to her smile as she placed them to the side of her having barely inspected them.

I could feel an uncomfortable pulling sensation so I took one pillow from under my head and shoved it under my belly on the right side. I lay there and I listened to the old house moaning and groaning. The wind was whipping across the already battered exterior and the waves were thrashing against the low wall at the end of the garden. I felt as though I were waking every half an hour. Ben was muttering in his sleep.

'Ben,' I called out softly. He didn't wake. His lips were still moving.

'Emma,' he mumbled.

'Ben.' I tried again, this time with a little more volume. Ben shot upright.

'What, what?' he said in a panicky voice. His breath was fast and he was grasping for something around him that wasn't there. I leant over to the bedside table and picked up a glass of water. The bright moon brought a sliver of light into the room and illuminated the white clock face on the bedside table. I could just make out it was about 3 a.m.

'Here, have a drink,' I said too curtly; the name Emma rang in my ears.

It had been the same every night since we had met. I had been convinced it was a one-off the first night we spent together but every night, with or without alcohol in his system, Ben would fall into a deep sleep and the mutterings would begin. They would never escalate to more than incomprehensible murmurs, but occasionally a name would escape through the strange sounds.

'So what was is it this time?' It was unlikely we would wake Annie all the way down the hall with our chatting, but I whispered as though the hour suggested I should.

'What do you mean?' Ben said groggily and lay back down facing the ceiling.

'You've woken me again with your chattering.'

'Sorry,' he said flatly.

'What was it about?'

'It's just a dream, Daisy,' Ben said through a heavy yawn.

'Well, what's the dream about?'

'Stuff. People.'

'Hmm, yeah? And? Am I there?'

'No. No. Definitely not.'

'Oh.' I tried to keep the offence from my voice whilst images of Ben with a faceless Emma flooded my mind.

'It's an old dream. A recurring thing. I think I've pretty much dreamt the same thing since I was a kid.'

'What? Surely that's not possible?' Although I knew it was. His unconscious mutterings were on a loop every night.

'Dunno.' Ben sounded as though he was drifting off again.

'So what's the dream about?' I persisted in a loud whisper, but he had fallen back into a slumber.

I couldn't get back to sleep after that so I flicked the duvet off me and padded out into the hallway. I headed for the bathroom, not bothering to shut the door; a habit from sharing a flat with Eve and continuing conversations whilst one of us peed. I sat down on the toilet and allowed my blurry eyes to focus on the items around me in the bathroom. Then I caught something out of the corner of my eye. I looked up.

'Oh, for fucking hell's sake!' I grappled for my pyjama bottoms which were around my legs and tried to cover my modesty as I looked at the figure standing in the doorway. I focused my eyes and realised it was Annie. She looked strange, because she was wearing a thin dressing gown that was open at the front and beneath that she was totally naked. She wasn't moving. Just standing. I finished up on the toilet and stood up. She was very still and looking straight through me. She must've been asleep. I remembered something I heard once about not waking sleepwalkers. Then, as quickly as she had arrived, she turned to go. I peered around the door into the hallway and watched her walk back to her room. Once I heard Annie's bedroom door close, I let out a long loud breath which felt as though I had been holding it in for some time. I walked back down to Ben's bedroom and got back into bed beside him where he moaned something in his sleep. I lay down but couldn't drift off, the image of Annie

standing in front of me would not leave my mind for the rest
of the night.

* * *

The next morning, I woke suddenly as though someone had
given the duvet a sharp yank. I opened my eyes, startled to
see Annie standing at the foot of the bed looking down at me.
It took a moment for me to come round and realise it was her
who had woken me. Had she pulled the duvet? Annie held a
steaming mug and all around me was an aroma of fresh
coffee which normally titillated my senses, but this morning
made me want to retch. I took a few deep breaths trying to
control the nausea which still caught me off guard every
morning.

'Good morning, Daisy.'

I felt instantly wary of Annie's tone. Did she remember
last night? Had she indeed been awake? What was the appropriate protocol, mention it or ignore it? The light streamed
through the curtains but I could tell it was barely eight or
nine o'clock. The seagulls were wailing their raucous calls. I
took Annie in for a moment and I was glad to see she had lost
the Christmas outfit and was back to her uniform of crisp
white shirt and trousers.

I had hoped for a long lie in with Ben before we drove
back to home. I felt for his side of the bed and found it
empty.

'Where's Ben?' I asked groggily.

'He's helping me with a small task I needed doing on the
computer. This internet stuff, I'm still so new to it all. I know
it's the age of technology, but I'm an old soul. So is Ben really.
Such a good boy he is. Always there to help his mama out,'

Annie said, apparently waiting for me to say something back.

'Well, yes,' was all I could manage. I started to sit up.

'Ben said it was okay to come in.' Annie was round by the side of the bed and was putting the coffee cup on the bedside table.

'Er, did he?'

'Yes he did, Daisy, are you calling me a liar?' Annie said, laughing as she straightened up.

I suddenly remembered I was wearing a thin cami top, so I pulled the duvet high up to my chest. Annie stood very still. Then she turned and walked out of the door. I opened my mouth to speak but realised it was too late. Suddenly I felt angry and somewhat violated at Annie's presumptuous behaviour. She had no right to wander in here and sneak up on me like that. I was about to holler after her but something stopped me. I took a long deep breath and exhaled slowly.

Ben wandered into the room looking annoyingly lively, and closed the door.

'Where have you been?' The breathing hadn't worked, the tension in my voice was apparent.

'Just sorting out my mum's computer? She asked me to do a couple of things. Are you looking forward to getting back home?' Ben was breezy as he skipped round to his side of the bed and hopped up next to me. We were going home today. He had yet to break the news to Annie but his sense of relief to be leaving the beach house was palpable.

'Your mum brought me coffee. Wasn't that nice of her?' I grinned inanely and heard the petulant tone in my voice.

'Did she? Oh right. I told her I'd bring it. Never mind, hope she didn't see you in your negligee,' he laughed. I frowned at him. Why was Annie so keen to bring me coffee herself, I wondered, as my mind flashed back to the incident in the bathroom.

Ben shuffled closer to me, placed his chilly hand under the sheets and began searching for bare skin. I pulled myself back down under the sheets and allowed my husband to caress me.

'There we go,' came a sing-song voice and both Ben and I shot up from under the sheets. Annie stood in the doorway where Ben had closed it moments ago.

'Mum!' Ben wailed. I grabbed the sheets around me again. I looked at Ben, my eyes wide with question. 'What are you doing, Mum?' The agitation was fraught in Ben's voice.

'Delivering you your clothes. You get the full service when you come here, Daisy.' Annie placed a small pile of neatly folded clothes on the end of the bed. I instantly recognised the T-shirt and pregnancy jeans I had been wearing yesterday and then, to my horror, I saw placed on top were my matching purple lace knickers and bra. I felt my face flush. Then I felt the anger rise.

'Annie, I really don't think this was necessary. Those...' I paused with embarrassment and pointed feebly to my underwear. 'They are very delicate.'

'Oh yes, dear, I know. Don't worry, I read the label and washed them accordingly.' Annie said and Ben placed his head in his hands and groaned.

'Right, who's for a delicious fry-up?' Annie said raising her eyebrows like an excited child.

I had the sensation of a watery mouth. I yanked my jeans from the pile at the end of the bed sending Annie's perfect folded washing into array. With Annie's huffing in my ear, I made it to the toilet just in time to throw up.

* * *

Half an hour later, we emerged into the kitchen where Annie was standing trying to conceal her annoyance at having waited a further thirty minutes to serve the breakfast.

'Well, your bacon will be dried up now. There's fresh fried eggs but that's the best I can do.' Annie's words were coarse as she stood wringing the tea towel between her hands. She looked hard at me. I was suddenly very glad we were leaving straight after breakfast. I felt like I'd over-stayed my visit here.

'How are you feeling now, Daisy? Too many rich foods last night. I always pace myself over Christmas, nothing worse than mince pies and brandy sloshing around your stomach.'

Of course, she was still refusing to acknowledge any real association with the baby. The baby I was having with her son. The baby that was still making me sick and want to retch again just thinking about Annie's fried eggs.

'Yes, it must have been that Annie,' I said playing along. 'I could have stayed in that bed all day though' I said wishing I were there now and not sitting in Annie's stark kitchen.

'It is a good bed, Daisy,' Annie said stiffly. 'Never been slept in by anyone except Ben. We will go for a walk later? I've got pancetta to make some turkey club sandwiches for lunch and a stack of board games just waiting to be played.'

I looked at Ben and then hung my head, leaving him to deal with his mother on his own.

'We're heading back after breakfast, mum. Daisy's got to teach a class later.' Ben heaped sugar into his mug.

'Oh,' Annie said, her disappointment obvious. I looked at Ben, who was looking at his teacup. 'And on Boxing Day?

Well, I say, you girls never stop. Who wants to work out the day after Christmas? And in your condition?'

'Daisy's perfectly fine to keep teaching right up until the birth, Mum, as long as she takes it easy. And Boxing Day is a very popular day for classes at the gym.'

Ben looked at me and gave me a quick subtle wink.

'Well, I never,' Annie said eyeing me up between serving the eggs and bringing the plates to the table.

'Breakfast smells great,' I said through a strained smile as Annie laid our plates in front of us. She returned with a full teapot, the very one she had burned me with at our last visit. Annie stared straight at me as she edged the tea pot between me and Ben. I folded my arms and laid them on my lap. She walked to the other side of the kitchen and when she was far enough away, I picked up the teapot and poured out. As I was pouring tea into Ben's cups I whispered, 'You're going straight to hell lying to your poor mother like that.'

'Not entirely lying.' Ben leant over the table and whispered, 'We'll be doing our own work out later.' He winked and I slapped his hand.

'Naughty boy,' I whispered and looked up as Annie returned our way carrying a plate of toast.

Twenty minutes later I pushed my plate away with barely half the food eaten, I looked over at Ben who had cleared his plate entirely. He was now standing up patting his pockets.

'Hey, Mum, did you find anything else in my pocket when you washed those jeans last night?

'No, son, why?'

'Oh, it's just I swore the flat keys were in one of these pockets.'

'You probably didn't bring them. We didn't lock up because Eve was still at home,' I said, picking up a piece of dry toast and nibbling on it. Annie who had been hovering around the table the whole time, looked down at my plate.

'Oh, Daisy, dear? Not hungry? I thought you had quite an appetite, young fit girl like you?'

'Sorry. It's just that, well, I'm not a massive eater first thing in the morning...' I felt sweat prickle under my arms. Was she doing this on purpose or had she forgotten what pregnancy felt like. 'It was good, thanks Annie. Just not as hungry as I thought, I guess.' I looked at Ben for some moral support but he was still frisking himself and looking agitated.

'So no keys, Mum?'

'No son!' Annie's bark rang loud and clear around the kitchen. 'I mean... really, could you not have just dropped them somewhere?' she said more softly. 'Stop badgering your poor old mum.' Annie gave a silly laugh, and then her attention was back on my plate. I flashed a look at Ben; his face was a myriad of emotions I couldn't fathom.

'Do you think it was that last mince pie you ate before you went to sleep last night, Daisy?' Annie said bluntly.

I counted to ten in my head and smiled.

'Maybe the baby likes mince pies.' Ben said, reaching down and stroking the bump as Annie picked up both of our plates. She looked as though she was trying not to look at us, but I saw her steal a glance at Bens hand.

'Maybe,' I said absently.

'Well, if you're leaving, I have a stack of food in the freezer for you to take home. I don't suppose you have time to cook, do you, Daisy.'

I felt the rage bubble up inside me.

'You really didn't need to do that Annie...' I began.

'Oh, I did. It's what a mother does for her son. Especially when he earns so little.' Annie looked at me and tilted her head to one side. Her eyes fell momentarily on my stomach. 'You'll see one day.'

'Thanks, Mum, I appreciate it – we appreciate it, we do.' Ben began and I felt my stomach drop in anticipation for what he was about to tell her. 'But things are looking up. I've got some work in the new year. Not like the few gigs I've had in the local pubs here, but real work.'

'Oh, really, son? A real job?' Annie scoffed. 'You wouldn't survive out there in the big bad world. Soft lad like you.' She looked at me with blame in her eyes. 'For how long?'

I gulped hard.

'A few months in the Outer Hebrides.'

I looked at Annie. She couldn't conceal the horror on her face. She couldn't control where she looked, her eyes flickered between me and Ben. Then she managed to compose herself. She took in a deep breath through her nose and turned on her heel, leaving the kitchen this time.

'Well, I hope they are paying you well,' she said as she walked out of the door. Ben's upper body seemed to deflate onto the table.

'That went well.' My voice was thick with sarcasm.

I looked at Ben for a reaction to my comment, an eye roll or a shake of his head, but Ben's expression was blank as he stared off into the distance. His mind was somewhere else entirely.

# 10

---

ANNIE

I could tell Daisy did not want to be here for Christmas. Did her mother never teach her any manners? I'm seriously wondering what Ben ever saw in her. Apart from the bleeding obvious. She struts around showing off every asset she has. And whilst carrying a baby. No shame.

I could tell she didn't like any of the presents I bought for her. I always relished a handkerchief set and soap when I was younger. And fancy not eating the breakfast I cooked for her. I'll be honest. I know breakfasts aren't my strong point. I've watched those cooking shows. I know it's the new millennium, I know these new fancy quick and easy Aussie-style breakfasts are in vogue, but I like a good, honest full English. And so does my Ben.

As for not stopping until the end of Boxing Day and leaving before lunch...! I spent the day taking down the decorations after they both left. No point keeping them up just for me, was there?

But then that bombshell from Ben about leaving to work away on the other side of the country? I bet the two of them had a good old chuckle about that. Ben won't be able to handle it, he's never been away anywhere before. How does he intend to manage a relationship with Daisy when he's all the way over there? And with a baby just months away. I've told him before and I'll tell him again, marriage is not easy. Who knows what that girl will be up to whilst he's not there? But there is the upside that he will come crawling back when it all comes crumbling down around him. I would have him back here in a heartbeat. I worry about him out there without me. People do terrible things; no one is really safe.

This was all Daisy's fault. If she hadn't wormed her way into his life, our life, probably making all kinds of demands of him, then we would still be plodding along as we always did. I wouldn't have him working himself ragged to support her and that child when there was plenty of room for the two of us here. I would have had the upstairs converted or even the cellar, so he could have his own space. Why did he have to leave me? It felt like it was happening all over again. I couldn't bear to feel neglected again.

I needed to get a grip and put a stop to all of this now. I spent far too long protecting my son, I needed to keep him where I knew he would be safe.

# 11

GRACE

During that first cooking lesson, the lady saw me staring at her little boy, a mere toddler.

'I had to bring him, his dad's at work. I can't get a babysitter. I know Emily a little bit. She doesn't mind.'

I looked away from the little boy who was contentedly playing with his toy train and then up at the woman. She was tall, her golden blonde hair tied neatly into a French plait. I noted how her skin was flawless and her cheeks were rosy pink.

'Oh. He doesn't bother me. He's very sweet. What's his name?' I winked at him.

'Michael. But we call him Mikee, don't we, love?' The lady looked down at Mikee, who continued playing with his train, seemingly oblivious to anyone or anything around, too engrossed in his toy to look at the desperate woman in front of him. 'Got two more, both at school, mind.' Then she patted her stomach and leant in. I could smell her perfume. It smelt like Chanel or something equally expensive, although I wouldn't really know. She whispered to me, 'And another one on the way. Haven't told the husband yet. But I just know, you know?'

I nodded. I knew all right. I had felt the perpetual ache of hope in my breasts, lulling me in, making me believe my body had created a baby that this time would stay in my womb long enough to develop.

She introduced herself as Jenny and held her hand out to me. I was presented with a beautiful green and gold vintage ring on the wedding finger of perfectly manicured hand. I took Jenny's soft hand in mine and looked up at her again as she smiled down upon me, almost regally. She had perfectly white teeth and a soft pastel red shade on her lips which complemented those naturally rosy cheeks. I tried to suppress the bitter feeling of jealousy that was stirring in the pit of my stomach but I couldn't shift it. This woman was like a golden goddess. How was it that some women got all the luck? They had looks to die for and could get pregnant without thinking about it. Here I was struggling to hold on to one baby in my womb.

'I'm Grace,' I said then realised I had been holding Jenny's hand for a few seconds longer than necessary, but Jenny didn't seem to mind or notice.

'Oh, what a beautiful name. Do you have any children?'

I released Jenny's hand and shook my head looking down at the counter. I began re-organising the recipe cards that were laid out neatly in front of us.

'Not yet. But we're working on it.'

'Oh well, you're still young! I know friends that had their first in their forties. When you do, you'll love it. They are a handful, I can't tell you they aren't. But they are worth every second of the aggro. It's all I wanted to do, to have kids. Started as soon as we were married.' She leant into me again, that scent of her clinging to me. 'Well, maybe just a little bit before if I'm honest. Don't tell my eldest though!' Jenny laughed and nudged me. It was all I could do to force a smile. 'I just can't live without the little blighters. But things are...' Jenny paused. 'Things change, don't they? All I know is, I need to touch up on my culinary skills. Especially now there will be another mouth to feed. My husband likes to cook and my mum, well you know mums, she was such a great cook. She could do anything with anything. That's what I want to be like, to be able to make something from nothing. Do you know what I mean?' Jenny smiled and cocked her head to one side. I nodded again, because I did know what Jenny meant, more so than she or anyone would ever be able to understand.

# 12

DAISY

The sound of the morning traffic was strangely comforting. I like to hear everyone rushing off to work knowing that I have a few free hours before I head off for my four back-to-back classes. Others might be up at the crack of dawn making the most of their time, but for me, this was making the most of it. I suppose I should have been one of those people fearful of their own company especially when time flows before you like an endless expanse and opens up opportunity for thought. Being alone with one's thoughts could be very dangerous. But somehow it didn't work like that for me. These times spent alone didn't fill me with fear or dread. I didn't sit and drag up the past or think about what has been done. You can't change the past. There is only now and I had been alone for long enough. I was a big girl. I could handle my own. When you keep all your secrets locked up so far away that even you can barely reach them, then all is well in the world. I was safe. No one knew the real me. The things I had done. The hurt I had caused. Not Ben, not Eve. And not Annie.

I was living for the present and heading for the future. I had wonderful opportunities in front of me. I had been working at the prestigious gym in town for over a year. Although I was self-employed, I would get some maternity allowance once the baby was born, and with Ben getting paid handsomely for his work on the album with this new band that were tipped to be the next Coldplay, we would do okay.

Then I hoped Ben would take some time off to be with me and the baby. The thought of being alone with a little person who was entirely dependent on me sent ripples of anxiety around my body.

Since I had been with Ben, he had begun to make me see myself properly again and I began to realise my potential. Something I had stopped realising I had. That's why Ben and I were perfect for one another. Just a few months together, but we clicked, we gelled. We were destined to be together. I had felt it in his touch the first night and he gave me a strength I didn't realise I had and I knew I did the same for him.

I watched him from my bed. He moved slowly around the room, folding jeans neatly and placing them carefully in the wardrobe, arranging paperwork, notes he had written, lyrics he had jotted down. Everything he did, he did with dexterity and a certain degree of softness that I had never before witnessed in a man. Other men before Ben had their softer sides, but there was always that obvious masculine way about them that they needed to assert; the way they would move from room to room or place objects down, all with force. But not Ben. He was tall and virile but soft and gentle. It was not something I had sought in a partner but when I met him I was drawn to him in a way I had never been with anyone before so I knew it was meant to be.

'Come back to bed.' I must have whispered loud enough for him to hear, he turned around with that yielding glow surrounding him, ready for me to take him and mould him exactly how I wanted him. He would surrender into me as he usually did. That I was certain of.

\* \* \*

Later that morning I had my bag packed ready for my classes and I sat at my laptop at the table in the lounge. Little waves of nausea pulsated around my body and I felt an over-whelming tiredness. But I needed to work. I began to check through a few emails as Ben hovered around. I had stopped asking him what the matter was whenever I saw a frown building. I had begun to leave him well alone when I could see he was somewhere far away in his mind.

Today was different though. That frown was nowhere to be seen and he looked very much in the present. He had brought mint tea and placed it in his usual careful manner slightly away from my laptop and elbow, out of harm's way but just within reaching distance. My concentration was brought from my computer to Ben's presence at my side.

I gave him an encouraging smile.

'We make a good team, don't we?' he said with a half laugh.

'I think so,' I said, wishing I didn't have to read between the lines. I had known Ben for such a short amount of time and I knew it would take a while to understand the way his behaviour could affect mine and how we could one day dance that seamless marital routine around one another to maintain harmony; meet each other's needs without upset-ting the natural balance of things. Right now, I was playing a delicate waiting game and I knew I would be for some time.

'You off to work soon?' Ben ran his hands through his hair and pushed one side behind his ears. I had noticed he was growing it even longer, probably to feel more like a rock star before he went off to record. I knew his question was rhetorical.

'Yeah, but I've got time if... you know... you need to talk.'

'You really should think about slowing down soon, Daisy. For the baby.'

I felt the surge of heat rising through me. I took a deep breath. The baby.

Then I waited for Ben to speak. I didn't want to force him to speak. I had been there with those kinds of conversations. I knew what it felt like to be trapped in a room with two pairs of accusing eyes upon me, waiting for the answers that would never come; eventually dismissing me, making me leave the room so I was out of their sight, my guilt following behind me like a heavy cloak.

I would have to let it come from him when he was ready. There was no hurry. We had all the time in the world. I knew the thoughts and secrets I harboured were packed so tightly away that they would not seep through my subconscious and disrupt our marriage. It was hard work, constantly analysing my own behaviour, but it was worth it.

'I was just thinking, about stuff.' Ben sniffed and rubbed his stubble with both hands

'Uh huh.'

'Like when you know something, but you can't be sure? Is that what you women call intuition?'

'Ha! Us women!' I sneered. 'Yeah, I guess it's called intuition. It's like a radar; a silent alarm that goes off in your body

when you think something isn't right; when danger is ahead.'
I grabbed his leg and pulled him in. 'Or in our case, when
something is very, very right.'

'Yeah.' He laughed. 'We are a pretty good match.'

'So, what's your intuition telling you today?' I tried to
sound light without dismissing the importance.

'Well, that's just it.' He placed his hands on my shoulders
and gave them a light rub. 'I just don't know. I think I'm only
just getting to grips with it, been reading a bit up on the
internet – they also call it gut feeling, don't they? Because we
have a primal connection between our brain and our gut –
they are connected by an extensive network of neurons and a
highway of chemicals and hormones.'

'Well, check you out, you've been doing your homework.'

'You know I like to read stuff.' Ben left my side and
wandered over to the large window. The part of the flat I
knew he adored – being able to have that light brought into
this room was a blessing we both appreciated.

'Yeah I do.' I took the moment as Ben's back was turned to
steal a surreptitious glance at the time on my phone. I had to
leave in five minutes. I think he knew that and he had chosen
his timing carefully; slowly introducing the idea that he was
mulling something over but knowing that we were short
enough on time that he wouldn't need to follow through if he
didn't want to. It would be parked, ready to take up again
when he felt ready. Who knew when that would be?

'I dunno.' Ben suddenly appeared less wistful 'I'll read up
a bit more about it. There's so much to know, isn't there,
about the mind and the body. I don't know how Eve does it,
where she stores it.' That was that then. Ben wasn't going to
divulge any more today. In a way I was partly relieved – who
knew what was coming? But through the pangs of paranoia, I

somehow knew it was Ben and not me that was trying to solve something. I had buried my demons, but as time passed and I got to witness more of Ben's foibles, the more it became abundantly clear how he had not even come close to putting his to bed. In fact, his had yet to be discovered and I had a terrible sinking feeling in the pit of my stomach, the gut sensation Ben had only just mentioned – for I knew I had married for better or for worse and with Ben, I felt the worst was still yet to come.

# 13

---

ANNIE

I decided to start the spring cleaning early this year. What with Christmas over and done with, I might as well start looking forward to the warmer days.

I began by clearing all the cupboards out in the kitchen. I made a right racket, but that was the great thing about living so far away from civilisation, I didn't need to worry about the noise. I could have a huge party, host a festival on the beach, and no one would bat an eye lid. People didn't care what went on here. I rarely had any contact with anyone. And I was glad of it. A remote setting was perfect for me. The less I saw of people, the better.

To be as far away from people, that was one of the tasks I had set for myself and I had done it. I had also set out to have a real family of my own. One that produced real love every minute and every second of the day. Even though I was a single mum and we weren't the family I had envisioned, I was still a mother. That was the most rewarding and special role any woman could ever hope to achieve in life. And I did it. I had to remind myself of that every day, to cover up all the other fears and frustrations. I had achieved what I had set out to do and succeeded.

Ben wasn't born here, we arrived soon after I realised the life I had been building with the man I thought I would spend the rest of my days with and I would raise my boy with, left me. Rory and I had originally lived together in a beautiful semi-detached house in a small village. But when he left, never knowing about Ben, I knew I could never raise my son there. Every crook and creak of that house bore a memory of Rory. And after he left me for good, I was practically walking around with my eyes shut and my hands firmly over my ears to avoid any reminders of him.

I remember the last day I spent in that house. The day I packed everything up and walked away for the last time with my son in tow. I was scared out of my mind. My heart didn't stop racing until I reached the beach house. For all the use my father was to me as a child, despite the lack of love he showed, when his useless cold heart packed up for good I inherited the beach house. I was under no illusions that it was an act of love, more practicality. There was no one else. Of course it would be handed down to me. It's just the way things were done.

I had loved Ben with such ferocity. I had mopped his brow and lain next to his bed through his high temperatures. But there was always the chance that one day he would leave me so callously, it was in his blood. He was his father's son.

As a child, Ben would ask the usual questions about life. Why is the sky blue? How do you get a rainbow? Can dogs laugh? He always accepted what was what. How I told him things. I enjoyed that power I had over him back then, the way he would hang on my every word. But as he grew, sentences like 'because I said so' were no longer accepted. He began to look at me differently. That look of determination grew stronger every day. I ached for the days of innocence where I could put my son to bed and know that he was going to sleep under the influence of whatever he had been told that day. Those days had slipped away too easily and the thing that was making me the angriest was that I hadn't even realised the enormity of it, until now. It was as though it was all for nothing.

It was Daisy's influence that had thrust him even more towards the world around him; towards the places that I didn't want him to go.

Ben had become independent. I should have felt proud, but instead all I felt was a twisted bitter hatred at the world that he had been taken from me, when I was the one who put in all the work, amongst all the threat and uncertainty.

I took myself off upstairs armed with window cleaner, kitchen roll and a feather duster. I began to work more furiously, the anger fuelled me, gave me the strength to reach high and bend low in one flawless sequence.

I found my way into Ben's room, as I always did at least once a day; to look around at all of his things that I wanted to keep, that he hadn't wanted to take with him. I was hurt to start with but now I was thankful that I could come and look at his certificates and remember all of his achievements, knowing I was partly responsible for him getting them. It brought me comfort during the times of the day when things were most difficult.

I got down on my hands and knees with the long attachment on the hoover and was ready to give the edges around his bed a good seeing to, when I caught sight of them out of the corner of my eye. A little round pink crystal-encrusted frame around a tiny mirror; a keyring holding a collection of three different keys. They were right in the corner by the furthest leg of the bed. Glaringly obvious to me but Ben wouldn't have seen them if his life had depended on it.

There was no way my body would fit under the bed so I had to get up, pull the bed out and reach down to get them. I held them in my hand looking at the hippy mirror keyring. Just the kind of pointless tat that Daisy would have scattered around their flat, classed as what young women called knick-knacks these days.

I held on to the keys and tightened my grip around them, feeling the cold sharp metal press into my skin; it felt strangely comforting.

Things had been spiralling out of control but suddenly, with these small inanimate objects firmly within my palm, I began to think I had a solution to the problem. I had been putting it off for too long.

I would love my son relentlessly until I drew my last breath. A relationship between a mother and son was a very special bond, but that bond was beginning to show signs of strain and I would do anything to keep it from breaking and to make sure nothing or anyone came between us.

I knew there was more to Daisy than what she projected; I could see behind the veil and it was messy and ugly. Now all I needed to do was make sure Ben and I were back together. Our secret party of two. And when we were, I would make sure I never let anyone come between us again.

# 14

DAISY

'I can't believe you're leaving us, Ben,' Eve said in a mock whine.

'I'm sure you'll be fine, Eve. A ballsy girl like you.' Ben walked past Eve giving her a friendly slap on her arm as she sat in her red Chinese silk robe at the dining table. It was her day off and her intention, she had informed me that morning, was to stay skimpily dressed all day. I stood in the lounge, cradling my herbal tea, dressed in my workout gear, ready for a class in an hour. It was the 9th of January, and all of my gym classes were packed with fresh-faced clients on a New Year promise.

I wanted to say goodbye to Ben first before he left for London where he was spending most of the week to go through all the formalities such as contracts for the album recording. It all sounded incredibly complicated so I put my faith in him that he knew what he was doing.

I smiled at Ben as he approached me for a final embrace. He gave the baby bump his usual tender touch just before I slipped from his arms.

'I'd make you some breakfast but it seems the cooker is playing up again.' I put my mug on the coffee table and ran both my hands through Ben's hair, and he responded like a dog being petted.

'I'll take a look before I go,' he said. Eve gave a splutter and a cough.

'You? Don't be daft,' she said placing her cup on the table.

'No,' Ben said firmly. 'I will.'

Eve and I looked at one another. Eve's expression was of amusement whereas mine probably resembled a lovesick puppy, overwhelmed at Ben's attempt at real domesticity.

Five minutes later Ben emerged from behind the cooker. Eve and I stood leaning against the wall of the kitchen waiting with anticipation.

'Nope. I mean, it's pretty old.' He stood up and brushed his jeans down.

'Told you,' Eve said and walked away.

'Oh, never mind, honey. At least you tried. It takes practice at these things. My dad didn't know anything about electrics and DIY stuff, but he just sort of learnt it along the way,' I said wistfully. Those sort of core memories were the ones I remembered the most.

'Well, he probably had a dad to learn from,' Ben said with a sniff.

'Well, perhaps. Anyway, cookers are tricky. Especially this ancient thing. We should leave it to the experts. I promise I will call the chap today. In the meantime, I don't think any of us should use it. We still have the microwave.' I put my arms around him, and thrust a thigh around his leg, pulling him in as close as I could with the bump between us. 'I rather liked you on the floor then, all manly and stuff.'

'Really? Is that what does it for you, cos I can do that a lot. Can't say I'll be able to fix anything,' he laughed.

'Do you need anything else before you go?' I released him and patted his rear.

'Nope. I should get going really. The meeting is at 2 p.m. Better give myself a few extra hours for rail problems and the walk from the station.' I walked him to the door. 'I'm sorry I won't be here for your birthday next week. But I'll be back two days after and I promise we'll celebrate big time.' Ben placed two holdalls next to the front door, took me in his arms and lifted my chin. 'I love you. I'm doing this for us okay? Me, you and the baby.'

'I know. And I appreciate it. I'm not saying it won't be hard. But it will be worth it when we can afford to buy our own place.'

'We'll be fine.' Ben kissed me again and then bent to pick his holdalls up. I opened the door for him.

'I shan't wave you off or I'll cry.'

'I'll call you later.' As Ben walked out of the door, I gave a small wave and closed it behind him.

The days without Ben passed fairly rapidly as I was busy with work. Ben called me every morning and evening, sent photos and even asked for photos of the bump. I eventually sent him one to shut him up.

Eve had been ill all week. One of her annual head colds. But at least it was a distraction from my nausea which, although it had subsided from all-day sickness, peaked during the morning and last thing at night. Eve moped about the flat with a box of tissues under her arm and I made her microwaved chicken broth and Lemsips. Soon enough Friday had arrived and despite her perpetual blocked nose and headache, she was unbelievably still badgering me about my birthday, which was three days away.

'So what are we going to do? Ben is away. We should have a party. It's Friday 13th! We should go out. You're turning twenty-nine on Monday, Daze. This is epic.' Eve was buzzing around me in the kitchen as I made lunch.

'No, turning thirty is epic. Turning twenty-nine is pretty boring and not something I wish to think about. Ben isn't here and I don't fancy doing anything until he gets back.'

'You're really boring.' Eve huffed, stuck out her bottom lip and blew her nose.

I looked at her and let out a sigh. 'Fine. We'll eat supper. Early.'

'Supper? I can't smell or taste anything Daze.'

If I was going to be dragged out on my birthday while pregnant, I wanted to eat delicious food first. 'You'll just have to watch me enjoying it.'

Eve pulled her mouth down into her best sad expression.

'Fine, I'll get takeaway and then we'll do that cocktail bar.'

'Okay, do you think they do a honey, lemon and ginger cocktail? I can wear that new dress. This is so exciting. See, you haven't abandoned me for married life.' Eve danced around me.

'I never had any intention of abandoning you, Eve. I'm still the same person. You'll see when you and Patrick make it official.'

'I'll never marry Patrick.' Eve stopped dancing and gave her nose a triumphant blow.

I grimaced. 'And does Patrick know this?'

'Not yet.'

'I thought you guys were like, solid. I presumed you'd be moving in with him, you know, when the baby comes. I know we've not discussed it, but...'

'It's fine, Daisy, of course I'm not going to make you move. Of course my room will become the nursery. I've already started looking. I'll make sure I'm gone in plenty of time for you to do all your nesting.'

I hadn't had any such instincts. I actually wanted Eve to stay, for everything to remain the same.

'And well, me and Pat, we're fine as far as two adults in a dating relationship go, but no. He's not marriage material. I need someone who will sort me out, put me in my place a bit.'

'And Patrick doesn't do that?' I was genuinely surprised.

'No way! I enjoy the thrill of a relationship where I have the power. But I won't want that forever, no way. I wouldn't make a marriage out of that.'

'Okaaaay.' I nodded 'That's fine. It's just news to me. I figured you and Patrick were, well, never mind. I know now.'

'So, we'll go out tonight?' Eve was standing in front of me with her hands pressed together in a prayer fashion.

'Yes, we'll go out tonight.'

'Yippee!' Eve squealed and ran out of the room. I heard her head into her bedroom and leap onto the bed. Twenty minutes later she emerged dressed in a short, black, tight-fitted, long-sleeved dress. She stood in front of me and twirled around. I eyed her up and down and rested my gaze on her feet.

'You're wearing my shoes.' I pointed down at the red shoes she was wearing, the ones I had in mind to complement my own outfit but doubted my poor swollen ankles could handle them.

'I know. Don't they look a-maaa-zing.' Eve continued to twirl and I couldn't help but smile.

That evening we left the flat, Eve dressed in my red high heels and her little black dress, me in a more sensible floaty number and flats. Aside from the fact I was exhausted, I had that fuzzy feeling in my stomach that something was brewing and it could turn in to a very interesting night.

* * *

'Come on then, I'll get the first round in!' Eve whooped and the barman looked at us with a small smirk, used to this sort of clientele in a town which hosted hen and stag parties every weekend.

'Well, okay then. Two of your finest cocktails barman.' I slammed my fist down on the bar. Now I was out, I fancied just one drink. One drink was fine. It wouldn't do any harm. I observed the way the barman took a moment to eye me up. I gave him a wink and threw my arm around Eve. 'My friend is paying.'

'Erm, well, I was.' Eve held her handbag and shoved her hand in deep whilst she screwed her face up. 'I definitely put my purse in here.' Her face changed to one of enlightenment. 'No, I remember, I took it out to buy something online earlier. I think I left it behind the chair in the lounge.'

'Oh yeah yeah! I see, drag me out here, to make me pay. I know your game,' I said, looking at the barman jovially.

'No no, I'm not trying to pull a fast one. I'll nip back and get it, Daisy. It's my treat. I promised.'

'Don't be daft. Pay me back later.' I yanked my bag from my shoulder and began rooting for some notes.

'No, honestly. Pay for these, enjoy. I'll be back in five minutes.' Eve turned to walk away.

I turned too, feeling an urge to grab my friend sternly by the arm and demand she stay and let me pay, but I let it fizzle away. I shrugged and turned back to the barman who was wearing a smarmy look, thinking he was now in luck. He was completely oblivious to the fact I was sporting a wedding ring and pregnancy belly which I must have done very well to disguise with my floaty dress.

He intermittently tore his glance away to focus on mixing and pouring the drinks and then would look back at me with a glint in his eye. I watched intently. I always enjoyed the artistic display of a cocktail being prepared, especially when the barman making it was so easy on the eye. I laid out two notes as the barman simultaneously presented the cocktails in all their cloudy multi-coloured glory.

'Keep the change,' I said as I picked up the drinks and sashayed my way to the nearest table.

It was almost an hour later that I finally tuned into my intuition. I had been chatting to a couple of Italian artists who were in town for a commission piece down at the seafront. One had finished off Eve's drink and had bought me another – this time I carefully opted for a mocktail – and all the while I was thinking about Eve. When Eve gets back, she will love these guys, we'll all have a drink together and Eve will impersonate the smaller one's accent and funny walk. When Eve gets back, everything will be complete again. But that hour of conversation came and went and finally I gave in to the nagging doubt that was building at the back of my mind and excused myself to call Eve. When it went straight to answerphone, my first thought was: daft cow, she's probably chatting to Ant. Ant was the bouncer at the club at the bottom of our road and whom we stopped and spoke to most evenings we went out. Then I got irritated. It was typical Eve behaviour to abandon me randomly, but it was not okay on my birthday. Not when she had organised and pleaded with me to come out. I threw my phone back in my bag and walked straight out of the bar, ignoring the raucous calls of the Italians behind me.

I hugged my arms around myself. The heat of the bar was a stark contrast to the icy January night air. It didn't occur to me to pay particular attention to the sirens echoing around the streets. It was a common sound and one I had become accustomed to hearing in my dreams. But as I turned the corner to the road that led to the hill where our flat was, the sirens became louder and I could see a vision of flashing reds and yellows. I could see Ant. He was waving at me. No, he was trying to get my attention. I quickened my pace, adrenaline filling my body. I wasn't sure what was happening but as I approached Ant, who was usually expressionless except for the mechanical movement of his jaw as he chewed his gum, I could see his brow was strained and his mouth was parted.

No chewing.

The club was directly at the bottom of the hill which led to the flat. Ant was talking, I couldn't hear what he was saying. I looked up the hill towards the flashing lights and crowds of people that were being herded backwards by firefighters. I could see flames and smoke. So much smoke that it was beginning to coat the back of my throat even as I stood at the bottom of the hill.

I spun around to hear the siren right behind me. An ambulance careered past me and swerved into the road and up the hill. It stopped next to the fire engine and crowds of people directly outside the building. Our building. Ant's arm was around me as he escorted me up the hill. I was presented before a fireman who took me aside and starting saying things to me which didn't make sense. 'Serious accident... explosion... tried everything we could...' There was a lady, perhaps a paramedic. She offered me a cup of water and tried to put a blanket around me. I tried to walk away, my mission was to get to the flat. Why was everyone getting in my way? I needed to find Eve, that was all. But I was grabbed by the arm and pulled back just as a stretcher was carried from the smoking building. A black material covered a body and I had a sudden urge to retch. I crouched down – or was I on my knees? I wasn't sure. There was a dull pain in my legs and I saw there was blood on my hands as I struggled to get back to my feet. But even as the two firefighters carried a body right past me, I still thought to myself, it was all going to be okay.

# 15

ANNIE

The thing about my son is that I love the bones of him. It's an instinct I thought I wouldn't ever experience and so when he came into my life, all I wanted to do was keep him all to myself because of the way we were deserted and let down. I tried so hard to make him feel loved with all the things I did, cooking and cleaning for him. So when someone else came and stole him away, and I didn't hear from him, it made me feel abnormal; like everything had been tipped upside down. I don't like disorder. I like to know what's what.

One thing I have learned is that you have to seize every moment that is drifting past you in this ever-changing life. There's no point waiting. It will only pass you by and then you've lost out.

Everything happens for a reason, there's no denying it. Take Ben, for instance. He came to me at a time when I thought nothing else good could happen in my life.

I know when someone is telling bare-faced lies, there's something about their demeanour, it's a slight shift in their body as they stand or a stutter in their speech, it's a twitch of the eyes to the left; searching for the truth that was never there. I've seen it all. Everything has to come to an end and her time is well and truly up. Those lies, all that covering up and pretending she is someone she isn't? I don't need to worry about it any more. Soon it will be as it was. Just me and my son.

# 16

DAISY

I hadn't felt that numb feeling for so many years. I didn't know this time if it would pass. Perhaps it wouldn't. Perhaps I would need drugs to make me feel something, to give me a lift. Or to just take me to where Eve was. Even easier. I didn't want to think about minutes, hours, days from now and how I might feel. Whatever was going to happen I knew it was going to be long, it was going to be painful and I was going to have to go through it without Eve. From here on in, every-thing would have to be without Eve. It didn't make sense. Not yet.

Ben opened the door to the incident room where I had been sat alone for... minutes? Hours? I didn't know. They had questioned me briefly, but nothing too heavy. I doubted that they thought I did it. I didn't care. They could lock me away and throw away the key.

Ben didn't say anything. He fell to his knees and threw his arms around my waist. His shoulders were shaking. I placed my hands on them and rubbed them. I found a strange release in giving comfort to someone else. As though my own loss was suddenly irrelevant.

'Shh,' I heard coming from my mouth. He was wearing his black leather jacket and I inhaled the familiar scent of him, mixed in with something foreign, brought from where Ben had been for the last few days. He pulled back and stood up then sat on the chair next to me. The blanket I had had on since nine o'clock last night had slackened and Ben pulled it back up and over my shoulders.

'I don't know what to say, Daisy. If you want to talk, then go ahead. If not, then I'm here anyway.' Ben paused and looked at me. Then he continued, speaking in a slow quiet voice. 'The guys excused me. From the meetings. I understand the protocol, signed all the relevant paperwork. They understand. I think they liked me, it's fine...'

I thought how it was funny how even in extreme cases, people carry on saying the most mundane and normal things.

'She's gone, Ben.' I interrupted Ben's ramblings. My voice sounded croaky. I didn't recognise it as my own. Ben put his arm around me and pulled me towards him as much as my limp body would allow.

'I don't know how, Daisy. I just don't understand. I don't know how this could have happened.'

'Me neither. It makes no sense. One minute she was with me in the bar and the next minute, she's dead!' I spat out the last word.

'You don't have to, but if you want to tell me...'

'I don't know, Ben, they're talking about an explosion of some kind. We won't know anything until a full investigation has taken place and... an ...autopsy.' My head fell into my hands. I was silently crying but then a small laugh found its way out, and then I was laughing louder. 'A fuckin' autopsy Ben! We used to laugh about that all the time, whenever we watched *Silent Witness* or, what's that other one called...? I don't know any more. Eve would joke about it... we would laugh about them waking up in the middle of it...' I trailed off.

'We should get you out of here.' Ben stood, walked to the door and poked his head out, looking either way along the corridor. 'Hi, yes, excuse me – can I borrow you for a sec?' Ben held the door open as a policewoman came into the room. 'Can I take my wife home now?'

The officer, who was tall with brown hair tied into a neat ponytail, spoke softly.

'You are absolutely free to leave, Mrs Cartwright.' She turned her attention to Ben. 'There is the issue of a formal identification.'

'Oh, right erm, I don't really have anything, babe, have you got your handbag?' Ben walked back over to me. I looked at him through blurry stinging eyes.

'What are you doing? She means Eve, you idiot.' I heard the manner in which I spoke and I felt as though I were witnessing someone else entirely. Ben appeared sheepish. The police officer looked down at her feet.

Ben tried to speak quietly as if I would not hear. 'I don't think she's up to the job.'

'That's fine, we've made an attempt to contact some family members,' she said in a hushed tone as though I wouldn't notice.

'That's pointless,' I interrupted. 'Her mother is a raging alcoholic, her dad is a complete couch potato and wouldn't get off his fat arse if it was on fire, which under the circumstances, is quite apt really.' The policewoman and Ben glanced uncomfortably at one another. 'And her brother is somewhere shooting at the Taliban, so really, it only actually leaves me.' I looked at Ben through red stinging eyes. 'And she would want me to do it Ben.'

'Well, I'll do it with you and if you know... you feel you can't, then I'll be there.'

'I'll be fine, I'll manage.' I stood up and the blanket dropped to the floor. 'Can I go now please?' I addressed the policewoman who quickly cast her eyes down to my belly then back to my face.

'Yes. Of course. I'll see you both to the front desk and I will give you the directions to the chapel of rest. It doesn't open for another few hours. There's an all-night petrol station just around the corner, you could grab coffees from there until it opens at 9 a.m.'

Once outside, Saturday morning had begun to greet us with a pale grey sky. Ben offered an arm around me which I neither accepted nor declined. He walked stiffly next to me until we reached the car, which Ben had collected before he came and got me from the police station.

'Daisy, I've called my mum. We're going to go and stay with her.' Ben delivered the news with an edge of wariness. He opened the passenger door and I barely nodded and got into the car. Ben walked around to the driver's side and got in. He looked at me. 'You don't have to do this, this identification. They can find someone else, they can look at her driver's licence for fuck's sake.'

'I'm doing it, Ben. She'd do it for me.' I felt the weight of Ben's stare as I turned to look out of the window.

* * *

I smelt death as soon I walked into the chapel of rest. So grimly distinctive was the smell of a body that had rid itself of a soul just a few hours earlier, I was tempted to turn around and leave. But I could feel Ben's hand squeezing my own so tightly that I feared I would never be able to release myself from his grip in order to run.

The coroner told us the procedure for viewing and said we could look through the window or enter the room. Ben went to speak and I shook him away, certain he would try to convince me that staying behind the screen and viewing Eve like an antique piece of jewellery was the better option. I walked towards the door and carefully opened it, fearful at what I may find, even though I knew that the lifeless body of my beloved friend was the only thing waiting for me.

The cold hit me, along with the smell and I rested my eyes upon a high bed where Eve lay with a blanket tucked right up to her chin, as though she was a bodiless puppet.

They had told me to expect the damage the fire had done to her face, but underneath the red streaks of exposed flesh I could still see the familiar outline of my friend's jaw, her hair-line, and those protruding luscious lips.

The noise came next. Loud and animalistic reverberating around the small icy room. It was a sound so unrecognisable that I didn't realise it was coming from me until Ben caught my weight when my legs crumbled beneath me.

'I just knew it would be too much for you and the baby.' Ben leant across my chest and clicked my seatbelt in.

'How did you get back from London so quickly?' My voice was grainy and low.

'The guys, they chipped in for a taxi. Cost £200. There were no trains.'

I gave a feeble nod. Then I felt it, two small but firm kicks. I knew this was the moment I was supposed to share with him, to take his hand and place it on my stomach so he could feel the life of his unborn child. But I let the moment pass. I looked past him out of the window.

'Just drive, Ben,' I said croakily after a few moments when it seemed that Ben was still leaning over me and watching me as though I were a pot of water about to boil over.

Ben pulled himself out of the car, slammed the door shut and walked around to the driver's side. Once we were out of the car park and driving along the road, he spoke again.

'We haven't got a home any more, Daisy.'

I looked at Ben. I nodded and blinked out the tears.

'But it's okay.' Ben touched my knee 'We'll be fine,' he said almost jovially. Then, as though he realised that his last statement probably sounded incredibly lame to me under the circumstances, he added, 'But I know things will never be fine, nor will they be the same again. I'm so sorry, Daisy. I don't know what to say... but in time you will know how much I love you and how much I am here for you. I promise I will do whatever I can to get us through this.'

'Stay.' I spoke softly. I wiped tears from my cheeks and looked at Ben. 'Don't leave again to record the album. I can't bear to be alone.' I began to weep. My shoulders shuddered. 'I just can't bear it, Ben.' Ben pulled the car over, unbuckled his own belt, leant right across and took me in his arms. He didn't answer me but his silence spoke volumes.

# 17

ANNIE

I was watching at the window when they arrived. The sun was just coming up. I hadn't slept all night. I was overwhelmed with tiredness and my anxiety levels had peaked. But I would have to try and bury those emotions so I could be the mother Ben needed me to be.

I pulled the curtain back another inch when I heard the tyres of their car crackling along the end of the gravelled driveway. I released the curtain and rushed down the stairs to open the door ready to greet them.

It was so strange that yesterday would bring so much revelation and tragedy at once. It was just terrible what had happened last night at the flat and I was only thankful Ben was in London at the time. Above all the terror in his voice, I heard how much my son needed me.

I greeted them at the door with a pained expression and a blanket. As Daisy walked through the door, I placed the blanket around her shoulders like I had seen on TV programmes. I was sure it was the right thing to do under the circumstances.

'When Ben said you had been out and about last tonight, I thought you might not be wearing much so I had this ready for you. I've run a bath and I've put some of Ben's old pyjamas on his bed for you. Come and sit down, you two. What a terrible shock for you both. I have brandy. Who will have a brandy? Ben?' I ushered Daisy through into the lounge as Ben obligingly removed his coat and hung it up on the peg as he always had done. All the while, I eyed Daisy, her presence ever more apparent.

I observed them uneasily as they settled themselves in the front room then I excused myself to fetch refreshments. I arrived back a few moments later with the tray I had prepared ready for them.

'I shouldn't imagine caffeine will affect you trying to sleep, I expect you are both beyond exhausted, so fill your boots.' I placed the tray filled with coffee and brandy and biscuits on the coffee table. 'I have plenty of whatever you need. It was so cold last night, wasn't it? Not much better today. Have you seen the frost out there? I don't know how you could have gone out in that weather. I suppose though, in a way, it was a good job you did.' I felt Ben's look hit me before I saw it. 'I'm just saying, son. It was very... lucky.'

'Mum. Not now.' Ben sat down on the sofa next to Daisy and poured two brandies. I watched as he handed one to Daisy. Interesting how they wanted my brandy now, but they weren't willing to stick around for more than twenty-four hours over Christmas and enjoy it then, when it was supposed to be enjoyed; when it really mattered.

Ben downed his brandy and then stood and walked to the window.

'It is cold though, I think it might snow,' he said as he nudged the curtains with his finger. 'Best not to drive anywhere over the next few days. I heard reports of a storm.'

'Oh, you know me, son, first sign of bad weather, I'm tucked up like a hermit. You wouldn't catch me driving anywhere in this cold.' As I spoke, my hand found its way into my trouser pocket and I curled my fingers around the cold metal of a circular mirrored keyring.

Daisy downed her brandy in one then flopped back into the sofa, her eyes staring intently at the ceiling, as though she could see something we couldn't. I pulled my hand out of my pocket

'If you need anything to help you, Daisy, you know, I have a vast selection, painkillers, sleeping tablets, the works. Just let me know.' I went to the opposite sofa and began to plump the cushions. I thought about these two people in my house, how it should only be Ben and me. Everything was off-kilter. As I moved along the sofa to the rest of the cushions, I felt metal shift inside my pocket and the slight sound of keys clinking.

Daisy reached forward and poured herself a second glass of brandy and I watched Ben's lips open to speak, then he closed them again. It only took a few more seconds to see that both shots of brandy had taken effect.

'I need air.' Daisy stood too quickly and Ben lunged to grab her. I began to pace the room feeling redundant.

'Oh son, this is terrible. Just terrible. Poor Daisy. What will we do? You have some of your things here still, son. I told you it was wise not to take everything with you.' Ben pulled Daisy into him, his strength and stature still surprised me sometimes. As he walked towards the door, he gave me a weak smile.

'Thanks Mum.' Just then I was reminded of the little boy

that would come home from school, famished and worn out, ready to be looked after by his dear old ma. 'Come on, let's get you some air.' He ushered Daisy forward.

I followed then both into the hallway. Daisy had lost her blanket somewhere between the hallway and the sofa so Ben grabbed his leather coat and put it around her. I saw the devotion that accompanied the action. Something stirred deep within me and I had to look away.

I sucked in my breath at the cold breeze that shot through the hall as Ben ushered Daisy outside. 'It's very cold son. You'll both catch your deaths.'

'We'll be fine, Mum.'

When they returned a few minutes later I was still standing there, not caring how it looked. I knew I had a purpose now.

Ben took his coat from Daisy and hung it back up.

'Should I get more brandy?' I asked, knowing I needed to at least look like I wanted to be of more help.

'I'm going to bed,' Daisy said with no emotion or tone to her voice at all. It sounded almost digital.

'Okay, I'll take you up.' Ben guided her up the stairs as I watched from the bottom.

I was hovering around the bottom of the stairs ten minutes later when Ben arrived back, as though I hadn't really left. I had plumped the cushions where Daisy had been sitting and hand washed the glasses, then I had taken up my post again by the first step.

'I don't expect you to look after us, Mum. I have my job,' Ben said. I followed him through into the lounge. 'I'll rent us a little place. The insurance money will come through and we can start to rebuild our lives. Don't feel like we are imposing. We are not. This is very temporary.'

I followed him through into the kitchen.

'Don't be ridiculous, son. I care about you.' We both stopped near the kettle. I laid my hand on Ben's wrist. He looked down at it then moved away to the table where I had left the brandy bottle. He poured himself a glass and paced with it. He seemed to be muttering to himself, but I couldn't quite tell. When he finally stopped, he looked at me. Not just at me, he looked at me as though he was looking right through me into my soul.

'Mum?' he said, with such an emphasis on the question that I was sure he was about to say something profound.

'Yes, son?' Then I waited, three, four, five seconds or so for him to speak.

'I'm going to bed.' He put down his empty glass on the table.

'Oh. Okay, son.' He went to walk past me. I put my hand out and caught his arm. 'Son?'

He stopped and bent his six-foot-one stature down towards me and allowed me to give him a little peck on the cheek; an act I had been doing for as long as I could remember. I watched him leave the room and I heard his heavy feet on the creaky wooden stairs. How I had missed that sound. I picked up his glass and cradled it.

I could have been stood for a while that way, for in my mind I was off somewhere else entirely. I was with Ben, we were walking through the park, his little podgy hand in mine. He had asked for an ice-cream. He had already had a bag of sweets that morning and usually I wouldn't have given in but there was something that resonated in me in his tone of voice that day; the way it went slightly up at the end of 'Mum' when he asked me could he have a white one with a chocolate stick. My heart thawed like the cold creamy substance on his little warm tongue. We walked together from the swings to the van, all the while Ben had his eyes firmly fixed in front of him, never wavering or stumbling once to point out a bug or an obscure-looking rock. When we reached the van, I leant down and Ben repeated his request too close to my ear; his voice broken and breathy in a manner which some mothers find endearing. I relayed his message to the server, still not ready to insert any independence into him, then looked on curiously as he consumed the confectionary in one tidy action – such a quiet, neat boy. I couldn't have hoped for a better behaved child.

The memory of my son as a perfect child momentarily faded as another memory filtered through. One from not so long ago and one that was of vital importance. Right now, there was a threat in my home. I had to admit, initially when I got the call from Ben, I presumed the worst had happened. But in fact the worst was here and sleeping under my roof; homeless and looking to me for support.

He said there was some sort of explosion. Girls are so silly and irresponsible these days. Not thinking about anything except their hair and make-up. No home sense and certainly no safety sense. Neither Daisy nor her silly friend had any of the instincts I carried with me daily.

With the two of them comatose by copious amounts of brandy and therefore safely out of my way for the foreseeable, I went to my bedroom. I felt a tingle in my stomach as I brought the box down from the shelf at the top of my wardrobe and took it over to my bed. Its presence under the circumstances was even more precious. It looked like it was once a vibrant duck egg blue colour but was well faded. I can't remember what it once held, but there was a darker blue spiral pattern that ran around the whole of the box giving it a regal affect and hinting that it once was the carrier for something rather precious and beautiful. Funny how what was inside now didn't bear quite the same splendour.

I carefully lifted the lid off and turned my attention to what was inside. I glanced at the stacked papers I had been collecting for weeks and thought how I now needed these more than ever. I lifted a few pieces of paper from the top, and my stomach did a double flip as my eyes scanned hurriedly across the contents once more for what could have been the hundredth time but each time felt brand new.

Things don't always go to plan; we don't always get what we want. Like the woman sleeping upstairs in my son's bedroom. I did not want her here. But I knew for sure that everything was going to work out because I had before me exactly what I required to make sure my son never wanted to go within a mile of that deceitful woman ever again.

# 18

DAISY

The next two days passed in a haze. I knew I spoke very little because when I did my lips were cracked and my throat was dry. I was sleeping a lot. One day rolled into the next. Each time I woke I would ask Ben the same thing. Was it a dream?

'No, my darling,' he would tell me as he stroked my head and I would feel my stomach tighten and my toes curl as a rush of adrenaline hurtled though my body. I would look at Ben – the blame didn't lie with him but there he was, the only face I could see, the closest person to me, and I felt an overwhelming desire to lash out. But it was fleeting before once again exhaustion overtook me.

Ben seemed to be carefully keeping Annie away. I could sense her lurking in a doorway and then I would hear tense whispers as her shadow followed her footsteps away.

He had soldiered on without me these last few days – I knew he had spoken to Patrick several times and it was Ben who had broken the news to him. I tried to imagine Patrick's crumpled face when he realised he would never see his beloved Eve breathing, laughing again. Even now, just a few days later, the regret at not telling Patrick myself, along with all the other tiers of guilt imbedded within me, lay heavy on my chest.

On Monday the police arrived at the house. Ben had been lying beside me – the position he had adopted since we arrived – waiting to perform a duty for me however small. Last night Annie had given me some tablets. They were just what I needed. I took one, and I had taken another an hour ago. I wanted to prolong this feeling of nothingness that they provided me with. We both heard the crunch of car tyres on the gravel as I was hovering between sleep and consciousness. Ben swung himself from the bed in one swift flawless movement.

'Coppers are here, Mum,' I heard Ben say at the bedroom door as Annie came scurrying past.

'What? Why?'

'To speak to Daisy. They called me yesterday.'

Annie made her way aggressively into the dark room and pulled back the curtains, an offensive stream of light flooded in. I let out a groan and began to sit up.

'Mum, what the... for Christ's sake.' Ben took Annie firmly by the arm and escorted her from the room then half-kicked the door to and approached the bed.

'You don't need to get up – you don't need to do this today. I can turn them away,' Ben said.

I looked at Ben, my head rolling from side to side, my eyes heavy from the drugs. 'No Ben, I'll do it.'

\* \* \*

They arranged me between two large cushions on one of the sofas and I looked around the room. I heard the voices of the police constables, but their words moved out of sync with their mouths. I started to imagine I was in a TV show and the sound hadn't caught up with the images. But this wasn't TV, was it? This was reality. Wasn't it?

'Ah, well, that's service,' said the burly constable with a goatee beard as Ben handed him a steaming mug of Annie's finest blend of coffee. His walkie-talkie that was attached to his shoulder, crackled and beeped and a woman's voice came through. He twiddled a knob and her voice faded.

'I'm only sorry it can't be with a smile,' Ben said as he perched on the end of the sofa I was sitting on and part of me wanted to laugh loudly at the bizarre way in which the comment fell out of his mouth.

'I know. We're so very sorry for your loss. It must be a terribly uncomfortable time for you and... your wife?' said the woman constable.

'Yes, my wife. We're married.' Ben reached for my limp hand and squeezed it too hard.

'Hello, Daisy,' the woman said brightly. 'I'm Police Constable Jones and this is Police Constable Burns. How far gone are you?' She motioned to my stomach. I made no effort to reply.

'She's almost six months,' Ben spoke for me. I sat up with some effort. Ben leaned over to assist but I shooed him off. Jones waited for me to get comfortable as she took a pen from the front pocket on her chest.

'Mr Cartwright. We're here to talk to you about the death of Eve Parker?'

'I can answer your questions.' My voice was scratchy and crackly.

'Let me get you some water.' Ben picked up a glass from

the coffee table and handed it to me. I took a sip and handed it back to him.

Burns cleared his throat and sat forward on the edge of the sofa. 'We're so sorry for your loss, Daisy. I understand your husband here had recently moved in with you?'

'Yes. That's right,' I croaked.

'And how long have you known your husband, Daisy?' Burns continued.

'Six... six months.' I heard the meek manner in which the line was delivered I never failed to feel a slight flutter of shame, admitting to strangers the foetus was as old as our relationship.

Burns seemed unperturbed and continued. 'We have the results of the post-mortem Daisy and they show that Miss Parker died of a blunt trauma to the head, now—'

'What? What does this mean?' I interrupted Burns. I could feel Ben squeezing my arm.

Burns carried on, unperturbed. 'We are yet to establish how it occurred and why. We're here because we need to get as much information from you as we can. We have stayed away for as long as we possibly could, giving you time. We want to eliminate any other possible reasons for her death. Once we get the full report back then we can make the best analysis of what exactly happened.'

I looked at Ben, trying desperately to make sense of what I was being told. Burns shifted on the sofa. He addressed his notes in front of him, licked his finger and flicked over the page.

'Were you and Eve close, Daisy?' Jones intercepted with a warm voice. I tried to focus on the woman in front of me. Her hair was alarmingly straight and tied neatly back in a pony-tail. Her lips were a rich red but surely she wasn't wearing lipstick? I was reminded of a shade I had at home that was called Ruby Woo. All the while her dark red lips were moving the words Ruby Woo kept falling through my head. Jones looked at me. Those lips taking on a form of their own.

Ruby Woo... Ruby Woo... Ruby Woo. Then a shocking thought struck me. I didn't have that lipstick at home, there was no home. It was burnt. Everything gone. I imagined my Ruby Woo, melted, the plastic outer casing dissolved to nothing. Those lips were moving again. I wondered if Jones had her Ruby Woo in her handbag. I looked down at her feet, of course she didn't have a handbag. She was a policewoman. Perhaps the lipstick was in one of the many pockets of her uniform, more than likely it was in the car...

'Daisy?' A female voice filtered though. Red matte lips were moving. Ben was up and coffee was being handed to me. A biscuit appeared. I bit into it. It was a golden crumble one with a soft sweet vanilla cream in the middle. It was very tasty. Very sweet. I took a sip of the coffee. Strong. Wet. Was coffee always this wet? I licked my lips, there were crumbs on them. The crumbs were dissolving on my tongue. Then things were happening around me. People were moving, standing up. Jones was gone. It was just Burns. He was slurping his coffee loudly, Annie was fluttering around the sofas, Ben was saying something to her, and she sat down in a chair that was slightly away from the sofas. I could feel her eyes on me. Jones was back. She rubbed her palms on her trousers and Ben was saying something to her. She picked up her pen; began writing something.

'Eve was a wonderful, beautiful human being. Inside and out. There is no way she would have ever done anything stupid. She was a bit reckless from time to time, rebellious even. But she was a psychologist, at the prison, for the prisoners.' I could hear the words. Had I said them out loud? Jones was still writing. No one was looking at me, could anyone hear me? Jones looked down at her notes in the palm of her hand. Such a small notebook. Barely bigger than her hand.

'Yes, we have that information here. You say she was reckless? Did she have any enemies? That she might have made as a result of her recklessness, perhaps?' She was talking to me.

'No, you misunderstand, she wasn't reckless, and I didn't mean that.'

Jones turned her attention to Ben.

'Do you have home insurance, Daisy?' Burns asked bluntly.

'Yes,' I said too quickly through a dry mouth.

'And you, Mr Cartwright. Where were you on the evening?' Jones looked down at her notes. 'From our initial discussion three days ago, you were away in London. But on that evening, you had returned to the hotel room. Alone.'

Ben looked down at me. 'Erm, yes. I was tired after a day of meetings, so I went to bed.'

'But you were back in town pretty sharpish when you heard the news,' Jones said without question.

'Of course. I had my phone on silent, but I woke in the night and saw the missed calls from Daisy. I came as soon as I could.'

'So what time would you say you arrived back in town, Mr Cartwright?' Jones continued.

'I can't really remember now. It was late, 3 or 4 a.m. maybe?'

'So what time did you leave London?' Jones' persistent tone caught my attention. I looked up at Ben with concern.

'I got in a cab sometime after midnight, 1 a.m.? I don't really remember.'

'So if you were asleep when you missed her call, you must have been in bed by what? Ten? Ten-thirty? That's rather an early time for a musician to go to bed on a Saturday night, wouldn't you say?' I looked at Ben, hearing the enormity of her accusations. I could see what was happening, but it was unfolding like a well-rehearsed drama, as though it was scripted.

'Look, do you mind? My wife has just lost her best friend...'

Jones closed her notepad. 'We understand that, Mr Cartwright, but there are some issues we need to iron out here. We can ask these questions at the station if you would prefer.' Jones raised her eyes and cocked her head in the direction of me. Ben looked at me.

'Yes. Yes, let's do that,' he said and stood up. Both Jones and Burns stood as well.

'What? What's happening?' I asked through my feigned ignorance. If this was what was happening then there was nothing I could do but let it. Ben took both of my hands in his.

'Let me just go and sort these queries out at the station, babe, and I'll be back home within the hour.'

'Actually, it will probably be a lot longer than that, Mr Cartwright. We need to go back to the station in town,' Burns said. 'That's a good hour and a half's drive there and back plus the interview time.'

'Fine, whatever,' Ben said over his shoulder. He kissed me. 'I'll see you in a while.'

I suddenly found strength and with Ben's help I left the sofa. I noticed Annie hovering in the doorway in my peripheral vision. I followed Ben and the constables to the door. Jones handed me a piece of paper.

'Here's the full post-mortem report Mrs Cartwright. You can probably call your doctor if you need assistance with any of the medical terminology.' I absentmindedly took the paper from her and glanced down at today's date that was glaring at me. 16th January 2008.

'Daisy, I'll see you soon,' Ben called over his shoulder as he took his jacket from the hook next to the door. I watched as the three of them walked away from the lounge to the front door. I summoned the strength to see them out. The wind was whipping wildly outside the porch. I took a step back and watched them head to the car. Perhaps the drugs were beginning to wear off or it was the sharp intake of sea air, which ever it was it caused me to shout to Ben before he disappeared into the car.

'Ben!'

Ben stopped just before the car and turned. I stepped outside onto the porch and hugged my arms around myself. 'Today is my birthday.' My voice was strained and I almost laughed at the absurdity of the words. How could we possibly celebrate anything, especially a birth, when someone I loved so dearly would never celebrate another birthday again?

Ben opened his mouth to speak but no words came out. Instead he offered me a pained expression and held his hands out in surrender of the situation that had literally taken him hostage.

I stood on the doorstep and shivered as I watched all three of their heads disappear into the car, feeling empty that no more words were spoken. But I knew there were no more words left to say today. And certainly not ones with 'happy' in the sentence.

# 19

---

ANNIE

Something had shifted in my world. Everything was different. In a strange way everything felt right. I knew my son was grieving and that he was probably experiencing some kind of pain that I wouldn't be able to relate to right now, but despite the circumstances, I felt glad. Glad that the woman who was responsible for creating such drama and hurting so many people, was lying down upstairs, weak and scared and vulnerable. Glad that my son had come home and now the time was right, I would use all the evidence I had to bring her down from her oh-so-very-high horse she had been residing on with my son so close in tow.

Soon everything would be as it once was.

Ben trundled into the kitchen. He looked tired. He had spent too long at the police station yesterday. It was night-time when he came home. I made him some soup and tried to get him to talk, but he barely said a word – instead he had finished his soup and then taken himself off to bed.

I heard him arrive behind me, the familiar scuff of his

shoes on the hard floor. He had been outside smoking a cigarette.

'Take those shoes off, please,' I said as I wiped the kitchen surface. I heard the tone in my own voice and I felt something inside tug, a warm familiar feeling. Here we were again, the two of us, as though those months of him not being here had never happened. Those subtle sounds of him arriving and leaving a room that had become the very fabric of our existence had stopped overnight and left a gaping hole.

In just a few days I was getting used to his smells and his sighs and his clanking around in the kitchen looking for something to eat. And slowly everything was falling back into place.

'Daisy's sleeping.' Ben went into the cupboard and pulled out a jar of coffee. He turned and shook the jar in my direction.

'Er, yes son, coffee would be great. Sleeping, you say? Do you feel like doing something today? With your old mum.'

Ben filled the kettle up, replaced it on its base and flicked the switch. He then busied himself with adding sugar and coffee granules to his favourite large brown mug; never removed from where I always hoped he would return one day to reach for it.

'I've got to keep an eye on Daisy. You know, make sure she doesn't veer off...'

'Veer off?'

'Yeah, you know?'

'No, son. I don't.' I finally turned to face Ben and saw his pent-up expression.

'Well, she lost her best friend and everything she owns is in smithereens. She's hanging on by a thread right now,

Mum. And you know, she's six months' pregnant. I need to keep a special eye on her.'

I moved to the fridge with a cloth and began wiping stray crumbs from the shelves. I let the tight feeling in my stomach disintegrate. There was time, just be patient. Ben dropped the teaspoon into the mug with a loud clash of metal on porcelain.

I heard Ben pouring boiling water into the mug, stirring it and then putting the spoon down on the kitchen surface. I didn't hear him make a second cup. I could feel the coffee seeping from the teaspoon into the work surface and staining it. It was something he always had done. I should have picked him up on it ages ago, but there had been years of removing those teaspoons from the counter. I had learnt to swallow down the frustration because I wanted Ben so much and to have him in my life was nothing more than a miracle. I had Ben and I would always be thankful for that.

But today I felt the rage of anger bubble up inside me – why was he still choosing her over me! I felt the urge to rush at Ben and throw his head against a kitchen cupboard. How could he have been so stupid, so naïve, as to get with a woman like Daisy? The deceit, the lies? But he was too tall and strong for me. I would have to make do with the only other weapon I had. My words. I had held my tongue for too long.

'You barely breathed a word about her until you were... married!' I spat the word out as though it were about to sting me in the mouth. I looked at Ben with disgust as he stood casually sipping his coffee. 'Now here she is licking her wounds, nursing her grief in my bed, under my roof. You barely know her for god's sake, son!'

'Oh right, so that's how it is, is it? I knew as much. This is why I never told you about us. You're so... precious! You don't own me! If you loved me, surely looking after the one I love shouldn't be a cross you have to bear?'

I sighed. 'Oh, son, you have so much to learn from life. Well, you have Daisy now, so you can simply wash your hands of me, can't you? But just remember, when it all comes crashing down, who are you going to turn to, hey?'

'What do you mean? This is ridiculous. Why are you so concerned with us? You barely even tell me anything about my own life. That's no fairy tale by all accounts. Where's my dad? Why did you not want me knowing him?' Ben asked with pain in his voice.

I felt my hand rush to my head and I began to fuss with my hair.

'Why are you asking so much of me today, Ben! You know it's hard for me to talk about such things. It was so hard for me back then, all alone without your father.'

'Exactly,' Ben threw his hands up 'Who is he? Did Dad have an affair? Is that why he left us? Can you tell me that? If he didn't do anything wrong to me, surely I have the right to know!'

'Ben! Son!' I moaned. 'Don't do this. Don't do this.' I fell into a chair at the kitchen table, weighed down with the past.

'This is what I mean!' Ben placed his coffee cup down with a force. A small amount of fear penetrated me. I had never seen or heard Ben act this way before and for a second, I wondered what he might do. He was a strong man like his father and I knew what atrocities his father was capable of and therefore it wouldn't surprise me if it was in him too. But I couldn't tell him that. Even after all these years and having not spent any time with him; blood was blood.

'This is what you do. As soon as I start to ask questions, you fall apart!' Ben shouted.

I threw my hands over my face 'Oh, son! Is this what being with Daisy has done to you?' I pulled my hands away and looked at him. 'All this doubt? All these questions? You were a good boy once. Kind, quiet, considerate. I did everything to protect you, can't you see?'

'I'm a man now, Mum, you can't keep treating me like I'm a baby. There are things I need to know! And if you won't tell me, then I will have to go and find out for myself. You really have left me with no choice.' Ben walked towards the kitchen door. I jumped up and ran up behind him. I had fought so hard to keep everything so perfect for us, it couldn't have all been for nothing. Yet here he was, a grown man, and my son was turning on me.

'Ben!' I called after him and he stopped in the doorway. 'Ben. I love you!' I said, my voice breaking, trying to force the words out – sometimes they didn't come naturally.

'Well, is that enough?' The words came from Ben and hit me like a bullet in my chest, but I knew I had the ammunition to fight back.

I took a deep breath. 'Ben, is Daisy sleeping?'

'What?' he snapped. 'Yes, why?'

'Good. I have something I want to talk to you about. I think we need to sit down.'

'Oh right, now you decide you're going to give me the big reveal, tell who my father is? He's not some murderer, is he? Is he in prison?'

'Ben stop, this isn't about your father. This is about Daisy.'

'What? Daisy? Why?' Ben was getting more agitated.

'Because son, she is not who you think she is.'

'Why are you so intent on telling me that Daisy isn't good

enough for me? I've known all the time you don't like her. Why are you choosing now to unleash your hatred when you can see how much we are both struggling with what has happened to Eve, to our home, our lives?'

'Because, son, none of those things would have happened to you if she had been honest with you from the beginning because, believe me, you would have run for the bloody hills. Daisy would be a distant memory and you would still have your piano, your guitars, your clothes, your song lyrics...' I could see the pain flash across Ben's face. He hadn't said as much yet but I knew the grief he was carrying was not all for Daisy and her friend, but also for his own personal belongings; the words he had written down. He was an old-fashioned soul never using a computer or making copies. Those words were lost. Years of work burnt in an instant. Never to be seen or read again.

'Son, please sit down. I promise you I am doing this because I love you, not to cause you more pain. I just need you to know that the woman upstairs, you think you know, is nothing but a fraud. We don't need to give her the time of day let alone shelter her through her grieving. These are her losses, not ours. We are one, son, you and I. Daisy, she is... someone else entirely, not like us. Sit, please. Hear me out. You will understand when you hear what I have to say.'

Ben shook his head, he pushed past me and pulled aggressively at the chair and sat down. 'I'm here, Mum, but I swear whatever ludicrous thing you have to tell me will not change my feelings for Daisy.'

'Okay, son, wait there.' I scuttled up to my bedroom. I stopped by Ben's room on the way to make sure Daisy was still sleeping. She was. Those drugs she so freely took from me were doing the trick nicely.

As shocking as the contents were, they were my key to happiness again. I left the box in the bedroom at the top of my wardrobe and cradled just the papers.

I arrived downstairs and laid the contents in front of Ben.

'Now, son, take a look at this and tell me that you know your wife and that you love her. Go ahead, take a good long look.'

Ben began flicking through the papers. I knew it would take a few minutes for him to piece the puzzle together the way it had for me, so I waited patiently for the penny to drop and when it did I could not stop the feeling of joy that spread through me. I watched Ben's head fall in his hands, sickened and shocked by what he was seeing.

# 20

---

DAISY

If it wasn't for the dawn chorus of the birds and the high pained shrieks of the seagulls outside the window every morning I would not know if one day had ended or another had begun. The trills and high whistles had become part of my waking ritual, as I had been asleep by 6 p.m. each night and woke naturally with the rhythm of nature.

Every day that passed I imagined Eve, and what she would look like now. How the natural decaying process of death was taking her piece by piece. As each day passed, I tried to claw it back, filled with despair because that time had already lapsed and despite my hardest efforts to imagine myself back with Eve over a week ago, there was no turning the clock back. Each day I woke with the heavy regret laying hard on my chest. Why didn't I stop Eve from leaving the bar? I had felt that pull to keep her with me. It was a brief moment, but it was there, that gut instinct that Ben had mentioned to me not too long ago. Now I thought how odd it was that he would be talking to me about such a thing, as though he could already sense something coming. I was in tune with my body. I too felt those gut instincts, yet for some reason, that night, I pushed it away.

And not for the first time in my life either.

Sometimes I wondered what the point to life was if you never learnt from your mistakes.

I let Eve down. For every piece of advice she had given me and every day and night she had been there for me with a wink, a smile, a joke, a song, or just a look, that said, I'm here for you, I will always be here for you, I couldn't be there for her when she needed me the most.

Eve was all I had. That was it plain and simple. I didn't seek out others at uni, I just saw her and she saw me and we had a conversation about a song they were playing in the cafeteria and that was it. I didn't let anyone else in. I never have done since. I turned down offers of work nights out, uni get-togethers, because I never once met anyone else I could connect with in the same way as Eve. I suppose now in hindsight I should have invested more time with other people who showed an interest in me. Then I wouldn't feel as alone. Of course I have Ben, but we've known each other for such a short space of time, I'm still figuring him out and vice versa. And then the baby will come. But it will need me.

Eve and I had over a decade of friendship. I would have to wait a long time to get that with Ben.

As I shifted to a comfortable position, something about this morning felt different. I was always pretty comatose by bedtime so I wasn't ever aware of Ben getting into bed, but as I lay my hand on his side of the bed, it felt cold. He had either got up very early or hadn't slept in there at all. It wasn't unusual because Ben was a thinker – a night owl. He would often stay awake long after me writing down his lyrics or watching a film for inspiration. But what was unusual was that he hadn't left my side since the explosion. I sat up and pulled my hair up into a bun on top of my head with the hair band I kept religiously around my wrist. There was a sharp pain in my head. I was dehydrated.

The stab of anxiety had already hit my stomach. Like clockwork it happened within ten seconds of opening my eyes. Those first seconds of consciousness, although deceiving, were the respite that I would take, no matter how short. I always let those waking moments lull me into security and make me think that everything was going to be okay, that I would wake and be able to face the day without feeling the depression creeping around my body. Only this morning, Ben's disappearance bought me an extra few seconds of solace as I was swept up in wonder. I looked at the bedside table. There was a glass of water and two tablets, left there by Annie probably. They looked a slightly different colour from yesterday but I couldn't be quite sure. Annie had assured me they were for the shock. She got them from the internet and they were not the sort of things the doctors would prescribe in this country. Normally I would question such things but all I wanted was to feel numb and they did just that. I put them both in my mouth and took a big gulp of water. For only a moment I let in thoughts of the developing life within me as I swallowed the strange tablets.

I padded across the hall in my pyjamas bottoms and T-shirt and made my way downstairs, my hand rested on top of my bump, the other against the wall for balance.

The cold downstairs bit at my arms and as I arrived into the lounge I could already see the oversized shape of Ben on one of the sofas; a large brown fleecy blanket covering him up to his chin.

I took a moment to steal a glance at the window; the

curtains hadn't been shut from last night. Or perhaps Ben had opened them. The waves were thrashing against the wall at the end of the garden. I could see a tiny dot of a boat on the misty horizon.

I walked to the edge of the sofa and knelt next to him. 'Ben,' I whispered.

'Uh... what?' Ben sat up.

'Shhh, it's okay.' I laid a hand on his chest. 'It's early. I just wondered where you were. You didn't come to bed?'

'I'm going to get a shower.' He stood up quickly and headed upstairs. I didn't have the energy to feel displaced by his behaviour.

By the time I made it upstairs I could hear him in the shower so I went to the bedroom to wait for him.

Despite the cold outside, I opened the curtains and the window an inch to let in some air. A fresh salty breeze hit my nostrils and I took a moment to gaze out to sea, I tried to decipher the ocean from the horizon but it was still too misty and barely dawn. I tried to feel something from the vast stretch of water just outside the window that went on for miles, as though it had no end. I could hear the waves through the small crack in the window. Such a simple and familiar sound.

Ben came into the room as I was settling myself back onto the bed which I had straightened out so it looked a little more inviting, rather than the tangled mess I had woken up in half an hour earlier.

'It's freezing,' Ben said and shut the window. I watched him dry himself and put on a pair of jogging bottoms. Ben had popped out a few days ago and picked up basic sport casuals for us. I heard Annie greet him at the top of the stairs and tell him to keep the receipts for when the insurance money came through. This sentence had been used many times already and I wasn't sure at what point I would drop the bombshell that Eve and I never once took out home insurance.

I had lied to the police.

Who lives their life with a sense of impending doom? Those were Eve's words. Apparently, we should have done. For it was certainly how I would live my life from now on.

I looked at Ben now as he was dressed and he had an intensely sad look in his eyes.

'I don't know what to do any more, everything is a mess.'

'I know,' I said.

'I know you've lost Eve, and I need to be here for you, but I have to go, Daisy. I have to go. If I don't go, I will lose the job. If I lose the job it will kill the career I have been working towards all my life. This is my one and only opportunity. If I lose it, that's it. You don't get a second chance in this industry.'

My heart started racing and I tried to swallow but it felt forced. 'So you're bailing? Five minutes in and you're bailing? Jesus, Ben, I thought you were here for me. This is it, for better or for worse. This is the worse and you can't handle it.'

Ben approached me, took hold of my shoulders and looked me directly in the eye. 'I'm not bailing. I have to go.'

'What?' I whispered barely able to understand what was happening.

Ben stepped away from me and rubbed his face in his hands.

'Who are you, Ben? I mean, you sweep into my life all melancholic and mysterious, not knowing what you want from life, always with that look in your eyes as though... as though, you haven't got a bloody clue what is going on?' I could feel the rage building and I continued. 'And then the police? What's with the police, hey? They drag you down to the station for seven hours and... and for what? You won't even tell me what they asked you? And then I get to thinking, Ben, that day at the flat, you with your head in the oven? We already know what happened here when you were a kid with the fire, I mean... would you? Is that your bag? Starting fires? Would you do something like that? Did you even care for Eve? Do you even love me...?'

Ben looked over at me. His eyes seemed ever darker with the shadows underneath. His stubble had grown into the beginnings of a beard. His hair was longer. Everything about him, down to the way he glared at me, was unrecognisable. He opened his mouth to say something, then closed it and simply shook his head. He pulled on a hoody and headed for the door. He paused and walked back towards me.

'Daisy. I have to go. I'll be back before the baby is here. I promise you that.' Ben leant in to embrace me but already I could feel something was missing. I pushed him away. He looked at me for a few seconds then walked out of the door. A part of me felt pure hatred for him right then, but another part of me ached to follow him out of the door and fall into his arms.

Instead I slumped down on the bed and soaked in the emptiness. Before long I felt weary again. I lay down on my side. As I did the baby began a short spurt of acrobatics. I felt the movements for a few minutes then closed my eyes.

* * *

I opened my eyes. Something had woken me. I was thrust from a dream where the echo of Ben's voice was all around me in the room still and it sounded as though a crash and thud had brought me to. I leapt up and looked out of the window. It was lighter now, the sea was less rough and was gently lapping at the shore. Further along the shore I saw a woman and a small dog walking along the shingle beach.

I walked downstairs, poked my head into the lounge. I called once.

'Ben? Annie?' I couldn't see or hear anyone.

I walked back into the hallway, and found the keys to my Renault. It was still early, barely 9 a.m. I felt a knot in my gut at the prospect of stepping outside, realising I hadn't done so since before, when everything was normal; as it should be. Where my life seemed once to seamlessly roll from one day into the next, it was now jagged and uneasy. Every breath or step I took came with an acute sense of awareness, as though I might break at any moment.

But I had an overwhelming urge to leave the house. To be somewhere, anywhere other than here. The last few days had been a mass of frustration and heartache. But most of all, I now doubted my husband, the man I had married for better or for worse. I realised I didn't know him at all.

I pushed the keys into my trouser pocket and headed for the door where I put on the plimsolls I had always kept in the car for when I had to drive and I was wearing heels. I instinctively grabbed Ben's thick blue winter cardigan which was hanging on a hook by the door and wrapped myself in it.

Forty minutes later I pulled up outside mine and Eve's flat. I looked up at the windows, which were broken. A thick grey smudge framed each one. I opened the car door and stepped out. There were yellow police banners plastered across the window, some had fallen away at one side and now hung there like discarded party streamers.

I closed the car door and began walking tentatively

towards the building that I once lived in with my best friend
and husband. As I got closer I could see a figure hovering by
the wall, looking at an array of flowers I hadn't expected to be
there. As I got closer I recognised the burley stature.

'Hi, Daisy.' Patrick raised his head slightly. He spoke softly
and without surprise. He was hunched over a bunch of flowers, reading a small card. He wore a heavy long black coat
and as he stood, he pulled it up around his neck. I mirrored
his behaviour by pulling the cardigan I had borrowed from
Ben tighter around me and the mound of baby inside of me.
Patrick motioned towards the flowers. 'I was just looking at
some of the things people had written. She was very popular,
our Eve.'

I bent down to a squat. Something that would normally
feel comfortable, today felt like hard work. I dropped to my
knees.

'I come here every day. I have done, since last week when
it happened. I have a bereavement counsellor, he said it's
called 'searching'. Common when, you know, someone,
goes... suddenly. Like our Eve did. He told me we find
ourselves returning to the spot where a person died. Hoping
to find something. Hoping to find them. That's what he told
me anyway. I suppose that's what you're doing, isn't it?'

'I... I don't know. I just came out for a drive and found
myself here.'

'Well, that sounds about right. Are you speaking to
anyone? A counsellor?' Patrick's tone was so matter of fact, it
felt as though we were strangers.

I brushed a piece of hair away from my mouth then
picked up a small blue teddy. There was no card attached and
I was overcome with wonder as to who would have left it. 'No,
no one. I've got no one,' I said, then realised the true enor-

mity of what I had said. Ben had gone. I knew it when I woke the second time. I had felt the echo of his presence. The words that I had said to him were still ringing in my ears.

'Well, you might think about it after the funeral. A week today. It seems like forever. But then afterwards time will fly by and this will all be... well, in the past.' Patrick remained together, focused. As though he was dealing with Eve's death like reading a textbook, whilst I wanted to curl up in a heap among the bouquets. I looked up at Patrick. He had lost weight and his face looked sunken. He reached down and helped me to my feet. We both stood looking at the floor for a few moments.

'Did she... did Eve ever...?' I looked up at Patrick and I could see his withdrawn cheeks flushing with colour. 'Did she talk about me much? About us? How do you think she... saw our future together?' Patrick looked at me with his mouth pulled to one side. He shoved his hands firmly into his pockets 'Cos, I know what you two are, were, well, like sisters really. You spoke about everything, I suppose.'

I felt my heart sink even further even though I didn't know it could, as I recalled the last conversation I had with Eve about Patrick.

'Well, she, you know... I can't remember.' I watched Patrick as he nodded his head and turned back to the tributes.

'Of course. I understand,' he said softly.

'I'm sorry.' I felt the rush of sadness and I put my hands over my face, trying to hide from Patrick who seemed so together.

'Hey, hey.' Patrick took me in his arms. Even though there wasn't much difference in height between the two of us, I felt Patrick take my weight and I felt safe and protected. I recognised the scent of his aftershave as the one that always lingered in the hallway long after he had come in and been escorted into the flat. I missed Eve. I wept and my shoulders shook. I didn't know how long I had been standing there in his arms, my mind racing with thoughts of Eve. Then it occurred to me, this was why Eve was with him. Patrick was caring, giving, strong and protective. Of course she was never going to leave him. She probably would have moved in with him for sure and even married him one day. Eve put on a front, but she had stayed with Patrick for over three years, which was a record. I remembered what she was like before he came around; she always made sure she was immaculate for him and I saw what they were like together as a couple. Eve may have not wanted to believe that Patrick was the one for her, but I could not imagine it any other way. I eased myself out his firm grip, to look at Patrick's face that couldn't hide the bitter sadness.

'She adored you.' I began. 'She couldn't wait for you to come over and hang out and she would always take that extra bit longer in the bathroom when she knew you were coming over. And she talked about you often, with fondness. Real fondness. She never slagged you off or called you all the stuff we women like to call you men. She genuinely loved you, Patrick. You would have had a very happy life together.' I felt relief. The last few days had been messy and fractured. I struggled constantly to hold one sane thought in my head. And now I felt I had said something that truly felt as though it made sense. Something real that would help ease Patrick's grief if only by a tiny per cent.

* * *

We had been sitting for over an hour, Patrick and I, with take away coffees from the café at the foot of the hill and we had left, both agreeing to keep in contact until the funeral. Apart from the support that it would bring, we had to converse between now and then as there were readings and flowers to arrange. Patrick would cover the cost; he had been adamant on that.

As I got into the car my thoughts were brought back to Ben and our argument. Despite the comfort Patrick had brought to me, I couldn't push away all the nagging feelings within me. Eve's death and my words to Ben. What had I meant by them? Was I truly blaming my husband for my friend's death? I sat in the car and mulled everything over and over until I began to feel dizzy with it all. But the uneasiness crept back and lingered long after I left and began the drive back to the beach house.

# 21

ANNIE

I heard the crunching of stones under rubber tyres and stood close to the door, waiting for her to enter. She opened the door and immediately I could see she looked terrible. Her eyes were bloodshot and red all around. She looked frozen having only been wearing Ben's cardigan. When I went to speak my voice was more controlled than I had anticipated.

'Daisy. Where on earth have you been? I have been...' I needed to say anxious, worried, but I couldn't force the word out of my mouth. 'The baby, Daisy, you need to be thinking of the baby. My grandchild. Come in, let me get you something warm to drink.'

Daisy closed the door and removed Ben's cardigan.

'I just need to lie down, Annie,' she said and made for the stairs.

'Okay,' I called after her. 'You just let me know if you or that little baby need anything.'

\* \* \*

A few hours later, I headed upstairs to perform my usual rituals of making sure all windows were shut having given the house sufficient airing, it was now time to warm the house for the afternoon and evening.

As I approached Ben's room I peered around the bedroom door. Daisy looked as though she were asleep. I approached her bedside on tiptoes. I should have stopped and caught my breath outside the door as my breathing was now laboured. Daisy stirred and moved under the duvet.

'Annie.' Daisy's voice was croaky from sleep.

'I was just coming to check on you. Do you need anything?'

Daisy pulled herself to sitting.

'Erm. No. I'm fine. I think.'

I watched as she began the religious act of tying her hair up with the band she kept around her wrist. Mounds of thick yellow hair, swiftly and confidently wrapped up into a bun on the top of her head.

'I will probably get up soon. I thought I heard his voice a little while ago.'

'Who, dear?'

'Ben's.'

'You know Ben has gone, don't you Daisy?'

'I... I thought he would wait... say goodbye'

'The taxi came and took him. He couldn't wait apparently.'

Daisy turned to look at the window where the curtains were open just a crack. I could see the tears welling in her eyes.

'Daisy' I began. 'You know as well as I do that you never really knew Ben. Think of everything that has happened:

marriage, a baby, a fire, losing your friend and home. How do you think that affected a simple soul like my Ben? Hmmm?'

Daisy didn't say anything, she just sat staring out of the window.

'Sometimes, Daisy, knowing too much about someone too soon is a recipe for disaster. Do you know what I mean?' I looked at Daisy and wondered if my words would impact her. They didn't. She was in shock. I looked around the room. It needed a hoover and a dust whilst I thought about it and there was a musty smell lingering. I looked at Daisy who was the centrepiece to the disgusting mess all around her.

I began to frantically pick up some clothes of Ben's which were lying at the end of the bed.

Daisy made a half attempt to lean over and retrieve a sweatshirt that was clearly not within reaching distance.

'Just leave it, dear, I'll do it. You need to save all your strength for you and the baby.'

I stood up straight and looked at Daisy who was eyeing me suspiciously. I knew I'd had had little to say about the baby until now – the whole seedy affair had disgusted me, the way she had got herself pregnant so soon – but with one parent absent in body and the other in her mind, it was my job to step up and be the grandparent that this child needed me to be.

'You're a guest, Daisy. You just stay put and don't worry. Everything is going to be just fine.'

I looked on at her curiously as I stood there with my arms full of clothes. I felt the irritation rise inside. Then I felt something familiar and I realised why Ben had fallen for her, because even in her depths of grief, the girl managed to look like a figure of elegance.

## 22

GRACE

At the second cooking lesson, Jenny was there as usual, in her place with Mikee by her feet. I watched Jenny from across the room; she was chatting animatedly to Emily whilst Mikee clung to her legs. I was captivated by her beauty but also at the prospect of having a friend. Someone I could call upon and vice versa. I had never had any sisters or brothers and just being near to Jenny made me feel something. She gave off a beautiful aura.

I looked on longingly. First at Jenny in all her golden splendour, then at the pair of them, mother and son; a tangled mess of love. I was lost in my admiration of her when suddenly Jenny was enthusiastically waving me over.

'Grace! Yoo-hoo!' As I approached the two women my eyes were once again drawn to Mikee and then to a large bruise that circled his cheek bone. I gasped and Jenny shot me a look.

'It's okay, he's just been falling over again, haven't you Mikee?' Jenny said with a reassuring tone and a wink at

Emily. 'Emily's got three boys at home, haven't you? Anyway, how are you, Grace? How's the cooking going?'

I nodded. 'Yes, good thanks, Jenny.' I placed my bag down under the counter and turned to the sink behind me.

'I must get on,' I heard Emily say as she went and took her place in front of the class. When I could see that Emily was out of earshot, I turned to Jenny as I dried my hands. 'So he got that bruise from falling over, did he?'

She looked down at Mikee who was pushing a car around on the floor. Jenny furrowed her brow and bent down and busied herself with straightening his jumper. 'Yes. He's very clumsy. He's not three until August. Boys, hey! You'll see, Grace, when you have children.'

I could sense the rawness of the subject, for I was a pro at brushing over things that didn't beg to be talked about, and decided not to mention it again. But I knew that boy didn't get that bruise from falling over. I understood the balance of power between adults and children. And the children always lost.

I arrived at her counter and wiped my damp hands down my apron. I smiled at Jenny and picked up the paperwork in front of me. I took a surreptitious peep under the counter at Mikee. He gave a cheeky grin. He looked happy enough.

I thought about the child Jenny was carrying and what sort of life it might have, born into a house where it wasn't wanted, with a father who had a temper and a mother who scuttled around covering it up all the while.

## 23

DAISY

I didn't know my husband. I had begun to understand his foibles and his awkward ways that sometimes disrupted my psyche, but that was a marriage; there had to be give and take. What I hadn't really known was what something so serious this soon into our relationship would do to Ben. I knew he had a tender soul and that he got affected by the world, so in hindsight I should have been prepared.

I knew I had broken us. I knew by blaming Ben for Eve's death, I had forced him away. We weren't strong enough to survive this. A baby, a marriage, Eve's death, not to mention Ben had lost everything in the fire. It was too much for one relationship to take so soon. But as I sat alone on the edge of the bed on the morning of Eve's funeral, I wasn't prepared for the sadness that engulfed me. Our relationship had barely done any mileage. Together we hadn't attended friends' weddings, had a holiday, weathered the storms of a marriage, waded through the tribulations of life. This tragedy should have been one we faced side-by-side. But it was too soon for him, as Annie often reminded me – he wasn't built for this kind of distress. I felt the lack of his presence hard.

I looked at myself in the mirror. Red was a colour that didn't do anything for me at the best of times, but now at almost six months' pregnant, it made me look hideous. But I was doing it for Eve. My sweet, funny Eve. But now that grief was muddled with my loss of Ben. There were moments of panic – what if something had happened to him, what if he was in trouble – but these just subsided when I remembered my parting words to him and what I had accused him of. Then there was the pain from losing Eve that kept rushing to the surface. And somewhere still within me, I had a nagging feeling that I didn't know the whole truth. As much as it filled me with complete despair to think my husband, Ben, the man I loved with such raw emotion, could lie to me, the doubt would not subside. There was something he hadn't told me. I was too familiar with how much strength it took to cover up the lies. And I could see it all too clearly in the man I thought I knew.

But today, I somehow had to compartmentalise it or I would fall down. I boxed it away, ready to deal with it after the funeral. My feelings for Ben were nudging me every now and again throughout the day, forcing me to ask myself the obvious questions, where was he, why hadn't he called, why would he say he had to leave so suddenly after Eve's death? But today my focus had to be with Eve, and saying goodbye to the most precious friend I had ever had.

Out of the speakers came the lyrics 'Read My Mind' by The Killers and all around me heads were turning. Smiles came through faces of tears and I watched as Eve's friends and relatives, felt the same mix of emotions that I was having. Suddenly the song, which had rapidly become Eve's favourite last year, took on a whole new meaning and I knew that from then on whenever I heard it, it would remind me of the day they cremated my best friend.

Once the coffin had arrived at the front of the room where about sixty people were gathered to pay their respects, I took my place at the front, next to Patrick. I glanced across to the other side where I saw Eve's mother sitting. Her shoulders and head were hunched over, and her arms were shaking as though she had no control over them. Her lank dark hair was long and hung around her face. She looked thin and malnourished. Her splash of red, as was the dress code for Eve's day, was a crumpled red blazer over a white shirt and un-ironed black trousers.

The humanist took her place at the lectern and welcomed the congregation. Just the mention of Eve's name under these circumstances didn't seem plausible and I felt the hot heavy tears coming. I felt a strong arm around my shoulder. It surprised me and for a sudden moment I thought Ben had arrived. I turned to my left and patted Patrick on his knee. He wasn't Ben, but it was a comfort.

I had opted not to speak as it felt too raw and, besides, I could already hear Eve's protests and see her rolling her eyes before I allowed the idea, suggested by Patrick, to embed itself in my head. Patrick read a poem, something about trees and wind, and it hardly seemed appropriate. Not very Eve. But then right at the end, he said a few words that were special and seemed to hold some meaning and I was thankful. He held it together well until just at the last moment his voice broke. I felt my body tense and wanted to reach out and grab him. Patrick cleared his throat, apologised and stepped down from the lectern.

As everyone left the chapel after the service, they each placed the white rose they had been given at the beginning on the coffin. I waited until last and Patrick and I slowly laid ours down together.

When I felt Eve's mother approach and touch me on the back, I jumped slightly.

'Thanks for being there for her all these years.' Eve's mum spoke with a lisp; I noted she had a few teeth missing. 'She looked up to you, you know.' She patted Patrick on the arm, casually tossed her rose onto the coffin and clomped unsteadily out of the door. Patrick and I gave one another a compassionate look. We both knew how hard Eve's mother's life had been and how Eve had struggled. It was inconceivable how a woman like Eve, so vivacious and confident, could have been born to 'a woman like that'. But neither of us had ever made judgement. For whatever had happened in the past, and in whatever way she was doing it, today a mother was saying goodbye to her child.

The reception was a blur. Sandwiches and crisps were passed around at the pub close to the cemetery. It felt wrong. There was no link here to Eve. It was simply convenience. The look of the bar staff and waiting staff suggested they did this at least once a week. All of Eve's favourite songs were playing in the background and images flashed up on the pull-down whiteboard of: Eve when she was five, Eve when she had graduated, Eve and Patrick huddled together in a tent at Glastonbury, Eve and I on her cousin's hen night wearing willy-shaped head garments. I walked from table to table. I chatted to people and they felt inclined to touch my growing stomach and comment on the life forming within me as we celebrated the end of another. People made small talk, no one mentioned the fire. No one talked of death, or where Eve was now. Everyone was careful not to slip into conversation about how Eve's body would be burning to a small pile of dust as they all sat and sipped their lagers and limes and chatted about the fact that 'at least the weather held off.' No one mentioned that that was that, Eve was gone and they would never see her again and how that in itself was the saddest thing that could have ever happened.

When it was time to leave and there were a few remaining bodies floating about the pub, taking advantage of the free drink, I approached Patrick who was leaning against the bar. I placed one arm around his waist. I was familiar with the feel of his body and it felt comfortable to do so. I laid my head on his chest, feeling the fascination at the new, sudden closeness I had adopted with my best friend's boyfriend.

'You did so well today, Pat. Well done. Eve would have been so proud of you.'

Patrick rubbed my back. 'Funny cos the only person I've wanted to see all day, to talk about it with, is Eve.'

I flipped my head back and gazed at Patrick. 'I know exactly how you feel.'

\* \* \*

It didn't seem right that Patrick and I should go our separate ways at the end of the day. Even though all I wanted to do was sleep and I imagined Patrick wanted to do the same, it seemed ludicrous that we should do it under separate roofs thirty miles apart on today of all days.

Patrick booked a car, and we wearily said our goodbyes to the bar staff and climbed into the waiting black taxi with its loud chugging diesel engine. Neither of us spoke a word on the journey back to Patrick's flat. There were no words that seemed at all appropriate. I was carrying a weight of disbelief and I knew Patrick was feeling the same. The word 'lost' is often used when referring to someone dying; people will regularly say 'I lost my husband' or 'I lost my mum.' I had lost Eve, yet lost was also exactly how I felt as well. We drove away from the pub that had no association with Eve yet all the while I felt a tug to return there. As though I wasn't ready to give up the day.

The taxi pulled to a halt outside the block of ocean-facing flats. Even in the low light of the taxi I could see Patrick pay the driver with several notes more than he needed to.

At the communal door Patrick gave a thin smile and motioned for me to lead the way to the second floor.

'I was going to go and try and get my old classes back tomorrow. I know it's probably too soon and everything but I need to do something. Now the funeral's over, there's an empty space and it's getting wider every minute. I need to start filling my life with something, or I know I will go mad. I can't sit around on my arse not doing anything. And I know it's a bloody cliché and I just hate myself for saying it, but it's what Eve would want.' I could hear the tired tension in my voice as I rambled on, casually walking around the lounge. Suddenly I felt very conscious of being here, alone with Patrick, having only ever been here with Eve. I eventually stopped my pacing and slinked into a spot on the sofa next to the sunken pit where Patrick obviously had a penchant for the area slightly left of the middle.

I let my head fall against the back of the sofa. Patrick sat down carefully next to me, his rear neatly filling the spot. Silence filled the space around us.

Patrick spoke first. Slowly and carefully. 'I'm going to mourn her good and proper.' He began. 'That's what Eve would have wanted me to do anyway. She said so once. "I hope you will grieve properly for me if I die. I don't expect you to get out of bed for a month". Didn't expect it to actually happen though, did I? Now I have to fulfil her wish.'

I smiled both at what Eve had said, as I could visualise her saying it the way Patrick mocked her voice, and also at the prospect of Patrick setting up camp in bed for a month on his dead girlfriend's wishes.

'I see you have supplies.' I nodded at the bottle of brandy in front of us on the coffee table.

'Ah yes, a gift from our girl. She gave it to me at Christmas. I was saving it for a... well, like you do. Course, those days never come. I've realised that now. Every day was special with Eve. Every moment a celebration.' He looked at me. 'I'll make you a herbal tea, shall I?'

I nodded and let Patrick's words hang for a moment, hating the reality of them. Hating that time couldn't be reversed and how we should have lived a little longer in those moments; felt them a little harder.

'It's nice in here. You've made it really cosy. I've not been here for a while,' I called through to the kitchen where I heard the kettle starting up. I looked around at several pieces of modern art hanging from the wall. There was a large red fluffy rug that spread the length of the room. Also, a small electric faux fireplace in the corner which Patrick had switched on when we arrived.

There were two framed pictures of Patrick and Eve on the small table next to the sofa and one on the coffee table. I imagined that Patrick had been looking at this particular one a lot recently as it looked out of place sitting amongst the coasters and books.

I liked the feel of Patrick's place. It felt like home. It felt like Eve.

'I can't take credit for any of it. Eve did all this.' Patrick pointed around with one hand as he handed me a steaming mug of peppermint tea. He clicked on a small black wireless radio, instantly soothing orchestral sounds escaped the tiny speakers and punctured the too-silent room.

'I like to listen to Classic FM,' Patrick told me as though I would question it.

'I miss music,' I said.

'Oh, how so?'

'Annie doesn't play music. I only heard carols at Christmas, from a record player. She has no TV, no radio. It's very quiet. I mean, in a way it's nice but I need the distraction of music.'

'Take that with you then.' Patrick gestured to the radio. 'I have another one around somewhere.'

'Thanks,' I said.

'It's really very Eve in here, isn't it' I looked up at the Oriental fabrics hanging loosely in sections from the ceiling.

'Sure is. Thought she was going to break her bloody neck trying to attach those things. She loved to take a risk.' Patrick looked at me. 'You don't think she did anything stupid that night, do you? To cause the accident?'

I immediately shook my head. 'No I don't. She was popping back to get her purse. That was all. What could she have possibly dreamt up to do that would have caused her death?'

'The explosion, that's what killed her.'

'Yes, the explosion.' There was panic in my voice, the blame was bearing down hard on me. I thought back to a few weeks ago when I had promised to get the cooker fixed.

'Well, they pretty much said so, Daisy. They can't completely be sure, but it's the only plausible reason. How much have you been told? I know you've been out of it a bit. Best way, I say. But I've spoken to the police. I've had my own liaison officer.' Patrick gave me a sympathetic look. I felt ashamed for being drugged out of my head for the last fortnight whilst Patrick carried on dealing with everything. 'But she might have been trying to do something. With the oven?' Patrick continued.

'I know, Patrick, I know.' I needed him to stop speaking about that night. I couldn't think about it. I cast my eyes over the bottle of brandy. 'Can I just have one glass? For Eve's sake?' I pleaded. I needed something to take the edge of the anxiety.

'Yep. Why not,' he grunted as he lifted himself from the sofa. 'I'll get some glasses.'

\* \* \*

Patrick got stuck into the bottle too easily, I cradled my one glass making every mouthful count whilst we chatted and reminisced about Eve. Every now and again I would cry and Patrick would instantly put a hand out to comfort me, seeming to refrain from showing any emotion himself. He must have been hurting, but the years at an all-boys school had taught him to hold everything in.

Patrick poured himself another glass. I swirled the dregs around my glass then took the final mouthful, letting the warm liquid trickle down my throat. I looked at Patrick. His eyes were sparkling in the low lighting of the room, his cheeks reddening from the heat and alcohol. His face looked more appealing with the weight he had lost over the last few weeks. He was watching me intently. I smiled self-consciously.

I held his gaze for a moment then held my empty glass out to clink with Patrick's. 'Here's to us and to getting through today.'

Patrick clinked my glass. Then he stood up and took me by the arm. I looked hesitantly at him. Patrick seemed to morph into a competent sober man in front of my eyes.

'Come on, I will show you to my finest suite, it's in the west wing. I changed the sheets just yesterday.'

I let myself be escorted but protested. 'Patrick, I couldn't. The couch is fine.'

'Me and that couch have spent many a cosy night together. Besides I could sleep in the kitchen sink tonight and I wouldn't know the difference, whereas you and that baby need a proper bed.' Patrick opened the door to his bedroom. There was a musky smell of deodorant that had been sprayed many hours previously, but besides that there was a perfectly comfortable-looking double bed. On the bedside table was another framed picture of Patrick and Eve.

'Do you think Eve will mind?' I said as I edged my way into the room, already looking longingly at the bed.

'She wouldn't have it any other way. Now in you get. You

need a straight head on you if you're going to try and do any business tomorrow.'

'I miss her,' I said as I felt my face crumble.

'I know. I know.' Patrick put his arm around me. 'It's so damn hard without her.'

I wiped my eyes and blew out a breath.

'You know sometimes, Daisy,' Patrick spoke soberly, 'I think I loved her too much. I mean if that's possible. I know she loved me and you said how she felt about me but I loved her furiously, with so much passion, sometimes I had to conceal it because I feared I may damage her.'

Patrick kissed me on the head, then turned and walked back to the lounge, leaving me with his parting words lingering in the air.

## 24

ANNIE

I missed Ben terribly. When he left me for her the first time, I was angry, then I felt there was hope. But this time I felt even more betrayed. If time away was what he needed then he could have it. Getting married so soon and then months away from becoming a father was all too much for him. It was a stupid mistake and he needed to realise that. I knew I had suppressed his innate abilities as a child by not letting him play with friends or have the kind of upbringing that you read about in an Enid Blyton novel: biking off at dawn with a ham sandwich and a bottle of ginger beer and returning when it was just getting dark. No, I kept him close by, watched his every move and made sure he was never in the way of trouble or danger. I had to. I had no choice. But somehow, he still felt he needed to prove himself he was capable without me.

Daisy thought she had shown him that in their short time together, but Daisy was a fool. She thought she could bring out his independence, make him feel he was capable. Then what did she do? She threw it all back in his face. I didn't hear exactly what she said to him that day before he left, but I got the gist of it. She pushed him away with her accusations. But he had already seen what she had done, I showed it to him in black and white. He was a sensitive soul. He can't handle that kind of stress in his life. No, he needed to be somewhere where she couldn't get to him and busy his brain with all her white noise and anxiety. My boy needed time alone and to be as far away from that wife of his as possible.

# 25

---

GRACE

On the third cooking lesson I arrived with a renewed sense of confidence for Jenny. She had perturbed me last time with the little one's bruises. It did upset me to think of tiny helpless tots who were mistreated and the thought of that happening to little Mikee made me very sad indeed. I wondered if the kids were happy. What kind of life were they going to have? I wondered about Jenny and how she could carry on as though nothing was happening and, what kind of person that made her. But today I allowed those thoughts to subside and instead I let the mellow aura that seemed to ooze from Jenny so naturally lull me back to a state of admiration.

The babies still weren't coming, so I satisfied my urge to create and nurture something through any form of cookery I could master. The day that Emily gave us a crash course on bread making was the day that I was saved. I was on the brink of crumbling. My husband was barely uttering any words to me and I had noticed that some of his larger possessions were gone. I knew it wouldn't be long before he himself became as elusive as his stack of classic films and antique encyclopaedias.

The day I got my hands on that dough and began kneading and winding it into different shapes was a good day indeed. I was able to completely forget about the troubles back home. The feelings about my husband, slowly moving away from the home we had bought together and planned to raise a family in together, were pushed into the kneading of that bread; you could almost taste the betrayal in the finished loaf.

I liked the experience of proving the bread the most. Placing it somewhere warm and watching that little flat bit of dough treble in size, knowing that I had fed it and kept it warm enough to grow, was almost enough to replace the desperate maternal pangs for just a few hours at least.

The only thing that cast a shadow over the day was Jenny. She didn't seem her usual sprightly self and as I tended to my bread dough like it was a small child, I could see Jenny fluttering about out of the corner of my eye. I was worried about her; she wasn't concentrating and was clearly taken with some other pressing matter. Once my dough was safely in the oven and I had cleared my surface down, I wandered over to Jenny's station. The woman had barely even reached the proving stage. Her stomach was slightly protruding out of her tight pinafore dress. Flour and dough were scattered everywhere and she had her handbag on the work surface, a clear health hazard, anything could have been clinging to the bottom of it and infecting her work area.

'Are you okay Jenny?' I asked.

'Oh, Grace, no I'm afraid I'm not today. I'm a little out of sorts.' Jenny continued to rifle through her handbag.

'Well, I can see that.' I looked under the table. There was

no sign of little Mikee. 'Where's your little one today?'

'Oh, my mum has come to visit for a few days, so I left him at home with her. I thought it would help. I've got so much on my mind. But I feel a little lost without him.' Jenny stopped rifling and looked past me into thin air. 'Truth is, Grace, they are like my limbs. I can't function properly without them.' Jenny waved away her last comment 'Besides, I'm thinking about a million things. Got so much to sort out. I don't know what I was thinking about coming here today.'

I leant in a little closer and that was when I saw it. Jenny had done a good job of covering it up but I could see the rainbow of blues, reds and greens hiding beneath a sheen of concealer and pressed powder. Jenny's hand was intermittently finding its way to her cheek.

'Well. Is there anything I can help you with?' I motioned to the cluttered workstation. The bruise was clear as day to me, but the mess on her counter was something I could fix right away.

'Well. Yes. If you wouldn't mind...'

Thirty minutes later, I had prepped the dough and it was sitting neatly in a bowl, proving. I cleared the work surface and left it as gleaming as if it were my own.

'How do you do that?' Jenny said from the chair she was now sitting in, relaxing with a cup of coffee.

'Do what?' I asked.

'Make it look such a breeze. You come in here every week and look like you haven't got a care in the world.'

My laugh came out like a tremble. 'Well, looks can be deceptive.'

Sometimes I felt ready to spill everything about my fairy tale dream that was unravelling back home. Jenny frowned at me and cocked her head. 'Surely not you, Grace. You have it all. A wonderful house and husband. No kids! God, all that time to yourself to think!'

'Well, sometimes having too much time to think is not good.' I wiped my hands on my apron and looked down at my feet.

Jenny took a deep breath in 'Well, yes. That's true. I would go mad if I didn't have my three to distract me.'

'Yes, it's a shame not to see little Mikee down there today.'

'Oh, don't worry. He'll back causing havoc next week!'

'Ah, he's no bother.'

'No, you're right. He's a good boy. I couldn't have asked for a better child.'

'You're very lucky, Jenny,' I said.

'Oh, I don't know, Grace.' Jenny smoothed her hands over her tiny bump and we both fell silent for a few moments; each of us immersed in our own thoughts. 'Can't wait to see how my bread has turned out! Although you will have to take all the glory for nurturing it back to life for me. You are very kind, Grace.' She leant forward and touched my arm. 'You'll make a wonderful mother one day.' And as though Jenny had just cast a spell over me, I suddenly felt an overwhelming sensation – a fire was alight in my belly. I knew I would be a good mother. I would often imagine myself pattering down the hallway to tend to the baby at all hours of the night, whilst my happy husband slept contentedly in our bed. The next morning he would tweak the cheek of his son or daughter and kiss me on the head before heading blithely to work, content that everything was as it should be.

Jenny was so good for me. She kept me going, she made me believe that one day I would become a mother I was destined to be. So I held on to that thought and never let it go.

## 26

I left Patrick's before 9 a.m., grabbing the radio and squeezing it into my handbag. The thought of having a little music, something familiar to listen to, was already bringing me a flicker of comfort. Patrick was sprawled on the couch when I left him, vowing to fulfil his promise to Eve and go to bed for a month. I hadn't slept well at all and I had a longing to get back to Annie's. I had thrown Patrick's words around in my mind for too long in bed, preventing myself from sleeping. As I walked along I gave myself a talking to – stop overthinking everything, Daisy, you're in shock and grieving.

I breathed in the bracing fresh air and walked the short distance to the gym where a few weeks ago I was teaching classes, when the new year had just begun and I had felt a great sense of positivity for the future. It frightened me just how quickly everything had changed.

Once inside the gym, I sought out the manager, Craig. He was sitting at a table in the café, wearing a crisp white polo shirt with his tanned biceps exploding out of the bottom of the short sleeves. I approached him from behind and kept my eyes focused on his bald head, which he shaved regularly to make it appear as though his lack of hair was his own choice and not nature's. I arrived next to him as he took a sip of his cappuccino from a cup that looked comically tiny next to his huge arms and hands. He looked me up and down. I knew I didn't look my best although I had made an effort with my hair and I was wearing something fairly sporty.

'I lost everything in the fire, Craig,' I said, noting his look of disgust.

Craig rested his gaze for too long on my protruding stomach.

'Come on, Daisy, you know as well as I do that this is a prestigious gym. People want to see... well... not that.' He motioned up and down to me with one hand whilst turning and sipping his coffee with the other. I narrowed my eyes at him and looked at how his comedy-sized muscles twitched and flexed even as he sat drinking coffee.

'So can I get my classes back?' I said in my best matter-of-fact tone. Craig had never got over my rejection after he brazenly tried it on with me at the staff party two years ago and it was apparent he was going to use his position of power to reap his revenge.

He pulled his lips in and shook his head. 'No can do, Daisy. It's been weeks. I didn't hear a word from you. Girls are falling over themselves to get work here.' He motioned to the other side of the room where a buxom blonde girl was chatting animatedly to another member of staff. Her pink Lycra leotard and matching sweat band made her look like a Barbie doll.

I rolled my eyes. 'Oh, please.' I looked at Craig as he sipped his coffee and eyed up Barbie. 'And by the way, do you have any empathy?'

Craig looked at me and then looked over at Barbie, keeping his creepy gaze firmly upon her rear end.

'I guess not,' I said, and turned and walked away.

It was all I needed to hear to set me back again. I looked tatty, I was tired, my skin looked rough. At this stage of pregnancy I was supposed to be blooming, preparing for a new life. A life that was relying on me to be strong. But I was a mess, I had already made so many mistakes and caused so much pain and now I was losing everything all over again. I felt hopeless and lost. My car was parked at Patrick's flat where I had left it before the funeral. I thought about the tablets Annie gave me so freely and how they made me feel nothing. I wanted to feel nothing. I thought about where I needed to be. I hurried back to my car and drove towards the sanctuary of Annie's beach house.

# 27

---

ANNIE

Knowing someone else was in the house was a comfort, especially now Ben was gone. I enjoyed the notion of cooking for someone other than myself. I didn't want to become one of those women who lived off a single cod fillet in parsley sauce with a boil in the bag rice; it was too depressing to even contemplate. It had always been the same. I overcompensated every time, with the amount of food I bought and the amount I cooked. I threw masses away every day, I just couldn't help myself. There was an innate need to cook for a family.

The notion that Daisy was going to be staying around for longer than initially anticipated should have perturbed me. The girl had always been a threat in my eyes; the enemy. She was, after all, the reason Ben was no longer here. What I knew about her made my stomach turn and she was never going to win any moral awards in my books, yet somewhere within me the thought of having someone around the house bore a comforting feeling. And I had a job as a grandparent to make sure that baby was born safely. I had no interest in the girl. The way she carried herself, even in her grief-stricken state, she still had an air of superiority about her that resonated deeply with me. But I could overcome that, look beyond her slim tall frame that glided around with her golden hair cascading down her back behind her which emphasised her effortless beauty. The words made me want to spit, but I couldn't stop them being true.

I had missed Ben terribly after he left to be with her. So I couldn't help myself if a smidgen of life about the house, however repulsed I was by it, was in some small way a comfort to me. Besides, now there was another reason I was needed. The baby Daisy was carrying was my grandchild. I had a purpose again. So however alarming and alien I had felt her presence initially it was better than being alone. I was never any good at being alone. It makes me slightly mad, I feel unhinged, and then who knows what I'm capable of?

# 28

GRACE

I arrived at the cookery school that morning as though I was carrying a glow around me. Something had occurred overnight. Just when I thought it was all over, that I would never become a mother and my marriage was truly ended, my husband was there beside me, He had been sleeping downstairs for some time, then just last night he came to me quietly. I had been asleep for over an hour when I heard the bedroom door open. At first I was alarmed. I sat up in bed holding the sheets to me for protection. Then he climbed in next to me. He embraced me gently and then with such vigour that I had never before experienced. He left as quietly as he had arrived. I thought he would stay and sleep next to me, but he picked up his pile of clothes from next to the bed and he was gone. The next morning as I tuned in occasionally to the pleasant ache between my legs, I couldn't keep the smile from my face.

\* \* \*

At Emily's house I kept thinking about my husband and I in bed. From time to time, I tried to push it aside, other times I played it out in my mind, toying with it like a cat with a mouse; attempting to hang on to every move and breath when he was next to me for those few brief minutes.

Then there was Jenny. Sweet, beautiful Jenny. Pregnant with her fourth child. I looked on at her with such hope and inspiration. I clung to the notion that there was a possibility that my husband and I had created another life just a few hours previously as I watched her swelling belly make its way around the room, receiving a stroke here and pat here from her fellow cooks.

I watched with hope and anticipation, that soon that was going to me. Maybe my husband coming to me was his attempt at a reconciliation. Maybe he hadn't given up.

That night as I lay in bed alone, I prayed.

# 29

DAISY

It seemed Annie was quite giddy to have me back. And it was a relief to be back amongst the few things I could call my own. I was a little confused as I'd presumed she would want me as far away as possible, especially with Ben not here. But I was starting to think that maybe the baby had had some effect on her, the idea of becoming a grandparent was becoming a reality and that perhaps I could be someone that she could care for. Now I needed to make sure the idea of me becoming a parent became a reality. For so long now I knew I had been pushing the idea aside and not truly accepting that it was going to happen. But it was hard. Even though I knew what I needed to do I still couldn't force the feelings to come. It was too reminiscent of my past. I was scared. And the one person I needed to be here, so I could off load all of my fears, was gone. Perhaps if I had been honest with Ben in the first place, then maybe he would have stayed, realised just how much he was needed.

Ben still hadn't answered any of my calls and I was at a loss to know what to do. When I hadn't heard anything from him on the day of Eve's funeral, well, I was trying not to think too hard about the words I wanted to use. I had already insulted him enough. Annie was right. I didn't know him. A few months isn't long enough to know someone you decide to spend the rest of your life with. I had been stupid and impulsive. But that didn't take away the ache that I felt, I missed him so much it hurt in my gut. It seemed no painkiller or pill could stop that.

I was still so unused to the whining and the creaking of the old house that I was really feeling the impact of the noise, far more than perhaps I would have done had I been living in the comfort of my own flat. I tried to focus on the other sounds the house offered but my mind always seemed to be drawn back to the high clanking sound. It was almost melodic, like a beat and, as a dancer, I automatically heard music wherever I went. Certain sounds like the creaking of a drawer opening, or the beeping sound of the telephone as it went back into the holster, always sounded like the beginning notes of a familiar song. It amused me and I would have the beginning of a song in my head for ages after hanging up after a call or shutting my old oak drawers. The thought of my drawers burnt to a cinder distressed me. Then I thought of Eve and hated myself for caring for an inanimate object.

Annie had fussed around me when I returned from Patrick's. She didn't ask any specific questions about how the day had gone, but I was grateful she was there. But I soon tired of her fluttering about me and I went upstairs to be alone.

I went to the plug socket in the corner of the room and took out of my handbag the small digital radio Patrick had kindly lent me. I tuned it into a local radio station and heard the beginning of a favourite R&B track. I nudged up the volume and began swaying gently to the music, allowing my hips to familiarise themselves with the beats I had so often become immersed in on a dance floor or during an aerobics class. I was instantly thrown back to my uni days with Eve and I closed my eyes as I remembered our many nights out drinking until dawn and stumbling home with the DJ's classic tunes still ringing in our ears. It had only been a few weeks, a matter of days really, since Eve was snatched away but right then, with the heavy insistent beat folding itself around me and bringing with it the euphoria I always felt when dancing, she could have been with me in the room. I even allowed a smile to creep across my lips as I felt a few firm kicks from the baby as it showed its appreciation of the bass line.

There was a loud bang and I turned around to see Annie making her way past me. She had flung open the door, which slammed against the wall in her haste to get to the radio on the other side of the room. When she reached it, she snatched the plug out of the wall socket.

I stood in the middle of the room, baffled by her raucous entrance.

'Annie, what are you doing?' I wailed – my body had been shocked out of sedation and I was bordering on fight or flight mode.

'I will not have radios in this house, Daisy!' Annie yelled as she stood in the middle of the room clutching the radio to her chest her eyes wide, her jaw tense. She was breathing fast.

'What? Why, Annie, I didn't mean any harm with it. I missed hearing music and Patrick lent it to me.' I took one step to approach her. 'I'm sorry if it was a little loud. I can keep it down or find some headphones.' I scanned the room.

Annie took in a deep breath and put her hand over her mouth as she let it out slowly. Then she smoothed her hair down and brought the radio down away from her chest, the thin wire hung limply next to her.

'I would appreciate it if you would not play it at all, Daisy.' Annie's voice was softer but wavering.

I narrowed my eyes at her, unable to work out what the outburst was about. But I was tired. It had been a long few days and Eve's funeral had taken it out of me.

'Okay,' I said bluntly. As I looked directly at Annie, I held out my hand for the radio. Annie locked eyes with me and then slowly handed the radio over.

'I cannot hear it again, Daisy. I must insist.'

I nodded and watched as Annie strode out of the room.

I blew out a breath. The tune was still in my ears, the whole incident had happened in a matter of seconds. I reluctantly placed the radio on the floor in the corner all the while churning over thoughts of Annie's agitation over it, and whether she hated electrical devices or was it just the music she couldn't stand. I wasn't about to ask her either. I checked my phone and saw two messages from Patrick telling me he would miss me and to call him soon. Then my mind was no longer on Annie and her rage over the music, instead I was thinking of Patrick and the last words he spoke to me last night: *I loved her furiously, with so much passion, sometimes I had to conceal it because I feared I may damage her.*

I put the phone down without replying. I undressed and put on a cotton T-shirt to sleep in. The pregnancy had begun to make me feel hot at night and I often woke in a sweat. I lay down on my side and allowed sleep to envelop me.

* * *

I was startled awake. I grappled for my phone, it said 3.33 a.m. There was pain in my arm that was radiating up into my shoulder and neck where I had slept awkwardly. I sat up and slid my feet out of bed, straining to hear. There had been a noise, some sort of ruckus that had woken me, an echo of some sort of a crash pounded in my ears. Still with memories of Annie storming into the bedroom simmering away in my mind, I felt a rush of adrenaline shoot through my body as I got up and headed for the stairs. I walked slowly down each step, not wanting the ever-growing weight of the bump to make me topple. I reached the hallway and looked through into the lounge. I could see there was a light coming from the kitchen.

'Annie,' I called out. I heard another noise. Another crash and then a sound, a deep noise like an animal in pain. 'Annie,' I said again as I walked towards the kitchen where I could hear thumping, and the deep throaty sound. 'Annie, are you okay?' I said with panic in my voice. Suddenly the noise stopped. I arrived at the kitchen doorway and peered around the corner. Annie was crouched down on the floor in her dressing gown, with the pantry door open. A large saucepan was half in the pantry and half out. 'What are you doing?' I wondered if perhaps Annie was sleep walking again.

'Oh, Daisy,' Annie replied, and I blew out a sigh of relief, I didn't fancy trying to assist her back up to bed. I came into the kitchen and stood rubbing my forehead; I squinted at the bright light of the kitchen and watched Annie crouched on the floor.

'What are you doing, Annie? Its three-thirty in the morning. I thought we had burglars.'

'I suddenly realised it's the end of January and I hadn't made my annual batch of Seville marmalade.' Annie's voice was high and strained. Annie lifted the heavy bottomed saucepan onto the kitchen counter. Even at three in the morning I could see how she lifted from her knees and not from her back. The strength of the woman was uncanny.

'You're not making it now, surely?' It wouldn't have surprised me though if she were.

'I'm just checking what I have. I'm popping out to the shops tomorrow.'

I rubbed my eyes. 'And this couldn't wait until the morning?'

'Oh, you know me, dear. I'm a night owl. Go back to bed, Daisy. I'm fine.' Annie's voice was strained. She waved me away with her hand.

Still half-asleep, I turned and walked out of the kitchen and back to bed.

* * *

I woke again about eight, pulled Ben's big chunky cardigan around me and went downstairs to the kitchen. I found Annie sitting at the kitchen table looking out of the window.

'Morning,' I said quietly, remembering how late Annie was up last night and that she probably wasn't in the mood for chit-chat. As she rose from the table and walked around to get to the sink, I took a sharp intake of breath.

'My God, Annie, your eye! What happened?' Annie slowly brought her hand to her face. She gently touched the area next to her eye that was blue and purple and swollen. She turned around and looked at me full on.

'I'm not entirely sure how it happened, Daisy. I think I must have tripped on that tiny step into the pantry and bashed my face on the shelf there. I was half asleep. Anyway, what about you? Do you need some—' Annie waved her hand about '—help with anything?'

I looked down at my bump. 'No. I'll be fine. I'm going to contact Ben tonight. I've drafted another text message.' Annie shot me a look from the sink.

I knew that I had let Ben down with what I had said and the way I treated him just before he disappeared and a part of me wanted to allow myself the punishment, but the other part of me needed to know what was happening. I was angry that he thought he could just walk out of our marriage and cut off all communication. I had been refusing to think that Ben was hiding something from me but I couldn't shift the nagging doubt. Why would the police question him so much and what if they needed to get back in touch with him again? But worst of all, what if I had made a horrible mistake and got myself involved with the wrong kind of man?

Annie cocked her head to one side. 'It sounds like you're talking about a work proposal, dear, not your husband.' Annie laughed. Her tone was brazen but she wasn't finished. 'My Ben, he's a free spirit. I had to learn to let him go several months ago and now I think you need to do the same.'

'What?' I could barely believe what I was hearing. 'You think he's gone? That's it, it's all over?'

Annie pulled her lips into an awkward half-smile and shrugged her shoulders.

'I'm just saying, dear, maybe you should concentrate on, you know...' She lowered her head and gesticulated to my stomach with her eyes.

'Well, I'm not ready to say goodbye.' My voice caught on goodbye, but I refused to let myself cry in front of Annie. 'He has to at least make that clear, people don't just disappear Annie! I will send him the message and if I don't get a reply I will...' I had no idea what I was going to do. What could I do? Ben had made his decision. I just had to wait.

'I'm going for a bath,' I said and headed back upstairs.

I ran a bath and once I was submerged to my neck in bubbles I reached up to the shelf above my head, for my phone. With my face hot from the bath water and the rage that was building inside me, I re-read the message laced with firm words and the odd expletive that I had assessed a thousand times and pressed send.

When I walked back into Ben's room wrapped in a thick towel, Annie had blitzed the room. The window was open an inch which had allowed a cool breeze to filter through. She had changed the bed sheets and there was an artificial floral smell about the air. On the bed were slouchy trousers, a soft cotton T-shirt and fresh underwear folded within an inch of their life by meticulous Annie. There was a cup of hot coffee on the bedside table. It was a thoughtful gesture and I was feeling tired, the most annoying of the many symptoms of pregnancy. I dressed and then drank the coffee which was by this point at optimum drinking temperature.

When I went downstairs, I found Annie sitting in the lounge flicking though one of her many home interior magazines, a cup of coffee sat half-drunk on the table in front of her.

'Better?' Annie asked looking up briefly. It was as if all those words she had sent my way about how Ben no longer loved me had never happened; evaporated and forgotten about. I wondered how she could simply switch her emotions towards me. More so, I considered how she really saw me, what her true thoughts were. She was becoming increasingly difficult to read.

I stroked the fine fabrics of the trousers and an image

flickered though my mind of Ben standing in the shops, picking them out for me. 'Yes. Thank you. And thanks for cleaning the room.'

'Well, I've always done it for Ben. He likes a clean room.' She cleared her throat. 'Did you get your coffee?'

'Yes, yes I did. It was the... perfect drinking temperature.' My words felt forced and unnatural as though I had to think about how to formulate them. 'I'm going to nip to the big supermarket. Go and pick up a few bits. Then, you know...' I rubbed my head which felt fuzzy.

'Well at least you don't have rent to worry about.' Annie's eyes remained fixed on her magazine.

'I don't know what you mean, Annie?'

'I mean, you can go and get your shopping, worry free. You don't owe me anything for staying here.'

I couldn't work out her tone, if she was being sincere or she was offended. But I could feel my head spinning. I took a deep breath, turned and walked to the coat hooks where my handbag was. I must have turned too quickly because I felt almost too dizzy to stand. I pushed my hand against the wall and regained my balance. I retrieved the handbag and walked back to the lounge.

Annie eyed me over her magazine. 'Everything okay, dear? You don't look too good.'

'No, I'm fine, I just. I'm sure I've got some cash in here somewhere...' I thrust my hand into my handbag as I arrived back in front of Annie. I pulled out a couple of twenty-pound notes and shoved them towards her. Annie looked at them, her expression one of horror.

'Good lord, no, Daisy. I wouldn't dream of asking anything from you.' Annie waved me away with her hand.

'Fine.' I thrust the notes back in the handbag. 'Just let me know if there's anything else I can do then.'

'Do you know when the insurance money is coming through?' Annie asked, with an edge to her voice.

I felt my heart quicken at her question. I thought of Ben's bed upstairs, the clean fresh room. I wanted more than anything to be away from Annie and her talk of money.

'Well, the truth is, Annie...' I began. It was now or never. I had to tell her for I knew she would continue to ask about it. I took a deep breath, my mouth felt dry and my palms felt sweaty.

'I don't know who suggested that there was insurance money, but there wasn't. Eve didn't believe in it and well, as ironic as that is now, it is what it is. Once the baby is born, I will make sure I get out of your hair.' My voice sounded as though I was in a tunnel.

Annie licked her finger and turned the page of her magazine. The noise of it filled the room. Her face was in a fixed nonchalant pose, her eyebrows ever so slightly raised. Annie waited a few extra seconds before speaking, all the while, my heart was beating faster than it should have been. She placed her hand in the centre of her magazine and looked up at me.

I gulped; my throat felt dry.

'I must say, Daisy, you look very sketchy. Why don't you go and lie back down upstairs?'

I found myself obeying without thinking. I headed upstairs with Annie in close proximity behind me and got myself comfortable in the bed.

'Well, we are in a muddle, aren't we? Death is a very destructive experience, Daisy. You can't just go rushing off expecting to feel fine a few weeks later. And look now, you have this baby to think of. You. Must. Rest.'

'Annie...' I could feel myself wanting to drift off. 'The money... I am sorry about the insurance... I didn't think.'

I closed my eyes and heard the last words Annie spoke to me that day.

'Well then, dear, I guess that means you're stuck here with me for the time being, doesn't it?'

# 30

---

GRACE

I looked at the letter over and over again as I stood at my workstation in Emily's kitchen. I had arrived a few minutes early. Emily had brought me over some tea and I sipped it whilst I mulled over the words my husband had written. It was short, precise and to the point. He had left me. He wasn't coming back and he was beginning the divorce proceedings.

I knew I should have felt more upset but in a way I felt as though a huge weight had been lifted. He had been silently threatening to leave for so long.

But now I had something else to occupy my mind. I had been there so many times before but this time it had an edge to it. Something extra that I hadn't felt before. My period was late by two weeks and it was all the evidence I needed. I knew this time I was going to keep this to myself. My husband would never need to know. He had already left the house, with all of his belongings. After that night together, I never saw him again. All I had left was this letter. And the growing life within me.

But he didn't deserve to know about my pregnancy this

time. I felt as though this was his parting gift to me. He had taken care of everything as he had spoken about in his letter to me so I knew I didn't need to worry about money or paperwork. The house was to be handed over to me. A result of his guilty conscience. But I knew I wouldn't be staying. The house was worth a fair bit now. I knew that and so I would leave. Far away as possible and start my new life, just me and my baby.

At last I felt in the same league as Jenny. We had a common ground that went beyond just being women.

We were like two teenage girls, giggling and wittering away at the back of the classroom. Emily glanced over regularly at us with a small smile of approval at our friendship and I thought my heart might burst with joy. I hadn't ever experienced the newness of a friendship before, the eagerness to be by the side of another woman and share feelings I realised you could only ever share with a female. This was quite alien to anything I had ever experienced with my husband. It felt natural and easy. I felt proud to be next to Jenny and that she had chosen me to confide in and trust. The high I felt to be pregnant overshadowed any grief I felt for my failed marriage and the love lost between me and my husband.

I didn't tell Jenny that I was with child. I kept that secret within me. I thought I would tell her when the time was right; when I was sure everything was going to be okay. This time, I knew it would be.

I imagined her face, how she would congratulate me with real sincerity and how when our children were born there would only be a few months between them in age and how they would play together. It was like a dream. I felt that I was the luckiest woman on earth to be given the chance of being a mother again even when my husband, the father of my child, was nowhere to be seen and busy making a life for himself somewhere else. I still had the opportunity for happiness. And who knew, maybe one day I would meet someone who would be willing to take on someone else's child as their own. I had read about it enough times, there was no reason it couldn't happen to me.

But right then, I didn't feel alone. I was growing something, one was becoming two.

A fresh start was all I needed. Me and the baby. My husband's punishment would be that for the rest of his stupid selfish life he would never know his son or daughter. I would be the mother to a child he would never know existed. Some might think that was cruel on the child, but I knew what my husband was capable of. He was a selfish man, who gave up on me because I wasn't as fertile as all the women his brothers married. That wasn't love. That was a convenient situation for him, whilst it lasted. Then he got bored of waiting for the thing he couldn't have and left me.

It was May and the trees were filled with blossom. I saw my life in those full trees, new life and hope. I was ready to let go of everything and start a fresh.

I was pregnant with my husband's child. It should have been a miracle to celebrate with him but I was facing my future alone.

# 31

DAISY

I allowed another week to trickle slowly by like thick treacle. I was finding it difficult to walk, each step becoming more obvious with the weight of the baby.

I touched the bump. I tried to feel some connection with it, but I just couldn't. Even when Ben was here, I couldn't do it. I was a terrible person. I tried not to think about what would happen when the baby was due in a few months. I tried not to think about how I had already failed this baby so much. I tried not to think how it wasn't the first time either.

Instead I let a blanket of hopelessness envelope me like a cloak. I wasn't counting the days, I was letting them pass and they skirted by. I mostly lolloped around the house like an unemployable teenager. Tiredness crippled me daily. I was so unused to it, it left me completely debilitated. I let Annie carry on doing everything whilst I tried to sink into the shadows, but I always felt as if I was being watched by her. She cooked and she seemed to be patient and at times it could even be perceived as kindness; I wasn't sure. But I was here and she hadn't told me to leave so I stayed. Although I felt in limbo. I needed to make a decision about my life, about where I would live. I couldn't keep putting off the inevitable. That I was going to be a mother and I was going to have to do it alone.

I laid in bed listening to the clanking of the pipes, deciding whether or not it was worth getting up. I knew eventually Annie would bring up a cup of coffee or tea if I didn't emerge downstairs.

Then my phone pinged the sound of a text message. And my heart leapt into my throat. I grabbed my phone and quickly navigated my way into the texts. Ben's name was staring back at me. I opened the text and straight away I felt my thudding heart slow with the despondency that filled my body.

One week since the last message to my husband, he replied. There were only three lines. Three measly lines.

Daisy, I have a lot to deal with over here right now and I would appreciate you giving me the time to do that.
I hope to be back in time for the birth but please in the meantime, let Mum look after you and the baby.
Take care and see you in a few months. Ben.

I read it at least six times, each time searching for the missing words, the meanings, something that meant he cared and that everything would be fine between us. To give me a reason to care for his baby I was carrying.

But there was nothing there.

I could still feel Ben, as though he wasn't that far away at all. I still had the smell of him in the room, on the cardigan that I perpetually wore and never washed. I thought he would have stayed to support me through this period, but he didn't.

Sitting still wasn't an option. I got up and as I arrived at the bottom of the stairs with my thoughts clearly written all over my face, Annie was passing through the hallway and stopped and exclaimed.

'Whatever is the matter, girl, you look as weak as a kitten!'

'It's Ben. He messaged me.'

'He did?' Annie's face matched the confusion in her tone 'Well, what did he say? Is he coming back?

I shook my head, barely able to say the words. 'I... don't know.'

Annie took me by the arm, walked me through to the lounge and got me seated on the sofa.

'But what did he say?' Annie stood in front of me with her arms folded, so I pulled out my phone and showed her the text with the words that had burned into my eyeballs by now.

Annie handed me the phone back. 'Well, at least he knows you are safe here. And he didn't say he wasn't coming back. He said he hopes to be back by the time the baby arrives. Do you have an exact due date? I know it's April.'

'From my calculations my due date is sometime in April. But I don't know exactly. I haven't seen a midwife. I haven't had a scan.' I blew out a big breath. I'd told Ben the 16th. I did some basic calculations, but I suppose the midwives have a better way of working it out.

'So we roughly have two months, possibly a few weeks more. Have you prepared anything?

'No.'

'No?'

'No.' Because I don't think I'm good enough. I don't think

I'm ready. 'Will... will I be ready?' I asked, knowing I had neglected the pregnancy.

'Well, no one is ever really ready, children come along and turn your whole world upside down. One always doubts one's abilities, more so when it comes to the most basic natural ways of motherhood.'

I nodded along with Annie's words but they meant nothing to me now Ben wasn't here. I couldn't help but start to imagine the worst, what was really keeping him away from me? The secrets I thought I had been able to keep buried had perhaps finally come back to haunt me. Already my life was in ruins. The only thing that I had left was the tiny heartbeat within me; this developing human waiting to be welcomed into the world by a loving mother who would give it all her love. But amongst the fog of grief and the doubt surrounding my marriage, the one thing I was clear upon was that I would not be a good mother.

## 32

ANNIE

Babies are a blessing. A miracle. They shouldn't be treated as though they are this disposable component that can be got rid of because circumstances don't suit.

I realised I was one of the few women out there who was willing to commit everything to raising a child. Our children are these tiny delicate creatures and we are the rock between them and the harmful effects of the outside world. I knew that the day Ben arrived in my world. Such an innocence. He needed me the most, and I was never going to let him down. I committed my life to raising him. And here it was again, Daisy's baby, another miracle. Another opportunity.

'You know, it's probably best that this baby business remains between us, Daisy,' I said as I fluffed up the cushions around her. She was in shock from the message from Ben. And rightly so. It was vague, impersonal, it was as though he didn't know her at all. 'I was looking into homebirths and how they are received now. Have you heard they are coming back? All the rage with new mums. Ben was born at home.'

I watched as Daisy looked up at me, a glint of interest in

her expression. 'You have gone through a great deal these last few weeks and becoming a mother, this is way more than you should be going through. And, Daisy, you know how many people are involved in a pregnancy, don't you? The doctors, the midwives, the health visitors? I mean we don't need all that palaver, do we?'

I paused to read Daisy's reaction, which was full of muddled emotions. 'Things aren't how they were twenty-five years ago in the early eighties when I was starting a family. There was none of this agency sharing information and every Tom, Dick and Harry sticking their two pennies' worth in. We were just left to get on with it. Of course, more of the poor buggers were slipping through the system, but now they watch everything, Daisy. They monitor you like a hawk. There's no hiding from them. They will pick up on anything, any emotion, any fault and it will all be recorded. They are all over everything these days, they know everything. All your past history...' I allowed that last comment to fill the air like a thick cloud of smoke and watch as Daisy inhaled it. She appeared to physically shrink down into the sofa. 'If you want to keep your baby, to not have anyone sticking their nose into your business, you need to have the baby here and not tell a soul.'

She looked as though she were thinking and then gave a small nod.

'But you know I'll look after you. I have my pharmacy experience. I can get hold of the right drugs.'

I edged a little closer to her and tentatively placed a hand on her leg. She looked at my hand. 'You should get rest. Now it is more important than ever.'

I went to stand and leave the room, I had a tonne of chores to do and there was so much to get prepared. I knew I had got through to Daisy and that she would comply. She really didn't have any other choice.

'Annie,' she called just as I reached the door to the kitchen. I tried not to show in my expression the inconvenience of having to stop when my mind was set on the tasks ahead of me.

'Yes, dear?' I turned back around.

'So you really think it's okay? If I don't tell the doctor, everything will be okay, here with you?'

I moved further into the room, but not close enough that Daisy would think this conversation was going to go beyond the next few minutes. 'Let me make myself clear on the matter, Daisy. I am just not comfortable with our current situation, with Ben not here and the inquest into your friend's death unresolved. I don't want people coming into our lives, my home and meddling. Under the circumstances, are you really the most ideal candidate for becoming a mother?'

Daisy's expression fell and she opened her mouth to say something.

'I mean,' I continued, ignoring her, 'these are not my thoughts, Daisy, you understand, I'm merely looking in from the professional's perspective, seeing it how they will see it. Seeing you all sad and depressed, grieving for your husband and friend who died in such a terrible accident. I read about it all the time, dear. They will take a baby off you for no other reason than because they can. They have all the power and we have none. So we keep schtum. Understand?'

Finally, she nodded firmly as if she understood. I felt as though I may have got through to her. I left her to her thoughts whilst I turned my attention to the more important matters of preparing for a new arrival, which was getting closer by the day. I could feel my nesting instincts kicking into full force. Daisy was a strong girl; she would carry that baby well and in about two months' time everything would be as it should be. Right now, she was merely the vessel to carry the child into the world and then I would have a beautiful new baby to care for.

# 33

DAISY

I woke to find Annie in the room with me. There had been no knock, or a 'may I come in', I was sure of it. She was just there. Yet again, fussing with the curtains. I could smell toast and coffee. I looked at my phone. It was almost nine-thirty. How had I slept in for so long this morning? I was rising later and later. I thought back to going to bed the night before and I couldn't remember falling asleep. My phone pinged and I leant down to look at the message. It was from Patrick. My eyes scanned his words.

Concerned... miss you... call me

'That smells delicious,' I said, trying to smile as I placed the phone back on the bedside table.

'You need to keep your strength up.' She placed the tray in front of me. 'You know, I have been independent for a long time now, Daisy, ever since... well, it has always been just me and Ben. And I've always done things my way. I would very much like it to stay the way I have become accustomed to.

And, if you feel you wish to, until we sort this whole situation out, you are more than welcome here. But under my conditions. I don't feel I am being unfair or unjust here, Daisy. I just like my life the way it is, without people poking their noses in. And I wish the same for my unborn grandchild. Once you involve other people in your life, it becomes their life. I don't want that.'

I looked at my plate of toast that was moments ago a temptation. My throat now felt dry. The tone in Annie's voice was apparent. We were going to do things her way. And once again, I was being left with little choice.

'I appreciate what you're saying, Annie.'

'Good.' She patted my arm. 'Then we'll get on like a house on fire.' She pulled her mouth to one side. 'Oops, I didn't mean that.'

'It's okay,' I said. It wasn't. It never would be. But it didn't bring back memories of Eve. It made me think of when Annie told me Ben had caused a fire. Then I thought about my accusations to Ben and how the two incidents now seemed so inextricably linked.

Annie plumped the cushion behind my head. I looked at her with gratitude as I couldn't keep thanking her. She knew my parents were absent, but she hadn't said anything else about them since our first meeting and that I was glad of. But Annie had suggested something yesterday. She talked about patient history and the fact that this baby could be taken away from me. Her words had alarmed me, but it was impossible that Annie could know anything about what happened before. It was so long ago. It was such old news you would have had to spend hours in library archives or trawling through the internet to find the stories. And I wasn't sure Annie was capable of that. When we were here at Christmas, she could barely use her computer and Ben had to do the basics for her.

'Right, you're all set. I'll bring you some fresh water up and then maybe a walk around the garden. You need to keep your blood pressure steady. None of this sitting around all day. That baby needs you healthy.'

Healthy I may be in body. But certainly not in my mind. I hadn't been for so long. I thought when I met Ben he would heal me, but all I ended up doing was losing him as well.

She would be thirteen now. A lump formed in my throat that was painful to swallow. Even after all these years I could see her, her tiny screwed up pink face, looking at me to care for her and tend to her. But I couldn't.

I didn't.

# 34

ANNIE

We had begun a very simple routine of sorts. I would wake early as I always did and make tea, orange juice and toast and take it to Daisy's room. She was getting the five-star treatment here, but I did it because it was innate. Hospitality was my forte.

A letter had arrived for Daisy yesterday, she hadn't said what it was but I was pretty sure I knew it was about the inquest. I was just waiting for her to confirm it.

Sure enough, as I entered the room this morning, filling the room with the fragrance of Earl Grey tea, Daisy was already sat up in bed looking at the letter again as though she hadn't put it down since it arrived. I observed her for a few moments whilst she stared at the letter. Her hair was long and tied back. Entering the third trimester now she was, as they say, blooming. My gut tightened at the sight of her, at her glowing aura brought on by her fertility.

I sniffed casually and walked to the bed, laying the tray to the side of her, eager to get a glimpse of what had taken Daisy's attention.

'It's the inquest date, for the verdict for Eve's death.'

It seemed she was finally willing to share as she waved the piece of paper about.

'Oh, okay, dear.' I feigned nonchalance.

'I'm surprised it has come around this quickly. I thought it would be a few more months yet.'

'Well, sometimes these things are a lot quicker.'

'Well yes, I suppose. Everyone seems to have got their shit together on this occasion.'

I winced at her language. 'So will you go? To the hearing?' I took an empty glass from the bedside table my hands clutched it tightly enough so the tips of my fingers began to turn white.

'Yes, of course.'

I stood and watched intently as Daisy grappled for her phone before it slipped through her fingers and landed next to the bed. I eyed her for a few more seconds and then bent down slowly. Daisy lifted her head to look at me.

'I feel so clumsy at the moment.' She took the phone 'I'm just going to text Patrick, check he has the same letter.' I heard Daisy let out a loud sigh. 'I wish I had more energy. Do you think I have that... that acute pregnancy sickness? I have felt tired for months now. I might need to be admitted to hospital?' Panic was apparent in Daisy's voice.

'Don't be silly Daisy,' I scolded. 'It's not forever, is it? Once that baby is out you'll be fit as a fiddle and off and about again. I suppose you'll be back to work and all sorts. You're not the stay at home type are you?'

'I... I well I hadn't thought about it really.'

'No, well there you are then.'

'At the moment I need to get everything into perspective, it will be easier once Ben is back,' Daisy began. 'Even after the way he has been, well, after everything that has happened. Even if, you know you are right and Ben has been scared off, I just can't have this child growing up not knowing anything about their father, the way Ben did.'

'You know nothing about our life!' I heard my voice resounding around the room as I looked at Daisy's startled face. Anger burned through my stomach and coursed through my veins.

'I... I didn't mean it in that way, I just meant...' Daisy stuttered

'I know what you meant.' I took a step forward 'I have known what everyone has meant all of Ben's life. People think what they think, but only I know. I know what Ben's father was like and he was not good. He would not have benefited in any way from knowing that man!' My voice seemed to reverberate around the room. Daisy hung her head.

'My life, Ben's life, before you came along, Daisy, was what it was.' I lowered my voice 'No one asked any questions and we got on with things because that's what you do. Ben had relationships with people and he remained my son, he stayed here with me. He didn't think to disappear off for months without contacting me. Suddenly he's with you and he doesn't call me any more. Then six months later, he's gone. I don't think you know Ben at all. He is in his own world and let's face it, you practically chased him away with your accusations.' I watched as the tears came from Daisy, but no emotion shifted inside me.

'I was in a mess then. I didn't know what I was thinking, let alone saying,' Daisy said through sobs. 'But he can't just have cut himself off completely?' Daisy said to my back as I walked towards the door. I paused and turned back around to look at her.

'For the whole time you and my son were gallivanting off thinking of no one but yourselves, I didn't hear a whisper from him. I think an entire month passed once before he replied to one of my texts.' I knew this was news to Daisy, and it pained me to have said it out loud, the memory of it. But the girl needed to know. I took the door handle in my hand, clutching onto the glass tightly again. 'Do you know Ben doesn't even have a driving licence?'

Daisy looked confused. 'But he drives...'

'Yes, because I taught him. I told you, Daisy, he's a free spirit. He didn't want to be bogged down with taking tests and laws. He likes his freedom. Sometimes, Daisy, people just want to be left well alone. And when they make that decision, it doesn't matter how hard someone tries to get to them, they will be fighting a losing battle. I'll see you downstairs.'

I walked out of the door and closed it gently behind me.

I stood and breathed slowly in and out and let my pounding heart return to normal before I walked down the stairs to the kitchen. Through her grief and exhaustion the girl was still a feisty little thing. If nothing else it would serve her well during labour.

I sat at the kitchen table and let my racing thoughts calm down before I could start assessing everything. How dare that girl say those things? Of course, she was all emotional because of the pregnancy, but good lord, did she think she was the only woman that had ever got herself pregnant? Ben was going to move on, he was already moving on. She didn't know my son when she married him.

I knew my son. More than anyone ever would.

I sensed the moment that I met Daisy that she was going to be hard work in one way or another and this incident with Eve's death had been a real burden on me and now I had the pregnancy to deal with as well. Now I had all these feelings I was harbouring about what I knew about her. But I couldn't say them. I didn't want to scare the girl away. I needed her. I needed the baby.

Babies were such a precious gift.

The situation was glaringly obvious. Daisy would abandon that child the way she had before. She would be long gone because Ben no longer loved her. She was no candidate for motherhood. She was given the chance once and she failed. Walking away would be that much easier for her a second time. She had done it once. I was certain she would do it again. And when the time came I would certainly not stand in her way. In fact, I was almost certain I could be the one to convince her to walk away from her baby for a second time.

# 35

DAISY

The beach house was beginning to feel like the only home I had. And with the birth not long away now, I relished a little in the way Annie made a show of fussing around me: getting me snacks and drinks, asking about the baby. It was all a novel experience to me. I had never felt that sort of care before.

I spent the morning in the garden, helping Annie lift a few weeds under watchful eyes hearing constant reminders to rest. It was an overcast day, spring not yet sprung, but Annie was keen to get ahead and begin preparing the beds. I took a breather every now and again and took a seat in the summer house to shelter from the sea breeze, which was at times uncomfortably bracing. Annie seemed to thrive amongst the harsher elements, she was completely immersed in the task, the myriad of thoughts that were usually etched across her face, gone and in their place a more serene expression.

'I'm fine,' I told her over and over again but eventually I tired of her requests and went upstairs to lay down. I wasn't fine. Nothing was fine. My head was swimming with thoughts. Thoughts of the inquest was currently prevailing. I was petrified about hearing the results. Teetering beneath that was what Annie had callously revealed to me about Ben's lack of driving licence and how he had lied to me, driven me around knowing I was pregnant, despite having never had any formal lessons. I was churning up inside about Ben and his text and Annie's words that hinted at my past were still lingering in my head. I turned them over and over trying to untangle them, trying to work out what she knew about me.

Then there was the baby; my thoughts rarely turned to the baby, or the birth. These were things I needed to concern myself with but I kept batting away the thoughts once they entered my head, a knee jerk reaction brought on by my past mistakes.

I pushed a pillow under my stomach and wrapped the duvet around me. I could hear the sound of the wind batting against the window and I imagined the force of it colliding with the noxious thoughts in my head and forcing them out. But it didn't. Instead I fell into a fitful slumber plagued by the words that made no sense and with the haunting image of Annie's placid expression at the forefront of my mind.

* * *

I woke suddenly to the sound of Annie placing down a tray on the bedside table. On it was a bowl of homemade tomato soup and some thick crusty bread.

'This will make you feel great,' she advised. 'Better to get those nutrients in you now, the baby will literally be sucking the life out of you, you'll be wasting away.'

The memories I had forced away all those years ago were

seeping back. I was young and the sickness knocked me off my feet. So used to flitting around without a care, suddenly I was burdened with the nausea from hell. I didn't know what to do with myself.

'Thank you, Annie,' I said and sat up. She gave me a weak smile and left the room.

Soon after I finished the soup, I began to feel tired again. The baby was growing fast, it was understandable I would feel this drained. I placed the tray on the bedside table and I lay down. I closed my eyes just to rest them for a moment.

* * *

I woke at dusk. I hauled myself out of bed with a groggy head and I forced myself to go downstairs. I found Annie in the kitchen preparing Tupperware boxes of food. She turned when she heard me come in.

'Just getting a few lunches made up for you. Soups and pastas and the likes. You slept for a while. I told you you needed the rest, didn't I?' I nodded. Sleep still enveloped me.

'Tea?' Annie flicked the switch on the kettle. 'I was just making one. Are you hungry?'

'Erm, not just yet,' I rubbed my eyes trying to bring myself back to the present. Everything still felt dreamlike; I had slept long and hard.

'Go and sit down. I'll bring your tea through.' Annie waved me out of the room.

I settled myself on the sofa, picked up a country lifestyle magazine and started to flick through. I tried to imagine the perfect country idyllic life that the magazine portrayed and wondered if anyone actually reached the point where they felt pure satisfaction with everything. Surely a checked throw or a cream Aga weren't the answer to everything. Surely the people that lived in these worlds still had problems. Didn't they?

'Did Ben come out when he was ready?' I asked when Annie returned to the lounge with the tea. I surprised myself with the question and realised I had been unconsciously thinking of the birth. Annie didn't reply straight away, she looked at me for a few moments and when she answered it was as though she were looking straight through me.

'Yes,' she said absently 'He always did what he wanted to do. Never in a malicious way, mind.' She handed me a cup. 'Here's your tea.'

I took the mug and smiled my thanks.

'It will be getting on for dinnertime soon, so I'll just go and get on.' Annie backed out of the room. 'There's some more new magazines there.' She motioned towards the coffee table. I looked at the neatly arranged pile of monthly glossies.

'Oh right, okay, thanks. Any parenting ones there?' I asked jovially. Annie gave me a tight smile. She had just turned to go when we were suddenly both startled by a loud clattering that sounded as though it was coming from the kitchen. Annie looked towards the door.

'Bloody feral cats again.' Annie jumped up and started ringing her apron between her hands.

'Are they in the house?' I asked.

'No... it's outside. There's an old tin bin, I leave out there to burn rubbish sometimes. They like to knock it over and it makes a racket.

'Who do they belong to?'

'Who?' Annie was distracted by looking at the doorway.

'The cats? Are they the neighbours'?'

'What? No, they're feral, like wild tigers. Stay away, Daisy, if you get scratched by one it will be a risk to the baby.'

She came over to the sofa and perched next to me and pulled up her sleeve 'I tried to shoo one away last night, and look what the blighter did to me!' There on Annie's left arm were three scratch lines, red and raw. I sucked the breath in between my teeth

'It looks sore.'

Annie shook off my comment. 'There's not long to go now Daisy, until the baby is born we don't want to risk anything happening to you. Don't worry about anything else except eating and breathing. The baby is the most important thing, do you understand?' Annie stood up 'Now let me deal with those cats.' Annie walked from the room and before I realised what I had done, I had lifted my hand to my stomach and let it rest there.

# 36

ANNIE

I had known the day Ben had told me about Daisy that he was smitten. I then saw the way Ben looked at his tall slim wife with her blue eyes and blonde hair, her long eyelashes and perfectly pink cheeks. The way her long golden hair cascading down her back so effortlessly. He was like a moth to a flame when she was near. She was always the one he was going to leave me for. I saw in Ben's eyes that look of pure love. It was true love, the sort of love that one only has for their mother. I feared I was going to be replaced. The relationship I had with Ben to date could be gone. Everything I had fought for and tried for could be finished because I would never be any match for such goddess beauty. Ben was putty in Daisy's hands. But I had put an end to that obsession. I had shown Ben what Daisy truly was. And now he was gone. It was the price I had to pay to make him see the truth. But he would be back, I was sure of that. Ben's absence would break their bond, though surely it was already broken? I wasn't a bad person for seeing the truth in the woman my son married and for wanting the best for my unborn grandchild.

I had thought of everything when it came to bringing my grandchild into the world, the birth being foremost the most important part to consider. I had my knowledge of pharmacy, but babies, that was a whole different ball game. But I had done plenty of research and preparation. I was sure Daisy was going be fine. She was a strong healthy girl and I had been feeding her all the right things. Once the baby was born, all would be well again and that baby would never want to leave me the way Ben did.

## 37

### GRACE

I continued with the cookery classes, in spite of my husband leaving. I had a baby to think of now. It was going to be just us.

When I arrived for one of our lessons, still with my secret growing within me, I saw Jenny standing in her usual place. She was beautiful and so tall it astounded me every time. Today her thick golden hair was falling naturally around her shoulders. I could see Jenny was fussing with it and patting her cheeks whilst holding a small compact mirror in her hand. When she saw me arrive, she snapped the mirror shut and her face stretched into a full beaming smile.

'Grace! It's so good to see you again. How have you been? Have you managed to practise any of the recipes yet? My husband is most impressed with the lasagne and he absolutely loved the scones. I think I might be getting rather good already and it's only been a few weeks.' Jenny wittered on. Every now and again her hand would rush to her cheek and she would try to turn her head but I had already seen it.

Another bruise. This one was too big to hide. No amount of make-up was going to fix that mess.

I realised that the woman who was standing before me was no longer the same woman I envied on the first week, with her perfect home life, growing brood and fertile ovaries. It was obvious that Jenny didn't want to share with me what had happened. Mikee had a bruise a few weeks ago, she had one on the other side of her face last week and now this. It was clear that she was the victim. I bent down slightly to see if she had brought with her the little boy. He sat in his usual place, playing quietly with the toy train and I gave him a small wave. This time he looked up and waved back and my stomach did a little somersault. It was a sensation I had never before experienced. He was incredibly endearing. He continued choo-chooing around under the table, every now and again looking at me and giving me a cheeky smile. I watched him for a few seconds longer and then stood back up and looked at Jenny.

'What a good little boy,' I said and Jenny looked forlorn. 'And your husband? What does he think?' But I already knew the answer. It was black and blue and shining across her left cheek bone. I saw tears spring to Jenny's eyes. She looked across the room for a second to blink them away.

'What a fool he is. Such an old man. Thinks we can't afford another. But what's one more I told him, when we already have three!' Her voice was high and strained. 'Better make this the last one.' She spoke softer. I looked at Jenny's stomach which after three babies was clearly showing the signs of a healthy baby bump. The baby that Jenny was carrying was obviously an inconvenience and whilst she appeared to be immaculately turned out, I now saw the tiny tear in the hem of her skirt and the scuffs on her high heels.

She was wearing the same outfit she had been wearing the week before. She was clever at making herself look well-presented, as the way she did her hair made it appear, but it was now obvious to me that Jenny and her family struggled. She probably wasn't even paying for the classes; she had made it clear that she knew Emily well and I had not yet noted Jenny's name on the register where everyone else had a tick under the word 'paid'.

I wondered if the baby Jenny was carrying was one created from love and would it ultimately be unwanted. It made me realise how life could be so cruel. How I had wanted a baby so dearly and how it would make my husband happier, how I would never be enough for him. Now I had what I wanted, I would hold onto this baby tighter, do as much as I could to make sure it stayed safe. Back then I actually had had daydreams where I thought the baby could be the glue to heal the marriage. Whereas in Jenny's case it was tearing hers apart. I reached over onto the counter and touched her quivering hand. Jenny looked at it and I could see in her eyes that she knew what I had seen, sometimes there is just no hiding things from other women, and we don't even need to say anything.

The lesson began and Jenny seemed to relax a little more into the moment. Intermittently, Mikee would show his face under the counter and Jenny would toss him a bit of pastry to knead in his chunky little hands, he grinned up at me and I did a peek-a-boo back at him.

When the class had finished, I touched Jenny on her arm. 'I'll see you next week?'

'Oh gosh, yes. Wouldn't miss it for the world. Look at us two, like a real pair of Mary Berrys.' Jenny chuckled and motioned for Mikee to come out of his play den under the table. When he stood up, he smiled at me.

'Say bye bye to Grace, Mikee,' Jenny said.

'Bye bye,' Mikee said softly and waved with his little chubby arm and if it wasn't for the foetus growing inside me, I would certainly have felt the crushing weight of a childless existence bear down on me even harder.

# 38

---

DAISY

Looking back now, I realised it was this very day that was the turning point. The point at which I became the most vulnerable and when I allowed everything to turn sour. To date I must have been living in some sort of dream. I hadn't been completely thinking straight. I think I was just sleepwalking through each day rather than allowing my feelings to surface, I was pushing them down, hiding them. From Annie. I didn't want her to see me at my most raw. I didn't want her to see me weak.

That morning, I got up and got dressed as usual, taking particular care over my hair, which had grown longer and unruly. Much like it was when I was a little girl and I would run wild around the vast garden in the family home.

I tied it back into a ponytail and then went the extra mile and pulled it around into a neat bun. I examined myself closely. I reminded myself of my old primary school teacher, not the aerobics instructor I had been months ago. The floral floaty dress which Annie had picked out for me last week, compensated for my hair that hadn't been shaped or cut for months. I applied a subtle shade of red to my lips, one of the few things I had left that had belonged to Eve. She had dropped it in my handbag with a cheeky grin and a wink on that night. The last night.

I picked up the letter again. I needed to check that it was today because my mind was all over the place, I couldn't seem to hold onto a single thought properly. I felt a sudden urge to be sick again. I ran from the bedroom, into the bathroom and allowed the retching to take over my body. There was nothing to come out because I hadn't eaten anything that morning even though Annie had stood over me sternly urging me to eat some of the scrambled eggs she had prepared.

Annie insisted on driving me to the court and I could tell she was quietly smug that I had allowed her to. Patrick had texted me a few times, offering his services in the gallant manner in which only he knew best, but I didn't wish to put him out. He was sad not to be nearer to me, that he couldn't step in and offer his help as and when. I tried not to think about his last words to me about his intense feelings for Eve. I had known Patrick for so long, I couldn't begin to doubt him as well.

Annie was obligingly quiet for the journey, allowing me to be alone with my thoughts. She parked outside the court and made quite a show of helping me out of the car in front of Patrick. She gave an awkward acknowledgement towards him and said she would meet me in the café around the corner in about an hour. I looked up at the bright blue March sky against the contrast of the dirty grey backstreet town building and thought about what was waiting for me on the inside.

Seeing Patrick was stranger than I had expected. He had

really lost a lot more weight and when he embraced me I could feel the bones in his back through his thin jacket.

'Darling, you look positively...' Patrick struggled with the final word.

'Shit.' I coughed out a laugh.

'No, just, well... you look tired. But you are glowing, blooming, and you are carrying a human inside you.' He placed his arm around my shoulder and escorted me into the coroner's court. A police officer greeted us in the doorway.

'Hi,' he said, looking at me.

'Daisy, this is Simon. He has been assigned as my family liaison officer. We've got quite a rapport going on, haven't we buddy?' Patrick slapped Simon's arm in his usual jovial manner. Simon smiled kindly and held out his hand to me.

'It's nice to finally meet you, Daisy,' he said. I placed my small hand in his large firm grip and let him shake it. 'So guys, the way this is going to work is, they will call you in in a little while. You will sit at the front. So far, it looks like it is just you two. When you get called I will walk you through into the room. You will hear the full report read out and you might be asked to say a few words, about Eve and the night it happened.' I felt my stomach drop and my face must have done something similar. 'Don't worry!' Simon reassured. 'Just basic stuff, just to clarify and it's mostly yes/no answers anyway. There will be some things that you might not want to hear.... like the way Eve died, but it's okay, you'll be fine. There will probably be a journalist sat at the back, taking notes for a small piece in the paper. It's so small...' Simon noted my expression again. 'Then that's it pretty much really. You'll be fine.' Simon looked at Patrick for encouragement.

'Yep, come on, Daisy, let's go and do this for our girl.' I allowed myself to be taken into the court room.

Patrick held my hand tighter than I had expected. I knew it was for his own sake and not mine.

Yet for the thirty minutes we were in the room listening to how Eve's head had made contact with the kitchen work surface when she was catapulted backwards during the gas explosion, and how the explosion was caused by a faulty gas appliance, I died a little more inside because I knew I was to blame. I was solely to blame because how could Eve be to blame? Eve was no more, so couldn't bear the burden. Neither of us had reported the fault to the landlord, so he certainly wasn't to blame. Of course, the coroner's report didn't at any time mention that one particular person was at fault, but I knew I was. I didn't cry because I felt I didn't deserve to cry. Instead I pinched my right thigh with my right hand and began to build the self-hatred within myself that would stay there for a very long time.

Outside the coroner's court, Patrick tried to comfort me over and over again, but I rejected his comments and his arms.

'I can't see you for a while, Patrick. I hope you understand. I just need to deal with this. I can't do that if I see you. Please, please don't contact me.'

'But, darling,' Patrick held his hand out even though he knew it was about to be made redundant. 'I need you. You're all I have left of her.' I pushed past him and rushed out into the bright morning and headed towards the café.

I stood in the middle of the brightly-lit room and watched as it began to spin about me.

I felt someone grab my arm and I looked around to see Annie.

'Come on,' she said and walked me outside.

* * *

Annie helped me to get my seat belt on and sat back in the driver's seat.

'Right, let's get you home then.'

'Should I go to the hospital, Annie, I feel… not well.'

'It's the shock dear. Nothing more.'

'But the baby,' I heard myself say for the first time.

'Now, Daisy.' Annie placed her hands on the wheel and looked straight ahead. 'You and I both know you are not feeling your best at the moment. Do I need to spell it out? As soon they see you in that hospital and see the state you are in, you know what will happen, don't you?' Annie waited for a response from me, when it didn't come, she continued. 'They will start making notes about you. Before you know it, you will be considered a high-risk case. Especially after everything that has happened with Eve. I presume the verdict was accidental death? I presume you are feeling the brunt of the blame? Do you know what the journalists will say about that?'

I looked up at Annie. 'But the family liaison officer said it would be a really small piece in the paper…'

'Yes, Daisy, small, but it's the words they will use. They will hint at neglect on the part of you girls. Did you ever get that appliance checked?'

'I know it's my fault, but I didn't do it on purpose.' I began to cry. I couldn't hide my emotions any longer.

'My dear, of course it's not your fault. Entirely. It was just a tragic accident. But these doctors, they talk to the social service people. They will start putting two and two together and coming up with all sorts. I've seen women have their babies taken away for far less.'

Annie's words were crushing me, I couldn't breathe. I willed her to start driving so I could feel the comfort from the motion of the car as she would take me back to the beach house, where I knew I would be safe.

# 39

ANNIE

I got Daisy settled under the bed sheets before handing her a chamomile tea. I concluded that extra iron wouldn't go amiss at this stage and I had stopped on the way home and bought a cart load of vitamins.

'Now drink this, swallow a couple of these; I've got iron, zinc and vitamin C and try not to think about that awful stuff. You will prepare yourself for reading what they print, but then you will put it behind you. This week's newspaper will be lining next week's bins, my dear.'

'I feel like I need something stronger.'

I watched as Daisy's teeth chattered and her hands shook.

'I'll run you a warm bath and get you a shot of brandy. One shot can't do any harm on a day like today.'

Daisy nodded and I left the room.

I went to the bathroom and began to run the water in the bath.

When I returned to the bedroom, I found Daisy crouched down on the floor. Fear catapulted through me. If Daisy was miscarrying, the mess would be horrendous. I wasn't sure I was able to cope with that. However, as I approached Daisy's bedside, I couldn't see any blood and there were no signs that she was in pain. She was however, weeping. Well, that was something at least. But to say she was inconsolable was an understatement. It took me half an hour to get one word out of her and then another half an hour to get her undressed and into the bath. All the while, Daisy was muttering like a drunk, talking about Ben and Eve in incomprehensible short blasts. Once she was out of the bath and dry again she had seemed to settle a bit.

'Shall I see if I can get something for you? Something to take the edge off it?' I looked down at Daisy sat up in bed with my fluffy dressing gown on, her cheeks were rosy from the steam and heat of the bath.

'You mean drugs?'

'Yes, Daisy. I mean drugs. I know what to get and where to get it. I have plenty of whatever you need here. I know exactly what will work for you.'

'What about the baby?'

'Oh don't worry about the baby, Daisy dear. I would never dream of hurting the baby.'

Daisy seemed to respond to the drugs very well. Just a little something to take the edge off it. At least there wouldn't be any more of those meltdowns. There was only so much I could take of that. But it wouldn't be long until she was completely dependent on them, so she wouldn't experience any of those horrible feelings again.

I was never one to respond well to a cry baby. Ben hadn't cried very much when he was a little boy. If he had fallen down and hurt himself, he would sit quietly for a moment, as though he were making the pain disperse back within him, and then he would stand up and carry on. None of this running to me to kiss it better. There was never any running to me for anything really, which at first had bothered me, until I realised the convenience of it. I was a mother with a son, but without all the silly soppy nonsense that went with it.

For the next few days Daisy took her meals alone in her room and came downstairs once a day for some fresh air and a walk around the garden. There was little interaction between the two of us. Which suited me fine. I was an excellent mother and carer. I knew how to make a house a home, I dressed my son to perfection, helped him with his school-work and cooked healthy homemade meals. I expected that to compensate for what I lacked in cuddles and all those other things I saw mothers do with their children. I think in the end too much soppiness ruins a child.

Occasionally Daisy asked questions, about Ben or Eve, or talked about police and hospitals, and when I could hear the worry heighten in her voice, I would increase the amount of the drugs, which would send the girl into a compliant state once more.

The swell to Daisy's stomach was increasing day by day as there was barely anything of her anyway. I could almost feel the tiny bundle in my arms. It wasn't going to be long now.

* * *

The pool arrived and I had already set it up in the dining room and looked at it daily and imagined the little purple bundle sliding out into the water, just as I had seen on the videos on YouTube. It was the perfectly natural way for babies to come into the world. Just like my Ben did.

Each week I had been ordering something from the internet to arrive.

I had showed the basic bits to Daisy, who had pulled her mouth into some sort of expression that neither indicated nonchalance nor excitement. But I had been secretly stashing away all the other little extra things, like mobiles, booties and cotton blankets.

This was what I was good at, being organised. I thought about Ben and for a moment I felt close to him again, as though he wasn't far away. We had come so far and achieved so much together as a team.

I just hoped one day he would realise it as much as I did.

## 40

DAISY

It was a topsy-turvy world I was living in. I couldn't stop saying the words. Topsy-turvy. They kept rolling around in my head. I couldn't remember when I had ever used the words topsy-turvy before. But they seemed appropriate and they seemed to have taken up permanent residence in my head like two uninvited lodgers. Yet they were the only description of how I was feeling. What if they never went away? What if every day was spent with those two ridiculous words stuck in my head? At the thought of this my mouth became very dry and the pit of my stomach churned. My legs started to shake on autopilot. It wasn't cold. In fact, it was too warm. So why was I shivering. I stood and looked out of the closed window. Below the sea was still and I could see the silhouette of a man and a dog in the distance. It was early, or so it seemed. The world had just been continuing around me and I had never felt so disconnected. I looked at the sand, the sea; the man in the distance and although I could see them, none of it felt real. It was all just... topsy-turvy.

I felt empty, even though I was brimming with new life.

Annie had promoted herself without any protest from me, to taking care of pretty much everything. She had told me there was no need to go for any scans or have appointments. It was a relief in a way, because since the day of the court, I had barely even stepped outside the front door. Patrick's words still haunted me and without Ben here I felt terrified. Since Eve's inquest result I felt the burden of her death even more heavily. It was an effort to do most things. Staying put felt right. I was safe here.

Besides, I was not entirely sure how I would have made it out of the house and have actual conversations with people. I had long forgotten what it was like to be functioning at a reasonable level. Didn't I have a life? A job? I couldn't remember what it felt like, I couldn't place those feelings again, the feeling of just being, without this weight of doubt and worry in the pit of my stomach. Suddenly my attention was drawn to a ticking sound in the room. I looked at the bedside table. There was a large round clock with a black base and a white face. It was just there. Had I noticed that before? I wasn't sure I had. It looked familiar yet completely alien.

My mind raced backwards and forwards to what I could see now out of the window, the ticking of the clock and the last day I saw Ben. I couldn't even remember what I had said to him now. I could see that clock face plain as day but I could not remember what Ben looked like. I had several photos of him in my phone but the task of going into the photos folders and scrolling through images filled me with dread. A mundane task which usually would require no thought suddenly seemed arduous and terrifying.

I just knew that this was all my fault. Everything that had

happened to Eve, the reason Ben wasn't here, it was all down to me.

The fragility of life was suddenly weighing down upon me. Something I had taken for granted, something I had rarely thought about, was now apparent. I was very conscious and aware of living. I could hear and feel the breath in my chest. It felt laboured and obvious.

Standing in this room, breathing, looking but not seeing, hearing the clock's heavy ticking. Those words, still falling about my mind:

Topsy-turvy.

Topsy-turvy.

Topsy—

'Daisy! What are you doing standing there? You should have flung that window open by now, it's so hot in here.'

I turned and saw Annie standing there in all her glory. Keen and excited for another day preparing herself for becoming a grandmother.

'Did I have breakfast?' I asked in a monotonous voice that didn't sound like me.

'No, not yet. I'm going to make you a sandwich and fruit. It's almost lunchtime. I just thought I would come and show you this!' She practically fell towards me with excitement. I stepped back slightly, feeling threatened by the energy.

'Look!' Annie thrust a white machine towards my face.

'It's so we can hear the baby's heartbeat! Would you look at that? It just arrived.' I looked at the contraption in Annie's hand. I was suddenly filled with dread. Was I ready to hear the heartbeat? I was feeling the kicks daily but to hear him or her would clarify it further. That I was to become a mother. A mother I failed at being the first time. I wasn't sure if I was ready.

Right then, dear, let's get you some lunch and then I'll be back to try this out.' Annie swept herself out of the room as quickly as she entered it.

\* \* \*

Sometime later she returned. It couldn't have been too long as I hadn't yet made it from the window over to the bed. Annie laid the tray out on one side of the bed and patted the other side. I obeyed and sat down like an old trained dog.

She handed me a glass of water and small white tablet. I took them both, placed the pill on my tongue and swallowed it with a large glass of water.

I had no idea what I was taking them for. But Annie said I was slightly unstable and to get me back on track I needed a little pick me up.

'I don't feel like these are working,' I said with a slight tremor to my voice. I still felt as though I was living life outside of myself as an observer.

'That's because you're carrying a baby. Your hormones are all over the place. But believe me, if you weren't taking them...' Annie stopped fussing with the tray and looked at me. 'Well, Daisy, I don't know what state you would be in. You have had such a shock these last few months. So much to deal with.' Annie whipped out the strange-looking machine again. 'Right, finish your sandwich and then shall we have a go with this thing then?'

I chewed and swallowed the bread which felt thick as a brick in my throat. Annie looked at me with what looked like irritation.

'Something wrong?'

'I've never been a big eater of bread and I don't know, it tastes strange today.'

'It's bread, Daisy. It won't kill you,' Annie said and all I heard was that one word. Kill. I looked at her and her stare seemed to penetrate through me.

I put the plate with half-eaten sandwich back on the tray and Annie placed it on the floor.

'This bit is the Doppler!' Annie held the base up. 'You put the headphones on and hear the baby's heartbeat. The Doppler goes on your stomach, I think... I'm not sure. Anyway, let's just muddle through. You are supposed to lie down and pull your T-shirt up. I've got this gel stuff, it helps move the Doppler bit around so we can hear the baby.'

I lay down and pulled my T-shirt up.

'Well, aren't you lucky not to have stretch marks Daisy?' Annie's voice sailed through a cacophony of notes as she fiddled with the device.

'Did you get stretch marks? With Ben?' I asked.

Annie stopped fiddling and her faraway look was back. 'Oh yes, as far as the eye could see. I'd never make a bikini model. Right, shall we get on then?' Annie's look was gone and she was back in the moment. I eyed the Doppler nervously. 'There's nothing to worry about, it's like listening to a song on a pair of headphones.'

Annie rubbed some gel on the Doppler and then placed it on my bump.

'Hold that in place whilst I get these things on.' I placed my hand over the alien contraption whilst Annie began arranging the headphones over her own ears.

'Aren't those supposed to be for me?' I wasn't sure I had said the words. It didn't feel like I had enough strength in me to say them. I looked at Annie getting the headphones arranged neatly over her ears. She pulled one foam earpiece away.

'What's that, dear?'

'I... erm... shouldn't I hear the baby first?' I repeated.

'Well, yes, dear, let me just get this thing going...' Annie began pressing buttons on the Doppler and moving it around my taut stomach. 'Then we can... oh right, that was easy, oh yes, that's it... oh...' Annie sat in front of me on the bed. She was sitting very still, completely in her own world, listening intently. I too sat quietly, not wanting to interrupt what seemed like a poignant and precious moment. I ignored the stirring pang that was suddenly there. A want, a need to hear what was alive inside me. A few minutes later, Annie pulled the headphones from her ears and let them sit around her neck.

'Well, that was... lovely.' Annie sat still for a few moments.

'Did it remind you of Ben?'

'What? Oh yes, it's so delightful to hear your baby's heartbeat for the first time, there's nothing like it. Here, here.' She pulled off the headphones. 'You try.'

She placed them on my ears.

'I can't hear anything,' I said, not even aware of the level of my own voice.

'Hang on a minute.' Annie moved the Doppler about. 'Little rascal is on the move.' A loud echoing punching sound was suddenly in my ears. With the noises of the room completely shut out, I felt as though I were in the womb myself. I closed my eyes and imagined a small warm cosy space, where the baby was cuddled. I too wanted to be transported there, to feel safe and unconscious. I was being lulled by the heartbeat into a state of meditation. I felt suddenly calm. I had completely forgotten where I was. I didn't know I was crying until there was a salty taste in my mouth. Suddenly the headphones were being pulled off my ears and I was catapulted back to stark reality of the bedroom. Annie was standing over me taking the Doppler from my stomach.

'Right that's enough for today. I read you shouldn't do it too often either, something to do with radiation.'

'Radiation?' I wiped the tears away and pulled my T-shirt back down and shuffled my body back up the bed.

'Well yes, Daisy, of course this is all unnatural materials. Didn't have this in my day. Got to be careful.'

Annie was packing the monitor away in the box.

'So how did you hear the heartbeat?'

'What?' Annie snapped and spun back around to look at me.

'You said you didn't have this equipment. But when I asked you a moment ago, you said it reminded you of Ben.'

Annie pursed her lips and then spoke curtly.

'It was something similar. Not as technical. It was a very old contraption that was much like a stethoscope if you must know.' Annie looked perturbed. 'At the doctor's surgery. None of these fancy at home machines.' Annie looked at me sternly. 'I'll be serving coffee downstairs in fifteen minutes if you can drag yourself out of this pit.'

Annie marched out of the room clutching the box with the heart monitor in it.

I lay back and closed my eyes again, waves of negativity flooded my body. Something didn't feel right about any of what just happened. It reminded me of another incident and I found myself thinking back to the first day I met Annie when I got burned by the teapot. I began to feel a glimmer of an instinctual feeling, a force that was pulling me closer to the life growing within me. I had felt safe until now here at the beach house, but Annie's behaviour towards me was increasingly alarming. This woman I should be thinking of as my mother-in-law was as much a stranger to me as my husband.

I tried to bring myself back to the feeling in the womb, imagining myself tucked away there safely. I even allowed myself a brief image of the baby in there all cosy and I felt a flicker of optimism that I was doing something mildly worthy. Even without the headphones on, I could still hear the heartbeat echoing in my ears. There was a baby inside me. Of course there was... It was natural, innate within me to be able to cope with being a mother. My senses were momentarily awakened by what I had just heard. I would ask Annie to let me hear it often enough to keep me thinking positively about the birth, which was now so close. The shift in my emotion was so slight, but it gave me enough energy to get up from the bed and go to the window. Outside a few clouds had gathered to create a grey tinge to the sky and the ocean looked wide and empty. It made me feel uneasy. I thought about the baby and the responsibility. I was incapable before, why would I be capable now. I would have no choice but to be its mother. That choice had been removed from me before, too easily when I look back now. But today I was a fully grown woman, able to make my own decisions and those for a helpless infant.

The baby would want to be, fed, cuddled and taken out. It would be solely reliant on me. The thought made the panic rise from my stomach to my throat. I slowly backed away from the window and the vast endless sea and went back to the security of the bed.

\* \* \*

It was dark, I was in the place somewhere between awake and asleep. Somewhere I was familiar with recently and it felt very comfortable to be there. I could hear banging. Was it coming from me, in my chest? I began to rouse myself a little more. The sound continued. It was a familiar noise something I had heard before. It was comforting, it was a sound that was pulling me towards consciousness. Bang bang bang... the baby. It was trying to get out? My eyes shot open. I could now feel my own heart pounding. I reached for my phone to see the time. It was just after 6 a.m. and starting to get light. The room was quiet. No banging. The window was closed. I had been dreaming. There was a glass of water and a pill on the bedside table. I had been taking them twice daily now, but for what? I accepted them because of how much pain I was in over Eve and the loss and anger I felt over Ben. A thought came to me. What if I didn't take the pill today? I had been taking them for so many weeks now, surely they couldn't be doing the baby any good.

But I was numb with them. The idea of experiencing a tsunami of emotions that related to Ben, Eve and the baby terrified me.

I rolled towards the bedside table, put the pill on my tongue and took a long gulp of water.

# 41

In hindsight it was a ridiculous thing to have done. I had wanted to hear the baby's heartbeat for myself, to check everything was as it should be. I had read so much online recently and checking the baby's heart at home was something a lot of mums were doing these days. It had been impossible to get anything out of Daisy in terms of what the baby was doing, how she was feeling or anything to do with the pregnancy, so the Doppler seemed the obvious option. I hadn't realised for a moment it would trigger some sort of maternal instinct in Daisy. All those tears. She knew she wouldn't be good enough for this baby and I didn't need to confuse her by letting her hear and think otherwise.

Daisy's pregnancy and imminent arrival of my first grand-child was making the memories of those early days with Ben come back alive, finally getting the boy I had hoped for. I couldn't ever imagine myself with a girl. I think I wanted a boy in the beginning for Rory. Every man hopes for their own son. But in the end, I wanted a boy for me. I wanted that tender dependency coupled with fearless adventure-seeking that boys were renowned for being with their mothers. But until Daisy came along, Ben was happy with just me. As a child, Ben was careful, thoughtful, never one to take chances. I always wondered if and when things might change. And they had. Things had definitely changed. I felt the longing for the innocence again.

These last few months with Daisy were reminding me so much of how it was with me and Ben, how becoming a mother for the first time was exhilarating yet scary. I wasn't sleeping well, I knew that. I was waking in the mornings feeling extremely fatigued. My muscles ached daily from the amount of hard graft I was doing around the house, always trying to maintain a tidy and hygienic one.

In the mornings I looked at the bed sheets and it appeared as though I had been having some sort of fight with the pillows in the night. I had clearly been experiencing fitful sleep. I looked at my arms and legs, they were littered with small bruises.

I knew it was the stress of it all. I might not be the one pregnant this time, but I was carrying all the anxieties. I needed to de-stress.

The beach. It called to me on days like this. I would leave Daisy in bed. It was still early. She was rising later these days with only a few weeks to go. I would walk along the rocky shore, the way Ben and I did when he was young. We would look for small stones to throw into the water and sit and watch the fishermen far out to sea and guess what they might be catching.

I pulled on a light cardigan as, even though it was almost April, the sea breeze always found its way to my bones.

I set out down the garden and strode over the small wall which took me straight onto the beach. Even though it was considered private land, occasionally people would wander past. It always unnerved me, but I turned a blind eye and hid in the summer house until they were out of sight, never really wanting to draw attention to myself.

As I walked I thought about Daisy sitting alone in the house, her purpose now clear in my head. I had muddled feelings of Ben, I was hanging onto the boy he was, yet he was a man now, with thoughts and feelings so far removed from me. I had despised Daisy from the outset, but now it was clear why Ben had brought her here: to deliver the new baby into my world.

A seagull landed on a piece of driftwood in front of me but flew off the moment I approached. There was no one on the beach today, so I took the time to enjoy and reflect on what I had created for me and my son. The vast space, the gentle sound of the rolling waves, the foaming froth of the tide. It was all so close to me and yet I rarely came out and enjoyed it these days.

These sounds and these sights of the natural waves and wind healed my doubts and insecurities as they seemed larger than the problems I had. They engulfed them and swallowed them down whole. I had worried about Daisy and her impact on my life but now I was starting to feel confident again, things were starting to click into place. There were certain things that were out of my control, that I had tried tirelessly to control for too long. I felt ready to let go. It was time for a fresh start.

# 42

GRACE

I arrived at Emily's house for one of the lessons in late May, ready to make chicken and ham pie and oat cookies. Jenny was in a particular flap. She looked anxious and kept touching her long blonde hair that was tied up in her usual French pleat. I could tell that something wasn't right about her, so I waited until she got little Mikee settled under the table and then approached her. I arrived at her side and touched her arm.

'Hello, Jenny.'

Jenny jumped and turned to look at me throwing her hand to her chest. 'Oh, Grace, golly, you gave me a fright.'

'You look bothered by something?' I frowned at the woman I now felt such a strong connection towards, a sort of nurturing protection. I felt as though we were sisters; that I could tell her anything. And I would of course. Very soon.

It was comforting to have someone else I knew who was also anxious, it took the focus off my own stresses and worries. I was feeling the beginnings of morning sickness. The tiredness had set in. The pregnancy was very real again.

I was worried about the life of this child. I wanted my body to hold on to it so much I was using everything I could to do so.

Jenny looked especially fraught that morning. She was wringing her hands and hunting through her handbag over and over.

'Is there something I can do for you? Cup of tea perhaps?' I quizzed, knowing it was tea I wished for myself. Tea and a chat with someone who understood me and the situation and the exciting journey of motherhood I was about to embark on.

'No, no, not tea. I've drank six cups already this morning,' Jenny said with her head in her bag. I looked on curiously.

'Have you lost something?' I asked her.

'No. I'm just checking...' Jenny tried to construct a sentence but was clearly too absorbed in her task. Then she suddenly stopped her searching to look at me. Her face softened and she whispered, 'Can you keep a secret?'

I touched my chest.

'Yes, Jenny.' I said and she nodded. My chest felt as though it might explode with the love I felt for her right then. 'I can keep your secret, Jenny, what is it?'

Jenny looked around the room and I followed her gaze. The class was still five minutes from beginning, some of the other women were still arriving and chatting by the door. Emily was stood at the front organising her notes. Jenny finished looking about the room and looked again at me

'It's my husband. I'm leaving him.'

My hand flew to my mouth. I had only known Jenny for a short time, and even then I only saw her for a few hours a day, but she was a part of my life. I felt as though we had become so close. I looked forward to seeing her every week.

She had never said that we were best friends, but I felt that was exactly what we were.

Then the shock of what Jenny had told me was as though it was happening to me. And it was, only my husband had left me. This was too convenient. The fact we were both married, Jenny on the brink of divorce, me with mine finalised. My husband had done a damn fine job of getting things moving swiftly with that one. And now with babies growing inside us. Something had brought us together.

Images started to fly around my mind of Jenny homeless, her three children and unborn child without a father. I felt like I now had a role and that I was slotting into Jenny's life. It all started to make sense: why I was here, why my husband had gone; Jenny needed me.

'Okay everyone, I know we're a few minutes early but can we get started as I have a pressing appointment straight after the class, so I can't stay and answer any of your questions today.' Emily's voice came from the front of the room. 'Although by now, you are all experts so I'm sure you won't need my humble advice any more,' Emily said with a knowing smile and sniggers of agreement circled the room. The class assembled themselves around us to begin the class.

'I'll talk to you during the break,' Jenny whispered and I gave her a firm nod. I knew my role now as Jenny's friend and I would do whatever I needed to do to help her.

Emily guided us through the class as usual with dexterity and I meticulously followed the instructions, although my mind was wandering to thoughts of Jenny. I could see little Mikee playing with his toys under the bench. I completed the task, as usual before anyone else in the group, and after I had cleaned my surface down, I moved closer to Jenny who had stopped her cooking to tend to Mikee. She had lifted him up to sit on the bench. I approached and looked at the little lad at eye level.

'Hello, darling,' I said in manner that I felt one should address a toddler. Mikee gave me one of his cheekiest grins and I felt a gap inside me fill up.

'I'm afraid we aren't getting anywhere today, Grace.'

'Oh well, I can see why, Jenny. He's a little cracker.' I leant over and tickled him under the chin. Mikee giggled and I felt an alien sensation in my chest, like an intense fluttering. I turned to Jenny.

'So you were telling me? Your husband?' Jenny looked at me shook her head and waved her hand

'Oh, that. No. I was being silly. I wasn't thinking straight. Forget I said anything.' She rubbed her swelling stomach. 'It's nothing, Grace. Forgive me, I was being rash.'

I felt anger surge through my body and a frown fill my face. I tried to lose it before Jenny turned to look at me. When she did, I was ready with a smile.

I couldn't understand. A few minutes ago, I was on the verge of being able to help Jenny, of being the one she confided in. I had invested my thoughts in her, worried for her safety and now she was brushing me aside, as though it didn't matter. I could feel something building within me, an anxiety, a bitterness. I didn't want to be made to feel anything but wanted and needed.

# 43

DAISY

There wasn't much of a change as the days went by. I had to keep talking myself round, telling myself it was going to be okay. Even though I didn't believe it, I told myself anyway. Occasionally I thought my heart was going to jump right out of my chest. If I wanted to, I could stop taking the pills, save them up one by one until I had enough to take at once and do permanent damage. Then I wouldn't need to wake up and still feel as though I were living in a nightmare.

Another morning arrived with another pill. I looked at it in my hand, ready to stash it away. I only needed to do that for a few more weeks and then everything would be okay. It would all just, stop.

The fear in the pit of my stomach was still there. The random thoughts, the guilt.

I took some time to walk about, spend time downstairs and absorb the hazy light of the spring evenings. I went through the motions. Doing all the things I felt I should do. But why wasn't it changing? All I had was the trust I could invest in myself. But I was never one to be trusted. Not by anyone. I thought of this time, these precious moments I should have been spending with Ben, each kick of the baby should have been shared with him, but I was doing it alone. As I had done once before.

I could feel the weight of Annie's stares as I wandered around the garden and lounged in the summer house. She always seemed to be there, around a corner pegging out washing or at the side of the bed removing used crockery.

I was in bed most days by 7 p.m. I had established some sort of monotonous routine. Doing things to distract myself from the feeling. The darkness that crept around my body and prevented any joy or happiness from entering. I wished I could wash it away. But I didn't know how. I tried to cast my mind back to the early days with Ben when I was completely obsessed with him and him with me. It felt so long ago yet we hadn't even reached our first anniversary.

That night I washed and dressed for bed as usual, taking extra care over my teeth. I had suddenly become panicky of them. It came from nowhere, but it felt like it was something very real. I was worrying that the pregnancy was going to make them all fall out. I'm sure I felt a loose one the other day. I imagined myself an unhealthy toothless woman and I had begun to obsess about it. Watching what I was putting in my mouth. Not consuming any sugar. Annie thought I was doing it for the baby and had praised me for my efforts. But she had no idea the lengths I was going to each day. The amount of time I was thinking about things that would never normally cross my mind. I looked at them now in the mirror. They didn't look like my teeth any more.

I climbed into bed and closed my eyes. It was strange how easy sleep came. That was something I thought I would struggle with what with everything my mind was doing, the endless obsessing and thinking and worrying. But each night I lay down and listened to the now familiar noises of the house. The faraway creaking and banging. I had become accustomed to the clanking I heard. They were just part of the house and I had grown to be comforted by them and they now played their part in lulling me to sleep.

* * *

I wasn't sure what I was experiencing at first, was it a dream? There was light and it was harsh and bright. Was I dead? Had I died in my sleep? Was the baby okay? Was I in labour? In the few moments it took for me to come round, all of these thoughts had already been processed.

As I started to come round from sleep I struggled to get to my phone and look at the time. It was 2.36 a.m. The light was on in the room and Annie was standing in front of the bed.

Stark naked.

I sat up, suddenly petrified. I pulled the duvet over my body.

'Annie, what are you doing!' I yelled. Annie didn't reply. She just stood still, her stare burning through me.

Then a memory returned to me. That Christmas night when Annie walked in on me in the bathroom. She had been sleepwalking. I leant forward and looked at her. She looked like she was in the same sleep-like trance as she had been that time. It was eerie to watch but I took a few moments to examine Annie in her most vulnerable state. She wasn't fat. There weren't rolls of flab hanging from her waist or thighs. Her skin was surprisingly taut for a woman in her sixties. I cast my eyes across her body. I was startled to see bruises on her arms and legs. On her left arm she had three bruises next to one another in a neat row. I got out of bed feeling a slight chill on my arms. Annie had already turned and was headed back towards the door. I thought I should follow her to make sure she got back safely. In the hallway her whole body was illuminated by the ceiling light and I watched each bottom cheek rise and fall as she walked slowly back to her room. Annie arrived at her bedroom and I stopped abruptly behind her.

That was when Annie turned round and looked directly at me, her nose inches from mine. I took a sharp intake of breath and stepped backwards. Annie turned back to face her door, walked through it and even shut it after herself. I stood for a few minutes taking it all in. Then I waited a few minutes more. I was intrigued to see what Annie was doing on the other side of the door, but I was terrified of what I might find. I tentatively approached the door and opened it as slowly as I could. The light was still on and there was Annie underneath the duvet. I crept over and listened for breath. I'm not sure why, it was a strangely maternal act. I heard the steady rhythmic breathing so I stepped backwards, turned out the light, left the room and padded back down the hall to my room, turning off the hall light on the way.

Back in my bedroom I turned off the big light and climbed into bed. The weight of my bump was now so uncomfortable, I was experiencing regular shooting pains and dull aches low down. I pushed a pillow under my stomach and felt the relief of the weight lifted. I lay there, still feeling the chill of the room and pulled Ben's cardigan around me. An eeriness to the whole scenario was filling my body. I kept playing it over and over, wondering why it was bothering me so much.

It took me a little while to fall back to sleep. The image of

Annie was on replay in my mind, the unconscious look she gave me before she turned back into her room, the speed at which she was back in bed and lying there as though she hadn't just been standing naked in my room a few minutes earlier.

* * *

I slept in until almost lunchtime the next morning; being woken up in the night had affected me and this morning I found sleeping in came a little more naturally.

I woke to the door opening and Annie walked in with a tray of food.

'You need to keep your strength up and that baby needs food. You can't just sleep all day.' There was an edge to Annie's voice that hadn't been there yesterday. It made my stomach go tense.

Annie placed the tray of food down next to the bed. I peered over. Annie had prepared a fruit platter and a glass of water. She perched on the side of the bed, clamping down some of the duvet so it went taught across my leg. I jerked my leg to move but the weight of Annie's backside had made the duvet too tight for me to release it.

'Here is your pill, Daisy.' Annie held her hand out and the little white pill was sitting in the middle. I looked at it for a moment and then at Annie.

'You know, Annie, I think I'm going to try a day without drugs. See how I feel.'

She looked thoughtful for a moment. She took in a deep breath before she spoke.

'You know, I got to know an incredible number of social workers in my job, you wouldn't think it, would you? I know two very well. Still keep in touch with them online from time to time. Sometimes it's hard to not talk about us, me and you and our little set-up. I'm such an honest person, you see. I dread to think what damage it might cause.' We looked at one another, Annie's stare was firm and rigid. 'Anyway,' Annie sing-songed and stood up. I moved my leg and felt the air circulating around it again. 'I'm sure you think you know what's best for you, Daisy, but things are different now. You're living here. This is my house after all.' Annie picked up the glass of water and pushed her open palm with the pill in it towards me. 'There you go, deary. Get it down you. Does you the world of good.'

I looked at Annie's hands outstretched one holding the water and one holding the pill. I felt the anxiety as it filtered its way around my body, I thought of my teeth and of the strange sentences getting stuck in my head like a scratched record.

'You're right,' I muttered.

I took the glass, popped the pill in my mouth, took a large gulp of water and swallowed.

Annie smiled and nodded. She placed the plate of fruit in front of me. I looked at the array of colours of watermelon, kiwi and grapes. 'Eat as much as you can. I'll be back later to collect it.'

I watched as Annie walked out of the room leaving the door ajar. When I heard her footsteps reach the bottom of the stairs, I put my hand to my mouth and retrieved the little white pill from under my tongue.

# 44

With so many tasks to keep myself busy with and how I was literally counting down the days, I found a whole morning had raced by having filled it with all the things I now did for Daisy. I would rise to make breakfast before her. I then cleared up and started preparing us both a healthy lunch whilst Daisy did whatever she did. I kept an eye on her mind, tried to get her out in the garden if it was nice in the mornings. Inhale some of that sea air that was so good for the baby. But she was clearly depressed. The tablets were helping her hold it together, I couldn't risk her coming off them yet. She could do all sorts of harm to herself. The girl was riddled with guilt, and so she should be.

Her acts were unforgivable, but she had the baby now and that changed everything. I was needed now more than anything.

After lunch Daisy was usually tired so she would nap. During this time I had been purchasing items for the baby online, looking on all the second-hand sites. It was amazing what I found for next to nothing. Daisy had not considered or talked about anything for the baby. I presumed she thought I would take care of it all, another sign the girl wasn't well. An expectant mother should be embracing pregnancy and looking forward to the baby arriving, buying little bits here and there. But Daisy had paid no attention to any of it. It was almost as if she didn't think there was going to be a baby. I was certain it was all going to work out just fine; as it should be.

When Ben arrived, I finally felt as though I had been awarded the most prestigious award possible. I felt as though I was the chosen one and Ben was the little oracle in my world. I didn't think I would ever get to experience that once more. Yet here I was about to embark on that journey all over again. The anticipation was almost unbearable. I wanted to feel the baby in my arms. I was ready to be a mother again.

# 45

GRACE

It was my last day at the cookery school. I hadn't thought it would be when I woke up. I was still signed up for another few weeks. I presumed I would see it through to the end and then afterwards, Jenny and I would spend more time with one another. Both of us with our new babies, and our newfound culinary knowledge. We had so much potential.

But she had fooled me. Pretended that she was going to confide in me and then changed her mind at the last minute. That wasn't what friends did. They told each other everything. Why didn't Jenny see me as a friend any more? I couldn't understand what I had done to deserve that.

I approached her with my concerns that morning.

'I'm sorry, Grace, I didn't mean to alarm you, it's just... well, you see, it's very complicated and I...' but Jenny couldn't finish her sentence. She was suddenly weeping, quite obviously and others were turning to look. I didn't want anyone else to come over and invade what we had. Jenny was on the verge of telling me what was going on. I needed her to tell me. To cement our friendship. She had to confide in me, and who knew, maybe I would reciprocate. Having never had that bond with another woman before. It was starting to feel like a friendship should feel.

'I'm sorry, Grace, I really am. You must consider me a total fool. I am afraid I haven't been straight with you because, well, my life is incredibly complex and well I just don't even know where to start. But I should enlighten you because you're nice, Grace. A real genuine person, I can tell.'

I smiled sheepishly and lowered my head as inside I felt my heart thump a little harder, swelling at the compliment. I touched my belly and looked at Jenny, waiting and wanting to know more.

Nothing could explain the emptiness one felt inside the womb whilst the mind still busied itself with the emotions of a pregnant woman. It was mental torture of the worst kind and it had happened over and over again. After so many miscarriages, to finally be awarded the precious role of a mother, felt like a prize I had been striving for all my life. Finally everything was falling into place.

## 46

It had been seventy-two hours since I took the last pill. I was going to hang on for another forty-eight hours. I was putting them under the mattress because I figured that I would need them, if things got too bad. I had a choice. A get out.

My eyes filled with tears regularly throughout the day, but it did feel different, I had to admit. Or maybe I was imagining it. The pain felt less dull and more real. I could actually acknowledge it and feel it as it was, rather than this surreal experience that was happening to someone else and not me.

I had thought so many times about the number of tablets I could stash and if I could use them to my advantage when the time was right. Without Ben here, was there really any point to me any more? And if there was no point to me, what would be the point of a baby?

Take the pills, take the pills.

I didn't deserve to feel numb, I reminded myself. I needed to feel the raw pain and take my punishment. Either that or finish myself off with them.

I caught sight of myself in the mirror next to the bed. My

face looked twisted and unfamiliar. My hair was unkempt. I had not had it cut since, well, I couldn't even remember when. It was almost touching my backside. A sudden image of me just a few months ago with Eve in our flat flashed into my mind and then there was panic rising though my chest. I ran to the bathroom and fell to my knees. I tried to breathe normally but I was acutely aware of my own breathing, my mouth filled with saliva and I found despite the heat, I was shivering.

There had to be answer to all of this. But I couldn't talk to anyone. I was clearly mad. They would lock me up and take the baby away from me.

I took several long breaths and blew them out slowly until I could feel the panic dispersing. I flushed the toilet and got myself straightened up and opened the bathroom door.

Then I was face to face to with Annie. My heart, which had begun to slow, was now galloping along at an alarming speed.

'Everything okay, Daisy? You were in there an awfully long time...'

'I'm fine.' I pushed past Annie and headed back to the bedroom.

'It's just, it's a rather nice day today. Not sure how many more of these we will get. I heard there was a cold spell headed. You should make the most of them. The baby needs sunlight for strong bones,' Annie was almost at my heels as she followed me into the bedroom.

'Yes, I will go out later.'

'Well. Just make sure you do, Daisy. I want my grandchild healthy.' She walked out of the room. I pulled my hair back into a ponytail. What had Annie just said? Her grandchild? Something about the way Annie had said 'her' grandchild made it sound as though she was making a claim over it and, through the dense pain and thick fog of depression that was still filling up around me, I felt a flickering of something that felt like a protective instinct.

Against my natural desire to crawl into bed and roll myself under the sheets, I took myself outside for some fresh air.

I could feel her stares from the kitchen window as I sat in the garden with my head tilted towards the sky and soaked up the healing rays of the spring sun. Annie must have been wrong about the bad weather that was due because the sun was as warm as it had been for weeks and there was blue all around me.

As I looked around at the cloudless sky and the vast endless flat sea. I felt a sensation, of something that felt like possibility. As I played with that positive thought, I felt a firm kick from the baby and I allowed myself to interpret that as confirmation. I laid my hand on my stomach and pressed firmly down on the little foot that was trying to burst out of me. I thought about the tablets I had been stashing. I would flush them away; I didn't need them. There was a baby in me desperate to live and it needed me to live too.

# 47

ANNIE

I was a serial mattress-turner, something that Daisy perhaps didn't know about me. I couldn't stand the idea of a mattress getting all squashed down in one place, they needed turning to keep them fresh all over. And what with the amount of time Daisy had been spending horizontal in that bed, it was all I could think about to get the thing turned every time I looked at her.

I was surprised to find what Daisy had been using the mattress for – to hide the tablets I had been giving her. I presumed I had got her into a state of mind where she believed she needed them.

And there she was, her face raised to the sun like she didn't have a care in the world. All the while, my son was somewhere else, forced away by her, everything had changed, because of her. I had encouraged her to get outside of course but for the sake of the baby. Vitamin D was important for healthy bone growth. And I needed my grandson to be strong.

Suddenly she was there, in the doorway. Her face had such a healthy glow to it.

'I need a drink.' Daisy picked up the water filter jug. 'It's warm out there.' She looked at me as I sliced the vegetables extra meticulously, my agitation manifested in the size and structure of the carrots.

'Can I help?' She poured herself a glass of water.

'You might chop off a finger, Daisy. No, not in your condition.'

'I'm pregnant, Annie, not incapable.'

I placed my knife down on the chopping board and turned and looked at her.

'No, not incapable, I have never said you are incapable. You were perfectly capable to get yourself into this situation. Tell me, how did you get pregnant in the first place? How does a bright young girl get herself into such a silly situation so early on? I mean, who could blame you, my son comes from good stock. Classically tall, dark and handsome, who wouldn't want to breed with him. No doubt that little baby of yours will be just as strong, healthy and clever as he is.'

I watched with pleasure as her face that had been so full of colour, drained to a non-descript grey.

'I forgot to take a pill – and I am married to him, Annie!'

'And what about your other pills, the ones to stop you going completely mad? I give them to you because I know you need them. You stop taking them then you are putting yourself in danger and I have allowed you to reside here even though you chased my son away. When will it end, Daisy, when will you have had enough of destroying people and peoples' lives? You think you are ready to become a mother in your condition? I have done so much for you. Do you think that by stopping taking your tablets you are helping anyone?'

I watched Daisy's face fall. She opened her mouth to say something, then closed it again. She turned and walked back out of the kitchen.

I turned back to the board and continued chopping the carrots into neat small square chunks.

# 48

DAISY

I felt as though I needed to run, but I had nowhere to run to. I began to pull at my skin as I paced the room. I couldn't contain the torrent of emotions that flooded my body. I felt as though they needed to be released or I would explode. And somehow, Annie knew. She must know all of it. I saw it the day I met her, the flickering of her eyes as she tried to place me. And she was right. Of course I wasn't capable of being a mother.

All the images I had worked so hard to forget were surfacing once again. The looks on the faces of the people I had hurt, the headlines, the gossip. The dreaded feeling in the pit of my stomach. The desire to end my life, even though it had barely begun. So young. So lost.

My life had been easy until then. Not perfect. But easy. Emotions weren't discussed, but if we all just remained civil, they never needed to be. It was no wonder my mother only had me. She suffered postnatal depression very badly, said she couldn't risk having any more after that. Raised in a large detached house on the outskirts of the city, I attended a very good all-girls school paid for by my father who worked hard at his business. He built it up when I was tiny so we could have everything we wanted and needed. Looking back though, what I wanted and needed was a real family, with my mum healthy and engaged in conversation with me and my dad throwing me around his waist and calling me his girl. He was always distracted. Never fully there. One foot was always already out of the door when he was saying goodnight; the books I held out to him to share with me refused with an empty promise of tomorrow.

School was a distraction. I did okay because I preferred being there to being at home.

Just after my fifteenth birthday, which came and went without a fuss from my parents, Callum arrived at school as the new English teacher, Mr Alderton. He had dirty blonde hair flicked to one side, piercing blue eyes and a shaven face revealing smooth flawless skin. All the girls were taken with him immediately, their voices dropping to a whisper when he walked past in his beige cords and slightly crumpled blue shirt. I opted out of their idle grotesque gossip, choosing to take in his beauty without comment. He offered the extra help I needed to pass my exams, I found myself drawn to him in more ways than just the father figure I was missing. I wasn't interested in English especially, but the world of literature suddenly became a whole lot more interesting with Callum there. But I couldn't concentrate in class. My thoughts were always somewhere else, usually on my dissatisfactory home life. I had my two close friends, Beth and Aimee. We did lots together, but I never really felt relaxed enough with them to fully open up about who I really was. They saw me as one of the tall, pretty, popular ones like them. But that's what I was on the outside. Only Callum really saw me, the person I was eager to become and with some nurturing would one day hopefully grow into.

He called me 'darlin'. His words were like honey warming my insides and I began to experience tingling all over whenever he gazed at me with his blue eyes.

I had stayed behind one day after class. I heard the scuffing and shuffling of the cleaner moving her mop and bucket down the corridor and when we felt we were totally alone, he turned to me and gently pressed his lips on mine, confirming every feeling I had been experienced in those weeks leading up to it.

He was seventeen years older than me, still a young man at thirty-two, finding himself and discovering things about who he was. He told me he felt pressured to be a particular person. He was recently married and they had started trying for a baby.

He told me all of this first, so everything was on the table, I suppose. It didn't change anything.

Our feelings remained. I was still a virgin and I gave myself to Callum two days later in a hotel room he booked specifically for that reason.

I didn't feel used, or dirty. It didn't feel wrong. It was all beautiful. I craved him, I thought about him night and day. We continued our relationship for four months. Four months of pure heaven. I didn't tell a soul. He was all mine and I was his.

Then everything came crashing down. It was so sudden. I couldn't have prepared for it.

One day, she was there. His wife: Karen. Small and bony. Her hard and bitter face pressed against the window of his car. She knew where we were. She had been tracing and following us for weeks.

She was livid. It was rage like I've never seen before. Certainly not in a woman. She was possessed with anger, spit falling from her mouth as she hurled the profanities at Callum.

I never saw him again after that day. He was dragged from the car by his tiny wretched angry wife and the next day at school he was gone. Relieved of his post by a man twice his age, with a beard so thick it looked positively inhabited.

I fell into a state of depression. Rumours circulated fast, Beth and Aimee deserted me. My parents were beside themselves. What had they raised? They questioned again and again, constantly looking to me for the answers, never once reflecting on their own position as parents and the lack of emotion that ran through our family. It was that barely-there kind of love that just about kept a family together, but we all would have been so much happier without it at all. Then the guilt wouldn't have been able to fester in the gaping holes which should have been overflowing with unconditional love.

But the worst was yet to come. If my parents thought they had been dealt a tough hand then they must have thought I had been given to them as the devil in disguise once the repercussions of my actions really came into play.

Just remembering the way things were for me as such a young girl, I wept for myself now. I could feel the baby was close to arriving. The pressure was building down below. I knew that feeling too well. I didn't know if I was ready to go through it again.

But I knew I had to and even after everything I had said to Ben and how much I hated him for deserting me, for not calling or texting and for not being here, right now in these last weeks when I needed him the most, he was all I could think of. He was all I ever wanted and needed.

As I clung to myself on the bed, I let the raw emotions fall out of me and tried to let the natural process of crying temporarily heal me.

# 49

ANNIE

I could hear the crying through the ceiling. Once or twice I hovered by the door listening. But I knew it couldn't go on forever. It wasn't good for the baby for a start and besides, I couldn't abide the relentless whimpering.

I prepared a simple snack of milk and breadsticks for her. She was still sobbing when I went in. She didn't turn. I laid the tray down next to the bed and perched myself on the edge. I put a hand reluctantly on her quivering leg.

'Daisy. This isn't good for you or the baby. I can't say I'm not sad too. I feel as though I have lost a son. But we just have to deal with it and get on with it for the sake of the baby.' I let those first words soak in and waited to see if they had taken any effect before I continued. Her leg stopped quivering under the weight of my touch.

'I have brought you a snack. You've not eaten all day. I've brought you something to take the edge off. I know you don't want to take the tablets any more. I know how much you favour a holistic lifestyle, but they might be necessary. Well, they are necessary. But for now, why don't you sit up and have a nibble on something?' I waited patiently for several minutes before Daisy finally turned and sat up. The mound of her stomach peeped out under her T-shirt.

Daisy's face was red and blotchy, her eyes puffed out.

'I know... I know I need to take the tablets,' she said between gulps. 'I don't think I was ever well enough. Even before Eve and Ben.'

'I know, dear, I know.' I patted her leg. I could feel the relief sweep through me. Finally she was succumbing. 'It won't be forever. It's just for the safety of the baby. You have a lot of responsibility for that unborn child. If your emotions are all over the place, you aren't really responsible for yourself. You just need a little help. That's all.'

She nodded compliantly as she took the plate from my hand and began nibbling lightly on the breadsticks.

I then handed her the tablets. 'That will help you sleep. Although you must be exhausted.'

She just nodded this time.

I tried to conceal my thrill at her compliance as she took the tablets.

Daisy raised her head and looked at me sorrowfully. She forced herself to swallow the breadstick which looked positively painful and pulled her face into a weak smile.

'Thank you,' she whispered so quietly it was barely audible. But I knew she was grateful, that poor pathetic girl only had me. There wasn't one soul left in the world who cared about her.

I didn't feel any sorrow for her as I left her in the room that night – although I made sure that all sharp objects were removed from her room and the bathroom, just to be on the safe side.

I had been where Daisy was. I had felt the utter hopelessness at life: over and over again the world had punished me.

In the end, we get what we need, not what we want.

## 50

DAISY

From that day on I stopped fighting. I allowed Annie to run things the way she wanted. She was right. Back then when I was just a fifteen-year-old kid, I took full responsibility for my part. Callum took his responsibility and paid the ultimate price in many ways too, but I bore the brunt of the guilt. I had so many more emotions that tormented me for years afterwards. That still tormented me to this day.

After Callum's wife found us, I took a week off school then I asked my mum if I could go back. I wasn't desperate to get back to classes, or face the torrent of subtle micro aggression that would seep from the mouths of those girls I had considered to be my friends a mere few days earlier. Nor was I in in any hurry to face the condescending look and tone of the teachers who would try and conceal their disgust but would always see a minor, a young girl who had had sex with the bloke they shared the staff room with. But to stay at home and be tortured by the look from my mother, who felt I had failed her in so many ways already, was the worst of the two evils.

But despite my contesting, my parents, whom I had never seen more united on any topic, told me I would never be returning to that school. If at the time I felt as if my life was completely ruined and that it was my punishment, then it was only because I had yet to discover what true misery felt like.

The first week after I left school for good, I missed Callum so much it became a permanent pain in my chest, rising into my throat and making it difficult to breathe. I couldn't think of anything or anyone else. He filled my every thought in my waking moment and haunted every dream. I couldn't be rid of him. I walked around the house feeling much like a spare part and endured the looks of disappointment from each of my parents if I would happen upon them on the stairway or coming out of the bathroom. If they were feeling particularly hard done by that day, they would ignore me altogether.

Of course, I had no idea what it was I needed or was craving from them; I was a mere child being treated like an incompetent adult.

To compensate for their lack of affection I ate more than I should have done and I became quickly podgy. I was never interested in sports. That came later. My puppy fat and their constant dismissal of me was how I managed to get away with it. I was barely touched by either of my parents prior to my disgracing them, but after Callum there was certainly no hint at them wanting to be near me, embrace me or comfort me, so they would never have felt the slow gentle swelling beneath my clothes. Only I interpreted the missed periods, the sickness, the tiredness and eventually my abdomen taking shape into a small perfect round neat bump, to be a pregnancy. A baby made by Callum and me.

Whilst there were odd uttered words to me about food
that needed to be eaten or waiting in to receive a package for
them, there was no real interaction. They could barely even
look at me. So I began to take all my meals in my room and
spend most of my time in there. They didn't seem to mind. In
fact they were relieved that I was out of their hair but not
getting into any trouble. To them, the teenage body and brain
was a minefield so the chaos and confusion that a young
hormonal woman brought to the house was finally removed.
They could almost go back to how things were before I acci-
dently came along.

When the small matter of me going into labour occurred,
I admitted myself into the local hospital, and revealed my
stomach to a quiet and compliant nurse who ushered me into
the labour ward.

I knew I would have to share this with my parents eventually but so far I had made little connection to the baby,
instead pretending for all those months that it wasn't
happening. The midwife, Heidi, looked after me like I was
her own child. She stayed by my side for those sixteen hours
and when I pushed out the little girl, Heidi congratulated me
as though I had won a gold medal at the Olympics.

Of course, my parents had to be informed and when my
mother arrived at the hospital, she was flushed and frantic.
This was all mainly due to the horror that she hadn't even
had one inkling that I was pregnant. Heidi tried to congratulate me further in front of my mum, but it fell on deaf ears.
She was quiet for some time, she even spent a few moments
gazing at the little girl and holding her tiny hand as she slept,
but once she had got over the shock she went straight into
practical mode, dictating to me the exact process that would
ensue over the next few days.

Once it was done, no one would ever need know.

The most important thing my mother needed me to realise was that Callum was never to know. This was not to get out to him. I suppose secretly a part of me had imagined a life with Callum, me and the baby all snug. Of course, I had revealed his name and the circumstances to Heidi in the throngs of labour, this burly woman who had a penchant for a few gin and tonics on a Friday night and an incompetence for respecting patient confidentiality.

Two days later the home phone rang and it was Callum.

# 51

ANNIE

I knew everything. The way she had destroyed that poor family's life. Wasted lives everywhere... who knew where Daisy's daughter was now, or the man, the teacher? As for the wife... All of it was pure tragedy, caused by the mind of one young callous girl.

I knew everything about her and I showed it all to my son. I told him his wife was not the woman he thought she was. This was the same girl I now treated like china, trying to protect the growing foetus inside her.

Just as she had done before, she was carrying the baby in a completely healthy way. Some people just had the knack of it and some days I couldn't hide my irritation.

I knew she had concealed that first pregnancy from her parents and she had carried that baby to full term, without one complication. The papers peppered their reports of the seedy love affair with these seemingly irrelevant facts, even risking printing a photo of her. It caused such an outrage at the time, but it made for a much more enticing read and to then hear about the lengths a young Daisy went to conceal the entire affair from start to finish. Even risking her own and the baby's lives by hiding her pregnancy. In some parts it clearly painted her as the malicious character I knew she was.

And to think that my son didn't have a clue about what dirty little secrets she was hiding when he married her.

The role of a grandmother is to nurture the grandchild as if it was their own and in many cases be the go-to proxy parent when the actual parent is absent in body or mind.

I knew Daisy was slowly losing her mind. She was a shadow of the girl she was when she arrived here at the beach house that day with my son in tow wearing those red high heels. She had already married my son without meeting me let alone considering I might have been inclined to witness the matrimony between my one and only son and his chosen life partner.

Now she was more inhibited, flinched when I entered the room, and seemed to retreat into herself. I was there to protect her body, make sure she was fit enough to carry the child. I had bought a blood pressure machine online and took her reading daily. I ensured she took her iron supplements and vitamins every day.

I found her this morning sitting in the lounge soaking up the warmth of the rays through the window

'Why don't you just get outside?' I said feeling the agitation in my voice. The sight of her just sitting there was enough to rile me up. Sometimes I thought I was almost looking forward to seeing her in immense pain. Daisy barely looked up at me. The conversations were few and far between these days. We were both aware that I knew everything about her sordid past.

The baby could be here within days. But there wasn't

anything I didn't now know about pregnancy, labour and newborns. I felt almost like a professional midwife. It wasn't going to be long now and I would finally be holding the child I had been waiting for.

# 52

DAISY

He only called me the once when I was back at home, and luckily both my parents were out, but I don't suppose that would have bothered him. He was beside himself, one minute throwing accusations at me the next crying over the baby.

After the phone call with Callum ended, I never saw or heard from him again.

I was on the brink of turning sixteen and I had just given birth. I stayed at the hospital for two more nights so they could monitor me, then the social services came and took her away.

Looking back, I suppose I could have fought harder for her. I allowed my mother, the woman who never showed me any compassion or true unconditional love, to convince me to give away my daughter. Whilst I may not have known it then, just having her with me for a mere few days was worse than letting her go without ever laying eyes on her.

It was only when the milk that was meant for her, to

nurture her and protect her, filled my breasts and leaked out uncontrollably with nowhere to go, did I feel like the world had slipped beneath my feet. My mother made an extra effort to give me as much space as possible. She was there for the practicalities, dropping painkillers at my bedside several times a day. But I was lost, my mind a whirlwind of emotions.

The midwife, Heidi, who betrayed my trust, but who knew I wouldn't be keeping the baby, warned me not to name her.

But I did. To me, she was Alice.

I thought about Alice every day. What she looked like, what she sounded like, how she'd be soothed when she cried. But I signed her life over to complete strangers and vowed never to seek her out.

Back at home, Dad busied himself straight away with work and was rarely seen and mum carried on as though I was recovering from a sprained wrist.

I turned sixteen. A milestone some parents may celebrate generously but I stumbled upon a few badly wrapped presents on the kitchen table and I opened them with no one around me to wish me a happy birthday.

Those few days after Alice was taken away, I felt that pull, that longing, like a constant feeling that I had forgotten to do something, there was always this nagging feeling. It never really went away.

'Hormones,' my mum told me when I tried to explain it to her.

Of course I would get over the baby. She was never really mine in the first place. Mum said with a high tone that she presumed would ease me.

But that wasn't how I felt at all. I felt she did belong to me and that she was taken from me without my proper consent. I was backed into a corner by agencies and authorities and my parents. But they neglected to realise that she was a part of me and would forever be so. I would never forget her. And I would always be tortured by her absence in my life.

Weeks went by and the pain lifted only enough so I could function. Mum found me a job at the local leisure centre mopping the changing rooms and clearing out the lost property. That was what got me interested in fitness. I used to stand and watch the classes through the glass. Realising I was never going to go back to school, I applied for a diploma in fitness and nutrition at the college and got accepted for the following year. But just as I felt that there might be some sort of hope for me, I read a headline in the local paper.

Teacher's wife commits suicide over affair with pupil.

I didn't even need to read the article to know it was Callum's wife.

After I finished the diploma course and left home to go to university, paid for with a loan I'm still paying back, I received a letter from my parents telling me they were immigrating to Australia. They gave me a forwarding address for practicalities, but what was missing from the letter was the part that told me I would be welcome anytime.

Thinking back to those days when I was a mother for merely a moment, it seemed obvious that I would become submissive once again when all my choices were removed. Here I sat in the third trimester of pregnancy, with just days to go, and I only had Annie. This time there would be no parents with their unforgiving looks of distain. I had never planned for a next time, but once I knew I was pregnant with Ben's baby, I thought we'd do this together. But then could I blame him for running hundreds of miles away? I practically accused him of killing my best friend. No one takes that level of accusation lightly. I knew he wasn't close to Annie, not in the way she tried so desperately to portray. Why would he want to stick around? What was there to stay for? I had, once again, managed to lose one of the most precious things in my life. I watched him go without a second glance. I felt that momentary pull. That familiar pang as he walked out of the door. Go after him, Daisy.

Bring him back.

Take your baby out of the hands of those strangers.

Don't let the most beautiful thing you have ever created be taken away.

Don't let Eve leave.

I ignored it.

The instinct.

The pull.

I let her go.

I lost her.

I'd lost him.

*  *  *

That night as I lay down to sleep, I listened to the low clanking sound of Annie downstairs as she washed up the dishes from dinner. I allowed myself to tune into the chiming of the pipes, the rhythmic sound that was now so familiar it didn't alarm me, but almost brought me comfort at a time when very little could.

I fell into a deep sleep that night and dreamt about giving birth at the beach house. I was outside in the dark and the cold, the labour was quick and painless.

The baby fell out of me and was swept out to sea.

The baby was Alice.

# 53

ANNIE

I woke with a start as though someone had shaken me violently. I jumped out of bed and almost ran to her room. I poked my head round the door and found her still sleeping. It was not yet 6 a.m.

She was almost ready to have the baby. There was no way of telling without scans and knowing all her dates, and I had no desire to know about the exact day she conceived with my son.

However, I had a feeling today would be the day that Daisy would go into labour. I had been watching her last night as she struggled with every step, stopping and bending over with the weight of the baby low in her pelvis.

It was a strange day all in all. It felt like a day of new beginnings in many ways. Watching Daisy last night and knowing she was so close to delivering, I decided that it was time to let Ben go. Neither Daisy nor I had been in contact with him for such a long time and I knew deep down that he had made his decision. If Ben truly wanted to be a part of my life he would be here with us now. But I knew my son and, regardless of everything I had done to raise that boy well, he had thrown it back in my face. And for that I could never forgive him.

So I pushed all thoughts of Ben aside and I instinctively began to prepare myself. I had the birth pool set up. It had been there for several weeks already. Daisy had noted it a few times but didn't really make any comment on its imposition nor importance as it sat there taking up the main space in the lounge. I had plenty of juice and teas, brought some local honey as I read it can be very good to take during labour as it gives natural energy. I had purchased several aromatherapy oils from the internet and I had even invested in some resuscitation gear online. I didn't want to tempt fate, but I had to be fully prepared for all possibilities.

Death was not on the cards. I had no intention of losing a baby in my house. That was why the baby was here, to bring me the salvation I had been relying on for all these years.

Images of Daisy in labour were racing through my mind, all the scenarios and possibilities. All the things that could go wrong, that I might have to deal with were prominent in my mind. I knew I was taking a massive risk, but this was my last chance. I still had plenty of life left in me. I could care for the child, give it everything it needed. I would make a wonderful parent for him.

I paced around the kitchen checking I had everything I needed to hand, I went to the pool and checked the exterior for any holes.

I had everything else prepared.

I went outside and stood and listened to the sea breeze whipping across the sea wall whispering to me. I could feel it in the air. It was tangible. I was both nervous and excited. Everything was prepared. Soon everything would be as it should be.

## 54

I woke with a dull ache in my abdomen and spent a few extra minutes on the toilet, trying to relieve it. But it remained there as I took the steps slowly downstairs and I realised it was the beginning.

Annie was there at the bottom of the stairs ready to greet me. She was wearing what appeared to be sports casuals, something I had never seen her in before as though she were about to run a race. Her face was fixed in a grimace she was desperately trying to pass off as a smile.

'Daisy, how are you?' She put her arm around me and chaperoned me into the kitchen. There was juice and fruit and cereal all laid out.

'I'm feeling some lower abdomen pains, but other than that...'

'That could be the start of the labour, does it feel like a period?'

'Yes, sort of.'

Something was preventing me from fully opening up and revealing my true thoughts. I had been here before, so I knew what was what. I had felt this same sensation all those years ago and I wanted to keep it to myself. But Annie was a like a wild-eyed creature fussing around me, as though she could sense it and smell the hormones that were slowly releasing themselves into my body, preparing me for birth.

'Right then, young lady, let's get you filled up. If this it, you're going to need all the energy you can get.'

It only took an hour before the first contraction came, which was soft and slow. I didn't call out to Annie initially. I hid in the bathroom first, crouching or on all fours. I wanted to keep those first few to myself because I knew that once I was in established labour I could lose control and I wouldn't be in the moment like I was now. I walked around the house a little before I then went and sat on the bed with my lower back very straight against the bottom of the headboard. I allowed myself to relax into the moment and tried to push out the sounds of the house. The creaking pipes of the hot water as Annie washed up downstairs, the slow whoosh of each wave through the window I had ajar. I closed my eyes and breathed in and out and allowed the soft contractions to come and go imagining them as the waves I could hear just beyond the wall. I did this for what seemed like a long time and when I looked at my phone, half an hour had passed. I didn't want Annie to be with me, egging me on. But I didn't want to be at a hospital either, where all the memories of Alice would come back. I had thought very little about the baby throughout the pregnancy because of how guilty I felt about Alice, the memory of how I had failed her played over and over in my mind daily. But one thing I had thought about was this moment, and I imagined I would share it with Ben, that instead of the scared little girl I was the first time round, this time I would have the strength of my husband to help me through.

However, Ben wasn't here and I knew I would need to turn to Annie eventually – but right now I needed to be alone. So I shut my eyes and took very long deep breaths.

I opened my eyes. Something had changed. There was a sensation taking shape within me. What was it exactly, I couldn't be sure. An excitement to meet the child that Ben and I had created together maybe? Wherever he was now, whatever he may be doing, we created the child out of love. I would always be sure of that. I would always be able to tell the child that. And maybe once the baby was here, everything would work itself out. Ben would come back and we would find a way back to how things were.

# 55

ANNIE

I found her eventually at the bottom of the garden. I don't know how she had managed to slip by me. I must have been so busy setting up in the lounge. She thought that I wouldn't know she was now in established labour, but I could tell by the way she had been walking from room to room, feigning interest in a magazine article. I could hear her breath, the way it had become laboured and I could see her mouth closing into a small 'O' shape and slowly blowing out.

I must admit it was a shock to see her trying to hide her contractions from me this way. But it just went to show what a determined little madam she could be.

I walked over to her and already I could see the look on her face. She was going to try and defy me.

She was on her knees by the wall, so far along towards the end of the garden I had almost missed her. I could see a few fisherman on the sea horizon and in the distance a couple of dog walkers. It was already gone 10 a.m. and Daisy had been up since seven-thirty so things must have progressed fairly rapidly. There wasn't much time to lose. I needed her inside, where I had everything ready. I needed her away from any prying eyes. I put my arm outstretched ready for her to grab it and lift herself up.

'Come on, Daisy, let's get you inside.'

'I don't need your help, thank you Annie,' she told me through gritted teeth.

'Well, I would say quite the opposite. You need me very much, dear. I am the only friend you have here.'

'Friend? Friend? You aren't my friend, Annie. Eve was my friend. Ben was my friend.'

'You're delirious and in pain, Daisy. My life has revolved around you these last few months. I suggest you start feeling grateful, young lady, if only for the sake of that child.' I let a long-awaited breath out of my body.

I watched as she struggled to get into a comfortable position. I realised that it wouldn't be long now as I observed the behaviour, she was definitely displaying signs that she was getting closer.

'Daisy, Daisy this is silly.' With my anger subsided, I could talk her round, I was sure of it. I crouched down. 'You don't want to have the baby out here, dear. It's too cold for him. He will freeze to death. You need to come inside. I have the birth pool all ready for you with the temperature just right. I think you are close now, aren't you? I'm right, aren't I? You can feel the push, can't you? We should get you undressed and into the water, you'll be comfortable there. Come on, dear.'

I reached out my hand again and this time she took it.

I got her undressed and helped her into the birth pool. The contractions were coming on stronger. I could see Daisy couldn't fight them off any more. She was making deep animalistic noises. My heart began to pound hard for the child that I was going to meet very soon.

# 56

DAISY

'Come on Daisy, that's right, you're doing great, now you just concentrate on your breathing and let the body do its natural thing. Don't worry about a thing, it's all going to be okay.'

The sound of Annie was like a faraway echo. I had transported myself somewhere else. But it would have helped more if she would pipe down with her ridiculous cheerleading.

Thoughts were rushing round my head. Where was Ben? Why wasn't he here? Had I really pushed him away with what I had said? As my body flooded with adrenaline and all the right hormones I needed to bring the baby into the world, so in turn did it replace any of the effects of the drugs I had been taking. Suddenly I felt more free than I had felt in months. Although my uterus was contracting and the pain was unbearable, I was no longer feeling any of the dark fears and thoughts I had been experiencing since Eve's death and Ben's disappearance.

If I could get through this, I could get through anything.

The next contraction came quicker than the last and I

couldn't repress the animalistic sound that erupted from my mouth.

'Arrrrrghhhhh!' I leant over the side of the pool.

After another hour of contractions that were getting closer together, there was nothing I could do, except hold on whilst I let out a long groan at the height of the contraction. It simmered away, as though someone was turning it down with a dial. I took the time to breathe in and out. I looked around the dimly lit room. Annie had closed all the curtains. There was a faint smell of lavender in the air.

'They are coming fast now, dear. Stand up so I can see your back.'

'What... why?' I cried

'Because your lower back will give me some indication as to whether the baby is coming or not.'

I wanted to get this baby out of me and as she and I were the only ones here, we were going to have to work together at it.

I pulled myself forward to expose a little of my back. Annie had a torch in her hand as was waving it around,

'Oh yes, that's it. I can see it. Baby won't be long now.'

'It's coming out of my vagina, not my back,' I wailed.

'Your back is stretching and changing colour, which means baby is on his way. Can you stay on all fours, so I can catch him? When you feel the next big contraction, can you push all the way into your bottom?'

For a moment I was back in the delivery room with Heidi and moments away from meeting Alice. I realised I was crying.

The next contraction came and I used all my energy to push very hard into my bottom as instructed, finding that it eased the pain. The more I pushed, the more I wanted to push the pain away.

'Oh look, I see the head, I see the head!' Annie cried out.

'Arrrrrghhhhhhhh! What do I do?' I held onto the side of the pool as the pain ripped through my body from my head to my toes.

'Just wait for the next contraction, then push again. Let's get this little baby out of you.'

It didn't take long; the contractions had been coming seconds apart and with the next one I did as I was instructed and pushed.

I wouldn't have known the baby was out except for the fact Annie was wailing. 'He's here. My son is here.'

I was so delirious I knew I wasn't hearing right. I turned around and let Annie lift him to the surface and onto my chest.

'We need to let the umbilical cord do its thing for a few more minutes, to keep pumping the blood. It's really good for the baby.' I could see Annie was shaking. I was shaking too from all the adrenaline racing around my body and for a few seconds both of us stayed there together silent, I cradled my son in my arms and Annie leant over the pool, perspiration around her forehead. She looked adoringly at the baby. It was a look similar to the one I had seen as she had tended to her garden, but a more intense version. All that coarseness was gone. Her face had softened and she looked almost unrecognisable. I could feel the joy creeping through my body and I was so overwhelmed I began to cry again. Annie took her eyes from the baby for a moment and looked at me.

'Ah, don't cry, girl. You did well. Bringing this into the world. I have scales, we can weigh him later. Shall we cut the cord now? I know how to tie it. I watched a video.'

I watched as Annie took the scissors and cut the umbilical cord, then clamped it with a plastic clip. The baby started to wriggle. So far, he had been silent. Then he began to cry a loud penetrating cry

'Good lord. What a set of lungs,' Annie sang. 'I'll wrap him up and hold him whilst you wait for the placenta.'

'What?'

'The placenta. It comes out after the baby. Shouldn't be long.' Annie held out her hands and for the second time in my life, I reluctantly handed over my newborn baby.

# 57

ANNIE

As I held the child in my arms for the first time I was filled with such joy. I didn't realise it was possible to feel such a way. Surely these sorts of emotions had to be paid for, they didn't come for free.

How was it possible to have such life in your hands? It was incredible. This little wriggling mass of particles was alive and letting the world know he had made it. Against all the biological complexities, he kept growing and changing and getting stronger each day until he pushed his way out into the world. I knew I was going to love this little life harder than I had ever loved anyone.

# 58

As I stood there in Emily's kitchen on that final day with Jenny, I praised myself for my ability to stay calm. I was able, I found, to not change the expression on my face even though I knew my world was already tumbling down on me. The sensation was familiar, as I had been here so many times before. I felt very hot, beads of perspiration appeared on my forehead and my mouth filled with saliva. I hoped it wouldn't be too painful. But I was lucky I was able to withhold emotions and not allow anyone to know how I was feeling nor know what was going on inside my body.

'I tell you what, Jenny, you get yourself settled, I'm just popping to the ladies'. When I come back, I'll get us a nice cup of tea.'

'Oh Grace, you're too kind.' Jenny touched my arm and her face compressed into one of real gratitude.

I walked with great composure to the toilet, never wavering or speeding up. I took my time. There was nothing about that moment I wanted to rush to get to. Yet I couldn't bypass it either, like skipping a few pages in a book or flicking straight to the article of interest in a magazine. I had to troll through the bits I wished to avoid, that didn't make sense.

I entered Emily's bathroom and the trickle between my legs was warm and familiar. I knew what to expect. The last few had been earlier and earlier. I wasn't even able to reach the twelve-week mark. But this, a mere nine weeks in. I didn't even know why I had allowed myself to feel even the slightest notion of hope. It was all over. I was ruined. No husband. No baby.

I pulled down my tights and knickers and I wasn't even alarmed at the vibrant red mass that engulfed the gusset. I simply tidied myself up as best as I could.

Aside from my heart racing, I knew I would appear completely calm. I walked out of the toilet and back into Emily's kitchen.

I found my way back to Jenny. Tea was what was needed.

'I'll get some tea for us, Jenny.' I spoke robotically.

Jenny was about to say something, thank me for my kindness perhaps, but then her attention was stolen from me as we both turned towards a ruckus at the doorway. One of the other girls had left her cooking station and was there with a man. The man was tall with dark hair. His face was covered in a grey stubble and he was rubbing the side of his head with one hand. Jenny's face had fallen into a look of horror. The man was making quite a commotion and was now trying to make his way into the room. Emily had been busy at the front, but her attention was now on the uninvited guests causing disruption. She began to walk over to him. I looked at Jenny, whose face had turned a sickly grey colour.

'So what are you going to call him?' Annie was sitting in the hard chair that she had positioned right up close to the soft chair, where I was now sitting, wrapped up in a towel and terry towelling robe. The baby was cradled in my arms. It had been a task to get him back off Annie who had been holding him for the time it took me to get the placenta out, get out of the pool, clean myself up and get into something dry. The baby was wrapped in a soft cotton towel, still naked.

'I've always liked the name Daniel. Or Isaac,' Annie offered.

I pulled my mouth down. 'Hmmm, I hadn't really thought about it. I didn't know if I was going to have a boy or a girl. How did you know he would be a boy?'

'Just intuition. I could feel those boy vibes.'

I looked at Annie. 'Did you get those boy vibes for Ben?'

'Um, yes I suppose I did. I bet you're desperate for a cup of tea. Toast? Shall I make toast as well?' Annie stood up and slipped out the room.

I lay my head back on the chair took in a deep breath

then looked down at the bundle in my arms. It was nothing short of a miracle to have something so small and helpless yet so alive in my arms. Here was my boy, ready to start his life. Could I possibly do it this time? Could I possibly be enough for him? Without Ben, I was all he had.

* * *

Annie returned with my tea and after I guzzled it down, she escorted me upstairs for a proper rest. I walked into the bedroom, carrying the baby, followed closely by Annie.

'Do we have a bed for him. I mean, did you—'

'Yes, yes, Daisy, I got all of that sorted. I thought we could use the front spare as his nursery. It's small and cosy. We could put his little basket in there.'

'But I thought...' I turned round to face Annie. 'I thought he would be in here, next to me.'

'Daisy, you've just given birth. You have been severely depressed and I don't know if you are better yet. I'm sorry. But I can't expect you to be on your own with him. You will be exhausted. It's just for a few days, whilst you get your strength back. Now look, you need to get some rest. He came at a good time. Just in time for an afternoon nap.'

'Annie, I must insist that my son is in the same room as me, it's not natural for us to be separated, and I have to be close to him. Surely you understand that?' I surprised myself at my own confidence.

Annie looked at me for a few seconds. I wondered if she would fight me again, make me believe that she was right and that I wasn't of a sane mind. I wasn't sure I had the strength in me to stand up to her a second time so when she backed down it was a complete relief. It had taken everything I had in me to tell her no.

'Yes of course, of course. Let me go and get you some muslin blankets, I left them downstairs.' Annie hurried from the room, leaving me and my son alone. I looked down at him, wrapped up in a blue blanket, with just his little round face and a sprout of dark hair poking out. He was watching me so intently with his little beady dark eyes. I didn't expect the wave of love that rushed up from my belly to my chest.

It made me think of Ben and that I needed him with me. I wanted him with me. Then I thought of Eve and how she would have adored this baby as much as I did.

I settled myself on the bed and watched as his eyes closed and he fell into a sleep.

I could still feel my stomach contracting a little. There was quite a lot of pain but I wanted to ignore that. I would try and feed the baby in a while when he woke up, that would help. But like me he was exhausted from the birth. I closed my eyes and let out a long sigh. With the hormones rushing around my body I felt suddenly as though everything was real. I could feel the weight of his tiny body pressed into the crook on my arm and could feel the warmth of him. He was alive. He was okay. He was mine.

My eyes were open and Annie was in the room. My arms felt different, lighter. It took me a moment to realise, I looked down, the baby was gone. Annie was fussing around the bedside table.

'The baby? Where is he?'

'Now, Daisy, I told you, you weren't in the right state of

mind for this. I left the room for a moment to collect the muslin blankets and you fell into a deep sleep with Daniel in your arms.'

I sat up and threw my legs over the side of the bed.

'Calm down, dear, Daniel is safe. He's in his Moses basket down the hall. Sound asleep. You have nothing to worry about.'

'But I need to be with him!' The desire to be with him was more intense than I could have imagined. Losing my baby again was not something I could allow to happen. I wasn't that teenage girl surrounded by people who never even asked my opinion but took it upon themselves to remove my baby from me. I could feel it happening all over again.

'Sit down, dear. You're too weak, you have just given birth. Daniel is perfectly safe in the other room.'

'Why are you calling him Daniel? He doesn't have a name. I haven't given him a name yet.' I could feel the panic rising in my chest and into my throat.

'Well, that's why I am referring to him as Daniel – it's perfectly better than baby, isn't it? Look, I've brought you some more tea... Daisy whatever are you doing?' I pushed past Annie with great force as the need to be with my son became animalistic. I sped down the hallway and into the next room on the left. The room was dark and cool. The Moses basket was stood in the corner with a large chair pushed up close to it and a small table next to that. As I approached, I could see an object on the table. It was a baby bottle. It had been filled with milk and was now almost empty.

'What the...' I stumbled towards the table and picked it up, holding it close to my chest, I spun around to find Annie in the doorway. 'What is this?' I spat at her.

'Now, Daisy, I suggest you calm down, Daniel – the baby was hungry, dear, you were passed right out!'

'I wanted to be the first, he needs my milk, not... this shit!' I threw the milk bottle at her feet. The baby stirred in his basket.

'I think you need to calm down, lassie, you are getting yourself into a pickle. This is not good for you or the baby. Your milk hasn't even come in yet, I was just trying to help.'

'Well, I don't need your help,' I snapped. I realised I shouldn't have said that last part. Of course I had needed her help, I hadn't been able to manage without her. 'I mean...' I cleared my throat and smoothed my hair across my head. 'I thank you for all your help,' I said calmly, 'but I really do need to take things from here. I'm his mother, Annie.'

I could see Annie's face, twisted and contorted like it was that day she laid eyes on me for the first time, when her words didn't match her face.

'Okay, Daisy. I understand. I have been a little hands-on. I will back off and let you take over.' She almost did a little head bow as she retreated from the doorway and left me standing there flushed with anger.

I stood and got my breath back and let the anger subside before I walked over to the Moses basket and looked in at my sleeping son.

I knew then that no matter how I had been feeling and no matter how much I still blamed myself for Karen and Eve's deaths, for giving away Alice and for letting Ben walk out on me, this little man needed me and I wasn't going to let him down. I wasn't going let anyone take him from me.

It was clear Daisy was not going to willingly hand over the baby as I had anticipated. It had seemed she had spiralled down so deep into a depression that she wouldn't find her way out. I could only presume it was those damn happy hormones from just giving birth that were stabilising her for a while. I needed her to fall back into a state of depression, which knowing her track record, how easily she fell last time, it wouldn't take long. The baby blues would surely escalate into full-blown postnatal depression and she would hand the baby straight over. But I didn't have that amount of time to waste. It could be weeks away and I needed to act now.

I gave her a tiny amount of time and space after the bottle incident. She was clearly riled. Now I needed to get her back into a compliant state once more. A little while later I arrived back in Daisy's room with a tray laden with hot chocolate and biscuits and my best smile.

She was sat up on the bed with the baby latched onto her breast. The natural maternal sight made my heart quicken with envy. I tried not to falter and continued over to the bedside table.

'There we are, some delicious hot chocolate for us and biscuits for your energy. I hope you're happy to have a little sugar now? Doesn't he look jolly happy there?' I said and Daisy smiled at me as she took the hot chocolate and took a few long sips.

I was clearly forgiven for offering the little man a bottle.

'Yes, he does.' She looked down at him with that maternal gaze and I had to glance away for a second.

'Four o'clock already? Where did the day go, anyone would think a baby arrived this morning.' I made a feeble attempt at a laugh but Daisy didn't notice as she was too engrossed in the baby.

'Any thoughts on names now?' I quizzed.

She shrugged. 'No, none. One will come in time.'

'I'm sure it will.' I settled myself on the side of the bed. 'Would you like some more hot chocolate, dear, it will give you some strength?'

The baby fell off her breast and his little head rocked back.

'Yes thanks.' She carried on drinking, her left arm cocooned around the baby. I had made sure it was at optimum drinking temperature. 'You know, I really need to get in touch with Ben again, send him some messages and photos of the baby. I'm sure now he's here, he will want to meet him.' She said taking big gulps I had made it extra sweet after all that exertion her body was probably craving the sugar.

'Yes, dear, you're right. We should try again and make contact soon.'

'What do you suppose he might say, after all this time?' Daisy's head was slouching to one side.

'I don't know, dear, I suppose he will have just been having a good long think and you would have thought given all that time he would have come to his senses. But I guess there's just no telling with that boy'.

Daisy took another long drink of the hot chocolate.'

'I miss him... that's all...' Her voice was small and sleepy.

'I know. We all miss Ben. But Ben has been a very naughty boy and disobeyed his mummy. Just you rest now, that's it, close your eyes, all will be well.' I reached over and took the tilted mug from her hand. I placed it on the bedside table. Then I stood up and reached down and took my baby.

# 61

---

DAISY

I woke up as though I had been underwater and I was taking my first gasp of air. My arms were light, no longer bearing the weight I remembered before I fell asleep. My naked breast was still out. I arranged it back inside my T-shirt.

The banging, it was there. Was it the banging that had woken me? It seemed louder than usual, as though it was in the room.

As I sat and listened to it, I started to place the beat alongside the lyrics that were suddenly in my head. Maybe they were always in my head. My mouth was dry and my heart rate had sped up. This wasn't like one of those moments I had where a mundane everyday sound, turned into the first few chords of a song. This was that song, I could hear loud and clear, it was there and it fitted with the tempo. Of course, the banging was too uniform to be just a random sound from the old house. I knew when I had heard it the very first night.

I started to hum along. Then I started singing. The tears were falling. Images of Ben and I singing along together in bed the day after I met him, flooded my mind.

I looked around to pick up the baby but he was gone. Panic paralysed me for a few seconds.

I tried to stand but I could feel the room spinning. Images were flashing in front of me. Memories from the last few months, the shouting I had heard the day Ben disappeared, Annie waking me up at 3 a.m. clattering about in the kitchen. The bruise on her cheek the next morning. Then I walked to the mirror. I lifted my T-shirt to expose my deflated stomach, wrinkled but stretch mark free. I thought about Annie walking into my room naked, her taut skin completely exposed. I cast my mind back to the conversation on the day we heard the baby's heartbeat, I could hear Annie's voice telling me her body was in ruins from stretch marks. I traced my fingers over the sides and front of my stomach and abdomen and my mind switched to Annie's body. I had seen enough of it, from all sides. Annie's body was taut and smooth. And did not look as though it had stretched to accommodate the space for a growing life.

I ran to the bathroom and threw up.

## 62

I had to work fast as I knew I couldn't keep her out for long with those drugs. And the damn baby was fussing, he was hungry, I would need to prepare another bottle.

I could have put money on Daisy losing the plot, handing the baby over to me and retreating back to her old life. But that wasn't so any more. Just in the same way as I imagined my son would comply and realise his place was here in his home with me.

So I had a new plan.

I pulled the blankets tighter around the baby and he settled down into the crook of my arm, the weight of his little body felt so right.

I stood in my bedroom and looked around for the final time. Everything was prepared, just a few more things to do now and we would be on our way.

Suddenly knowing I was running away again brought it all back. The face that loomed down at me from the electric shop that day in the village was once again prominent in my mind. I checked my handbag for the essentials. I had plenty of cash to keep me going. I would empty more from my account over the next few weeks. I didn't want to draw attention to myself by withdrawing the hundreds of thousands I had in there which was all the money from the house Rory and I had lived in. I had barely touched it. Living in my father's beach house and working for most of my life I had never needed it. Ben and I lived a very simple existence. And then my pensions came in and, well, the house sale money just sat there gaining lots of interest. It had been earmarked for a day like today, when I needed to leave, and so as I checked the handbag one last time, I pulled out my driving licence to double check it was still in date. I glanced at my name, the full name I was christened with: Marianne Grace Cartwright. I had never once liked the name Marianne, so formal. I immediately dropped it to Annie when I divorced Rory. I had always liked my middle name, Grace. It was the name I used from time to time. However, I could never go back to using again. I stuffed my licence back into my purse. Then my eye caught something else in my bag. A slim black phone. With curved edges. What sort of ridiculous name was Blackberry anyway? I needed to be as weightless as possible with all the extra baby paraphernalia I would be carting with me, so I took the phone that once belonged to my son and dropped it in the wastepaper bin next to my bed.

## 63

GRACE

As that final day at Emily's unravelled it was to be the day my life finally became whole.

Jenny had reached out to grab my hand and I took hold of it.

'That's my husband,' Jenny said with trepidation pointing to the man at the door that had caused so much commotion. I looked at the man who was making his way over to her. Jenny looked at me. 'You must forgive him, he's... he's not well. The bruises, he doesn't know what he's doing. I was going to leave because we couldn't take it any more, me and the kids... my stuff, I had things... I was going to take them to my mum's for a while.'

Jenny's husband was grinning and cooing at Mikee, who shied away initially but then after a few seconds, responded with giggles. Then Jenny's husband turned to her.

'Hello, love, I've been wondering where you'd got to?' I heard an edge to his voice that resonated deep within me, easy words peppered with malice.

'Darling,' Jenny sang. 'How on earth did you find your

way here?' She placed an arm around her husband. Emily was now at the bench looking intrigued. All the other women had stopped and were staring in the direction of Jenny's workstation, some of them huddled together whispering.

'And who's this, love?' Michael looked at me.

'This is my friend Grace I was telling you about, she's a wonderful cook, she helps me all the time...' Jenny's voice was wavering.

Michael's eyes were drawn to Mikee again.

'There he is, my wee lad. Miracle this one, popped out at home, did Jenny tell you? Middle of summer, midwife got there just as his head came out.'

'Yes, yes. She told me,' I said. Jenny had told me the story enough times, it was etched in my brain, but when I would recall it later, I would switch some of the details to suit me better.

'Emily, you remember my husband, Michael? Could you possibly see about getting him to sit down for a cup of tea and some of that Victoria sponge? Victoria sponge is your favourite isn't it, Michael?' Jenny said through a strained smile.

'Ooo yes, Victoria sponge, yes that would be wonderful!' Michael said with unnecessary enthusiasm. He turned to walk away with Emily, but before he did, I saw the look he flashed at Jenny, a vile wretched look I recognised from my own childhood.

As I watched more colour drain from Jenny's face, she turned to me and I saw her physically shudder.

'I just need you to do something for me, Grace.' She placed her hand on my arm.

I listened intently. Jenny did need me after all. Of course she did. I was silly to ever doubt her.

I began to feel overwhelmed with excitement at finally being able to help, to be able to do something that meant something. All the horrors of the moments in the toilet were evaporating around me. I had been there so many times already, but it never stopped hurting. I felt as though I was being physically lifted up by Jenny's request. Sweet kind, beautiful Jenny, who needed me. The words came at me, but not in any order, I felt giddy with all the emotion.

'Mikee... help me... favour... keep him safe...' Jenny was looking at me and smiling then she walked to Mikee and gave him a kiss on his lips. The child, still seated on the bench worktop, responded by throwing his arms around Jenny's waist and squeezed her with his eyes shut tightly and then Jenny was gone. She was making her way across the room to her husband.

I thought of my husband taking his last items from the house, without a care for anyone and I thought about the baby that left my womb before I'd barely had time to acknowledge it.

And I realised how lost I was going to be.

I didn't deserve that. I deserved better. I deserved to be a mother if nothing else. And that child deserved better.

I began to edge closer to Mikee. Jenny had asked me to take care of him. The husband, Mikee's father, was a mess. I had seen those bruises for myself they had been on both Jenny and Mikee's face. It wasn't fair on anyone. Certainly not the little one.

As I arrived at his level, Mikee was clinging to a blue crocheted blanket. I could see he now recognised me from the weeks I had grinned at him under the counter. He gave me one of his special smiles.

'Hi, Mikee.' I held my hand out and Mikee thrust out one chubby arm to greet me.

'Hi,' he squeaked.

I knew what Jenny was saying to me, even if she didn't speak the exact words.

I knew what I was meant to do. The messages were all there.

I bent down and put my handbag over my shoulder. Then I lifted a compliant Mikee into my arms from where he closed his legs around my waist. I took a last look around the room and saw Jenny and Emily to the side of the kitchen. Jenny was standing next to Michael with her back to me, her hand tentatively placed on his shoulder as he sat on the chair sipping his tea. I headed for the door with Mikee taking one last look over my shoulder towards Jenny.

'Mummy,' he whispered into my shoulder as I walked out of the door and I tightened my grip and squeezed him harder.

## 64

I could feel palpitations fluttering deeply in my chest, I felt sick. My mouth was dry from whatever Annie had last given me; it was obviously more than I had usually taken, but it wasn't enough. My body wasn't going to take it today. I could feel the empty heavy dragging feeling in my belly, where my son had been but a few hours earlier. I found my way downstairs and allowed my instinct to take me through the lounge, past the kitchen door and down the hallway that I had had never needed to walk down before, towards a back door that led out to the side of the house. Then I heard the noise, the clanking, I put the light on and found I was standing on a heavy red antique rug which I had observed many times over from a distance. My attention was brought to the clanking I had heard in the bedroom, a sound I automatically associated with the age of the building and due to the amount of drugs I had been taking, I never really fully acknowledged it. But now I knew better. All those nights I had lain there and been lulled off to sleep stuck between depression and a drug-fuelled state, I presumed I was imagining the melodic structure to the sounds because I heard music so often when it wasn't there.

But now, I suddenly felt more free, the birth of the baby had heightened my senses, and my mind and soul surged with maternal instincts and oxytocin was flooding my body, my instinctual urge made me fall to my knees and I pulled back the rug. It was heavier than I anticipated, and I felt every part of my body ache as I did so. I was still surprised when I saw the large metal bolt and round handle. A cellar. No one had ever mentioned a cellar. I was merely following a hunch. The bolt was heavy and didn't shift easily but with one hand on top of the other I was able to pull it and lift the handle.

I stood up and took a step backwards so I could use my full body weight to release the door and lay it down on the floor. I walked back around to where I had started. I saw a steep staircase leading down into darkness. I was breathing heavily from the exertion of the lifting. Already I could feel blood leaking out of me on to the thick pad I was wearing. I felt dizzy and weak. I tried to control my breathing and my racing heart. I paused and stood still for a few moments. Then I placed my foot on the staircase. I didn't know what to expect as I took the first step into the darkness.

The baby had begun to fuss. He would need a bottle before I left. I knew Daisy would be well out of it so I threw my handbag over my shoulder and rushed across the landing and down the stairs. As I did, memories of Ben were flooding in and out of my mind.

I wondered how I had managed all those years, none of it was plotted or planned, I just went along with what I thought was best. I often told Ben the story of Mrs Keeley with the two children who helped us out. Then when he was old enough his original memory of a kindly woman with two small children, one girl and one boy and a woman he referred to as mama, merely morphed into my new memory which I had spoon-fed him. Eventually in his mind his own mother evolved into Mrs Keeley. It was my saviour for many a moment when Ben referred back to something in the past that I couldn't account for during my time with him.

'That must have been when you were with Mrs Keeley,' I told him. And like everything else I told him during those innocent years, he swallowed down. Until my job was complete. He had erased her from his memory. And all the new memories that we made from then on took precedence. I couldn't help it if my womb was inhabitable. I did the very best for my Ben when he came to me. Those first few months had been torturous for me. I didn't stop looking over my shoulder until we had travelled the 400 miles to the beach house. Then I went about creating a new identity for myself. I simply dropped Marianne and became known as Annie. No one at that cookery class had known a thing about me. They didn't know where I lived and twenty-two years ago, they didn't have CCTV on every corner. No one batted an eyelid at a young mother with a toddler walking down the street hand in hand. But I went out as little as I could in those early days. Keeping oneself to oneself all my life, had paid off for me. It took a while, but eventually I stopped looking over my shoulder. I was always acutely aware though. Forever checking the papers, but never able to listen to the radio or TV for fear of hearing or seeing something I wasn't prepared for. And then there she was on that ridiculous oversized screen, all these years later, making some plea or another.

She told me to keep him safe. I had done what she asked.

The little mite didn't stop asking for his mama. Never mind that I kept telling him, I was his mummy now. Crying at every opportunity. I wondered if the tears would ever stop. I was just beginning to grow tired of looking at his red eyes and wet cheeks, when one day, he stopped and he gave me his first proper smile and I knew I was made for this job. I was always careful not to let anyone get close to him. I invented a new memory for him. A fire that destroyed vital paperwork and photographs. And he was to blame. He held onto that memory so tightly and I knew he felt the brunt of the guilt, but at least he would never suspect why there were no legal documents in his name.

I taught him to drive, told him lessons were a waste of money. We had a mile-long road leading to the beach house, so once he was old enough I allowed him access to the driver's seat, and we went up and down that road every day. I then let him use my little car to drive to and from his gigs. He never questioned not getting a licence, because to him it was normal. He didn't seem to strive for anything more than what he knew.

I knew we were running out of time once he met Daisy. She began to show him everything about the world that I refused to show him. I kept him sheltered for his own good. That night in July last year when he didn't come home, well... then I knew. It was the beginning of the end.

But then he brought her here, into my home, pregnant! And she reminded me so much of her, of Jenny with her long golden hair and her perfect complexion. Of course he would fall for a woman like that, the image of his mother was imprinted on his brain.

How could Ben not be attracted to this golden beauty who bore so many traits like his own tall, handsome mother's. The one whose face lit up the whole sixty inches of that TV screen that day in town. A mother who just wouldn't give up. I refused to have a television or turn on a radio. I didn't want to live my life on the edge. Out of sight, out of mind. Ben accepted it, never even questioning it once he started school and all the other kids had TVs. Such a good boy.

I changed Ben's birthday from the 12th of August to the 17th of December. Just a few months' difference. He was a tall lad anyway so it was never going to make too much difference. Besides, I adored Christmas and I wanted Ben to share his birthday with the most magical time of year. Pity he never really appreciated the season as much as I did.

I knew Daisy wasn't everything she tried to present to me, which was why I needed to search for evidence, to prove my case, prove that she wasn't this golden glamorous, innocent woman she was portraying herself to be.

I thought about the papers, everything I had discovered about her and printed out. I had thrown them in the fire days ago, when I realised it had all been for nothing.

I showed it all to Ben, all the news reports, the evidence of the lives she had destroyed and when his head fell into his hands I thought, finally, he would see her for the manipulative girl I knew she was. He would end this silly infatuation with her. But after a few moments he sat up straight and looked at me shook his head and said, 'You are not my mother.'

He looked at me with such repulsion. I couldn't control what happened next.

## 66

DAISY

I stood and breathed heavily on the first step. There was a thin wooden banister about three steps down. It was pitch-black but I could see a thin sliver of light stretched out across the floor at the bottom. I needed to find my baby, I had no idea where Annie was, an urge to find my son overwhelmed me, the need to be with him was overpowering, yet the sounds I was hearing that had been flooding the house and my mind for months were driving me down the steps. Fear pulsated though every vein. I looked back into the kitchen before I tentatively took the second step.

I stretched my hand to the right and found a light switch. I flicked it and the basement was suddenly illuminated by a pale yellow sea of light. My legs felt as though they would give way at any moment and although I knew in my mind what I thought I might possibly find, I really didn't want to know.

As I reached the bottom of the stairs, a vast space stretched out in front of me and to the right of the staircase, the room continued round the corner. I took my final step,

onto the cold concrete floor, looked to my left and saw a
canvas sheet covering up a large pointy object. Next to it was
a box that said 'Christmas decorations' written neatly in
black pen. There was foam coming out in pyramid shapes
attached to all the walls from ceiling to floor. The basement
was sound proofed. I guess it had always been this way from
when Ben used to use it to play his instruments. All along the
wall to the left were stacked boxes and an old dusty-looking
wooden bookshelf. I left the security of the last step and
walked around the corner to the right. The smell hit me but I
still couldn't see anything else until I was still further around
the corner, practically under the stairs I had just walked
down. Then I saw something – something that initially my
eyes could not accept. In the furthest corner there were
several blankets piled on top of one another. There was a
bulge in the blankets. An obvious body shape. And from the
bottom of the blankets came a chain which was attached to
an old iron radiator. I let out a gasp and whatever was underneath moved. It started to sit up, its face partially covered by
the blankets and by a mass of hair. An arm came out of the
blankets stretching its way to me. My feet felt as though they
were stuck to the ground. I could neither run nor walk
towards the stairs or towards the body. With pain now
resonating through my pelvis and into my legs I bent down
on all fours and moved my hands and legs one at a time, the
position eased the pain in my abdomen, until I was so close
that my face was just inches away from a nose... a mouth. My
brain was refusing to make the connection, but there was no
mistaking those deep brown eyes that were staring back
at me.

# 67

ANNIE

Last night I had packed the car with everything I would need to start me and the baby off. It felt the same as it did the first time with Ben. I had no plan, I simply went with the flow and it had all worked out. Until now.

As I walked through the lounge towards the kitchen, I could see straight away that down the hallway the cellar door was open. I thought I had given Daisy a double dose to knock her out for a good few hours, she couldn't possibly be up and about? Perhaps in my haste I had miscalculated. A surge of panic stalled me. What was I doing? It had been twenty-two years since I had walked away with a toddler clinging to me like a baby monkey. And now, here was a baby in my arms, a mere few hours old. Could I do it all again? This time would be easier though surely? The baby would be like a blank canvas. There would be no memories to erase. He would only ever know me as his grandmother who raised him when his parents died in a tragic house fire.

There wasn't much time left, the baby was beginning its pathetic mewlings. I went quickly to the pantry, tripping on the step and banging my shoulder against the doorframe. Another bruise to add to the many my body was already littered with from when Ben had attempted to fight back. The ungrateful little sod. I was feeding him, the way I had always done throughout his childhood, trying to care for him, yet he kicked out, bruising me and scratching me like a feral cat with his uncut fingernails. I reached up with my spare hand and fumbled about on the top shelf for the box, I flipped the lid off and my fingers slid around the cold metal handle easily. The memory of watching my father polish it once a week was etched in my brain. I was brave enough one day to ask how it worked. It was the only time he and I ever shared a moment, as he carefully talked me through each cylinder and barrel and finally the trigger.

I held the old revolver in my left hand, adjusted the baby in my right arm and walked out of the kitchen towards the open cellar door.

'Ben. Ben is that you... I can't believe it.' I stayed on all fours, tears poured down my cheeks, my hands and arms shook trying to hold the weight of my contorting body. He was trying to sit up. He was wearing a woolly bobble hat, and his face was a mass of beard. I looked to the corner to where a wretched smell was coming from. There was a bucket. I could imagine what was in there. Finally, Ben began to sit up.

'Darling. My darling.' A flood of shock and relief cascaded through my body. My breathing was ragged and laboured. I pushed myself onto my knees and gently touched his face, his matted beard. Leaning on one arm as he took my hand in his, he opened his mouth to speak.

'Darling,' I continued. 'What is it?'

It was Ben's voice, but he sounded drunk. Or drugged. He entwined his fingers in mine and I leant into him.

His voice was small, croaky and rough.

'Daisy,' he said.

'I see you found him then.'

I swung around to see Annie standing a few feet away holding a gun and pointing it directly at us.

I could see the baby in the crook of Annie's arm. I could hear the tiny whimpering coming from my son. I could see these three people around me and none of it made sense. I pulled myself to standing.

'I'll take the baby. He needs me, he needs feeding,' I said, trying to conceal the panic in my voice.

Behind me I could sense Ben trying to sit up even more.

'Ha! You think I'm just going to hand the baby over to you. Look at you. Look at him. Do you think that either of you are fit to bring up a baby?

I inched closer to Annie and she shoved the gun out further towards us both. 'Don't think I won't. I will do whatever I have to.'

'You don't have to do this, Annie.' I tried to take another step without Annie noticing. 'Just let me take the baby. He needs me.'

'He needs me, Daisy. This is how it was supposed to be. This is what all this was for, what all this has led up to. Haven't you ever felt that something was supposed to be for a reason? Can't you see that everything that has happened is so I can have him?' I watched Annie's hand clutching my son too tightly. His mewling was becoming a full cry which penetrated my body filling me with fear and anxiety.

I could feel the hysteria rising through my body as I thought about my baby boy of only a few hours being snatched away from me by a woman that wasn't speaking a word of sense.

A million thoughts were already racing around my head. What would Annie do to him? Where would they go? I would never see him again.

'Annie. Please.' I held my hands out in a prayer fashion.

'No!' Annie shouted and the baby began to cry a full loud wail that resounded around the basement.

'Mum,' Ben tried to shout but his voice was small and hollow. 'Don't do this. I love you!'

'Ha! You think I'm falling for that after everything you have said to me. I tried so hard with you, Ben. I thought eventually you had succumbed to me, that you had accepted me as yours. I raised you! I saved you! God knows what would have become of you if I left you with that madman of a father.'

I rubbed my hands ferociously across my face.

'Ben does love you, don't you, Ben?' I looked down at Ben, pleading with my eyes to keep saying the words Annie needed to hear but I could already see he had given up. He had slouched back onto the floor, and his eyes were rolling.

'Ben was my son. I had him. He was given to me. I saved him! You took my son away from me. I would have been happy, just me and him, but no, you had to come along, take him and fill his head with ridiculous ideas. Well, you are welcome to him now. I'm done with the pair of you. I have what I need. What I was destined for all along. And I will take, him. Daniel.' Annie pointed the gun at the baby. 'Baby Daniel, I will take him.'

'No, Annie. No!' I screamed and walked closer to Annie. Her eyes were wide and wild.

Annie pointed the gun. 'Stop. Or I'll shoot you both now!' I stopped. Annie took a deep breath. 'Now. I'm going to go. Be good children and stay here. It won't be long. Don't try and follow me.' Annie started walking backwards, around the corner until she reached the edge of the first step. I followed her slowly. 'I mean it. One move to these steps and I'll shoot you.'

I stood at the bottom of the steps and watched Annie walk up them backwards until she reached the top. Then suddenly, I found a surge of energy. Even though I had given birth just a few hours ago, even though I was bleeding, my abdomen still contracting, I put one hand against the wall then launched myself and leapt across as many steps as I could to reach the top just as Annie's legs were disappearing. All the while I could hear Annie screaming her threats and the baby, who had been quiet for a while, started wailing again, innately aware of the dangers. Annie tried to slam the door shut. My fingers became trapped under the heavy wood and I cried out, but before I knew what was happening, I had managed to push the door, the strength of both of my arms against Annie's one arm, meant I was out, crouched down on the floor inside the kitchen, staring up at her. I pulled myself from my knees to standing.

'Give. Him. To. Me!' I was fighting for breath, I could barely stand, my insides felt as though they were being ripped from within me, but I could see my son, my son who had been safe inside my body just a few hours ago, now in the arms of this crazy woman.

'Annie. Give. Me. My. Son!' I could see Annie was edging back from me. 'Annie.' My voice was louder, the hysteria palpable. I took a step forward ready to snatch him straight from her arms when I saw Annie's left hand rising high into the air, holding the gun.

# 69

ANNIE

She had some strength, I'll give her that, but even with one hand holding onto the baby I had been able to knock her back down again with the weight of the gun. She had slumped to the floor like a rag doll and I used my feet to kick her back down the steps.

I raced out of the house with baby Daniel in my arms. He would have to take the milk cold, I didn't have time to heat it now. He was crying hysterically and the sound was driving me to distraction. The baby seat was already fitted in the back seat and so I clipped him in as I had watched on the internet several times. I went round to the driver side, turned the key in the ignition and with the shudder of the car engine his crying subsided.

I turned back to look at the house I grew up in, it held all the memories I had tried so hard to forget and then rebuild a new life again with Ben.

I walked round to the boot and took out a can of petrol. I went to the front door and poured the contents on the floor of the hallway. One last image of Ben flitted though my mind as I thought of the many years we managed to have together. I allowed a brief smile to etch its way across my lips, then the image of his face melted away as I struck the match.

I opened my eyes. My head was throbbing so hard I thought there was something about to burst out of it. I touched the side of my head and felt the damp through my hair, I brought my hand to my face and looked at the bright red blood on my fingertips.

'Oh god.'

'It's okay.' Ben's voice reached me, I turned. He was still lying on the floor.

'You're still here... we're still here?' I looked around the filthy cellar, it was all beginning to feel incredibly surreal. Surely I'd wake up in a moment and be somewhere safe with my Ben and the baby. 'I... I was standing in front of her?' I went to try and stand and realised I couldn't, my leg wouldn't work. I slowly dragged my way back towards Ben.

Ben held out a chewing gum grey towel frayed at the edges. I picked it up and pushed it hard against my head.

'Why didn't I try? I should have tried harder. This is hopeless, we'll never get out, we're trapped.' The hysteria in my voice was rising.

I looked at Ben and thought about his time down here, how he must have suffered.

I tried to stand again, but I couldn't, my whole body now in agony from head to toe. My trousers were soaked in blood around the crotch.

'The baby, that was him?'

'Yes' I sobbed. 'I need him, Ben, I can't let him go, not again.'

I dragged my useless body towards the bottom of the steps – each movement sent pain searing through my body.

'Annie, come back, wait! I just need to talk to you. Can I just give him a kiss? Let me just...' I had lost all energy to call out and my words came out feeble and pitiable. I flopped down on the bottom step and lay my head on my arms. 'What have I done?' I breathed out the words into the crooks of my arms.

Pain was resonating through my abdomen. I crawled on all fours back to Ben. He had managed to pull himself fully upright and I could see how one of his legs had a thick circular bracket around it and a thick chain running from it which was attached to the radiator. The sight of him in that way, looking like an animal, made me feel sick.

'Ben... what the... how did this happen?'

Ben lips were dry and cracked. His skin looked grey. His breathing was ragged. 'That day Daisy... that day I spoke to you last... I went to the kitchen to talk to Mum, she tried to show me all this stuff about you... but I already knew about *her*. I had been tracking this story about a woman who had lost her son. I only had to look at the photos of him as a baby and a toddler, photos I had never seen from my own mother. I just always knew, Daisy. And then she told me, the other day, she told me the whole story. She stole me.'

Ben's words made me realise the true horror of what was happening, and as the panic overtook me, I felt as though I couldn't breathe. 'We need to get out, Ben' I began looking frantically around. 'There must be a little window or hatch somewhere?' I forced myself to focus and breathe.

'I know this room.' Ben coughed. 'I used to play in it when I was a kid.'

My head fell into his lap. 'I'm sorry. I didn't know. I thought I knew, but I didn't know.'

'How could you know?' he whispered.

'I promise you. Everything will be okay, it will.' I grabbed his hand and pressed it to my chest. It was easier to soothe someone else than feel my own fear.

Ben's eyes were flickering. His breathing was uneven.

I let out a big breath and looked around the room again.

'I'll start hitting the hatch. It could take a while, but I'm sure I can break it open.' I didn't believe my own words, the reality was I wanted to lay with Ben and hold him, but I could see he was falling in and out of consciousness, his head dropped to one side.

'We have to get out of here.' I said taking another frantic look around the room.

I looked down at Ben, still slouched but not moving. His mouth remained fixed. He was dying. I had to do something.

* * *

I had managed to drag my way back to the top step, every movement sent splintering pain through my body, but finally I got there.

I touched my stomach, where my son had been just a few hours earlier and tears fell down my face. I leant on the top of the step with my head in my hands realising I was done for. I was ready to give up. But somewhere, still ignited, was the desire, the maternal instinct to get back to my son that Annie had stolen from me was there. I couldn't give up until I drew my last breath. Then I smelt it, smoke. I turned around to see streams of white smoke seeping through the cracks in the door. Automatically I let out a cough and terror surged through me, along with images of Ben and I suffocating to death.

Then I heard them. Loud footsteps and voices far away but they could very well have been above me. Annie? She was back. She had changed her mind. Realised she couldn't do it alone. Seen sense. I banged the door with my palm.

'Help! Help! Annie, we're down here. Open this door. Ben is sick, Annie. Really sick!' I used so much force that I could feel my skin splitting. The smoked was billowing around my face now. I gave the door one last hit. 'Open this fuckin' door you sick, sick mother—'

I could see a sliver of light coming through the door as it was being lifted and opened. Then a bright light from a powerful torch was pointing right in my eyes. I shielded my face with my arm. As I did, more plumes of smoke caught in my throat and I started to cough. I peered out from behind my arm and I saw a mass of smoke and a figure in a mask illuminated by a bright light

I coughed again as the smoke entered my lungs. A large gloved hand reached towards me and as I reached out to grab it, everything went black.

* * *

The next twenty-four hours went by in a blur of paramedics,

firemen, ambulances, doctors, police, questions, questions, questions. The last thing I saw before I was knocked out was a surgeon's eyes, his mouth covered with a surgical mask. Something had gone wrong when I gave birth and pieces of the placenta were still inside me. Ben was whisked away somewhere else.

When I came round, Patrick was sitting next to me.

'Patrick.' I held my hand out and Patrick took it in both of his.

Patrick looked down at his feet.

'The op went well. They were able to stop the bleeding. You've broken a rib and your ankle. You're in a bit of a mess, Daze. Ben is not so good, he's going to need a bit more time, but he'll get there. He will. I don't know much else, but they are monitoring him. You're both strong.'

'My baby!' Realisation then panic swelled from the pit of my stomach. I tried unsuccessfully to swing my legs out of the bed.

Patrick stood and put a hand on my shoulder. 'Hey, stop, you're in no condition to go anywhere.' He squeezed my shoulder. 'I haven't heard anything about the baby yet, I'm afraid Daisy.'

I leant my head back against the pillow. I felt the familiar feeling of tears soaking my cheeks as though they had never stopped. 'How? How were you even here, Patrick?'

'I had been trying to text you for days, Daisy; you kept ignoring me. I know you said you needed time, but that was ridiculous. I needed to see you. I missed you. I knew the baby was due. I drove to the house and when I arrived there were ambulances and fire engines, smoke was pouring from inside. Someone from the beach, a dog walker, alerted the emergency services when they saw smoke.'

Patrick's voice turned hollow and my attention was now on the door of the hospital room. Everything felt as though it had slowed down, Patrick was still talking, but it was as though he was a record player playing at the wrong speed. I could see the doors had opened and two policemen had walked in. My eyes were locked on them, willing the scenario to change, I looked away. I could hear myself crying out.

I put my hands over my ears and started shaking my head. My legs felt like jelly and were shaking uncontrollably. 'No!' I shouted again. I wasn't ready to hear it yet. It couldn't happen again.

Patrick had his arm around me, attempting to console me in some way. 'It's okay, Daisy, look.' He was gesturing to the doorway. I looked up at Patrick and then at the door. As I did both policemen stepped aside and a policewoman walked through the gap between them. In her arms, she was carrying a little blue bundle.

* * *

I held the baby tightly in my arms. I nuzzled my face into his little face. The nurse was at my side.

'Let's try and get him to have some milk. I've bet you've got plenty of it?' She helped me lift up the nightgown. Patrick had headed off down the hall for some coffee. I looked at her and the nurse winked back down at me. 'Come on, let's try this. You can do it.' Under my gown, my swelling breast fell out near to the baby's lips. He turned automatically and began to root for the nipple. The nurse gently nudged my breast and held it in place until the baby was latched on. 'There look at that. Pair of naturals.' She smiled down at us.

I let out a small nervous laugh. 'He'll be wondering what's been going on.'

'Well, babies are more resilient than we give them credit for. They have short memories at this age,' she said through a smile. 'I reckon he's forgiven you already. Got a name for him yet?'

'I thought... Jasper. Obviously I'll have to discuss it with Ben.' The name had been creeping in and out of my mind for weeks but with no one to discuss it with I kept pushing it to one side. No girls' names had come to me. I had been struggling to imagine a life with a girl after Alice. I felt a small glint of hope as I spoke his name out loud, something I had never been able to do with my first child. I had yet to see Ben, but the idea that we were a family and that we were all here, safe and alive created a small spark of joy. I acknowledged it and held on to it.

'Well, I think that's a perfect name for him. Lucky little chap.'

The door opened and a young doctor in a smart sky-blue shirt walked in.

'Mrs Cartwright. How are we doing?' he said brightly.

'These two are doing just great,' the nurse said.

'Good. I have news about your husband. Ben is now in what we can consider to be a stable condition. He is slightly delirious and he still needs a lot of rest. He's extremely dehydrated with multiple fractures but I think, if you are feeling up to it, you can pop up and see him later.'

'Yes, yes I want to,' I said looking up at the nurse who nodded enthusiastically.

The doctor smiled. 'Okay, well, I'll let you finish off here and I'll arrange for someone to take you up shortly.' He smiled again and turned and walked back out of the door.

*　*　*

The nurse wheeled me down to the lift and took me up two flights to where Ben was. I stayed sitting in the wheelchair, cradling Jasper, adamant I would never let him out of my sight. The pain from my broken bones had been numbed by morphine.

I was alarmed to see a policeman sitting outside Ben's room.

'Why does he need the police here?' I asked him.

'It's just precautionary,' the young officer said.

'Could she come here?' I increased my grip on Jasper who was sleeping soundly.

'She's in police custody. We don't know the facts yet. If there were more people involved,' the policeman said, looking down at me.

'No. No one else was involved. She did this all by herself,' I scoffed.

'Okay. Shall we go on in and see Ben now?' the nurse said and the officer stood up opened the door for us.

Inside the room was dimly lit. Immediately I was taken back at the machine beeping, and the tube coming from his arm to a bag. My hand was in my mouth when the nurse patted my shoulder.

'It looks worse than it is.'

'I'm sure I don't look much better myself,' I said, touching the bandage on my head and knowing without needing to look that my face was swollen and probably covered in bruises and scratches.

'Ben,' I said as I was wheeled up close to the bed. Ben was raised up slightly. He opened his eyes and looked at me then he looked down at Jasper. He blinked a slow blink and smiled.

'Say hello to your son,' I whispered with tears spilling down my face.

'Hello, mate,' he croaked.

'I'll leave you to it. I'll be back shortly,' the nurse said and walked out.

'They got her Ben,' I said when I could finally stop crying to speak. I could see how weak Ben was still, but his smiled remained static and his gaze was fixed on Jasper. 'You're going to be okay,' I said and I grabbed his hand and squeezed it. Ben linked his fingers through mine and I felt the urgency in his grip. The raw emotion and love I felt for him flooded my body and for a second I felt as though I couldn't breathe. Ben had never left me. He was there all the time through everything.

## 71

ANNIE

The officer who had arrested me was removing items from my handbag and listing them out loud to a policewoman behind the desk who was inputting the data into a computer. I stared blankly ahead.

'One mobile phone, black, Nokia. One blue and green patterned diary. One set of keys with round pink crystal frame around a mirror.'

I lifted my head and looked at the keys he was describing and I thought back to the day when I found them under the bed in Ben's room. I had meant to throw them away, it was careless of me. A schoolboy error. Now here they were, retrieved from the inside pocket of my handbag.

I had sat in the car for long enough and watched two carefree women cackling and heading out to enjoy themselves. I was drawn to the flat that night where I knew my son lived but I had never been invited.

I watched a pair of red heels disappear around the corner and then I walked up the hill and let myself in to the flat. It was a cold night and I had on my thick coat with the big

buttons. I entered the hallway pausing to take in all the paraphernalia: stacks of paperbacks, photos in mismatched
frames littering the wall, shoes left where they were thrown
off and then found my way into the kitchen. The kitchen
counter was a mess with empty take out cartons. I saw a
scrawled note above the cooker and I leant against the hob to
read it. I didn't recognise it as Ben's writing. 'DO NOT USE'. It
was an old flat and so were the appliances. The cooker was a
small gas one, the sort of one I had when I was a young
woman. The kind of one that needs lighting with matches.
Then I heard keys in the door and instinctively went to pull
back but as I did my buttons had become caught on a knob at
the front. I yanked it forcefully and stepped back against the
wall of the kitchen just in time to see a pair of red shoes flash
past. I had seen all I needed to see. The mess they resided in.
I slipped from the kitchen and glanced into the lounge where
I saw another flash of the red shoes, I could just about make
out a body on all fours, reaching behind a chair. I thought it
was her. I thought it was the girl who had taken my son and I
paused for a brief second to imagine all the possibilities of
the two of us alone in the flat.

Then I smelt it. Gas. My button had obviously forced the
knob to one side and turned the gas on. Then something else
took over, it was as though I was having an out of body experience. I walked back over to the oven and turned all four
knobs on full so I could hear the gas hissing out. I wasn't sure
what sort of damage would be caused but I pulled back and
crept silently towards the door, opening it just enough to slip
through and out into the street. Later that night when Daisy
and Ben arrived, I felt nothing. I just thought it was all a
terrible shame. I had often brushed against my own old
cooker in my younger days and seconds later smelt the gas.

That's the trouble with old appliances, I suppose if you were full of a cold and lit a cigarette many minutes later you would be none the wiser.

The police officer had my handbag on the counter, the entire contents now sealed up in a clear plastic bag.

'Cell F12.' The policewoman behind the counter looked at me and spoke coldly, her eyes locked on me.

I felt the firm grip on my arm as I was escorted down the stairs to the cells. When the heavy door slammed and locked I stood motionless in the small stark room. My mind flashed back to the days with Ben when it was just us two, when he was so young, so influenced by me. I had a purpose. I was needed. I was wearing a cardigan but they had removed my shoes because they had a small heel and my feet, through my tights, could feel the chill coming up from the floor. I saw there was a blanket on the bed so I made my way towards it and wrapped it around my shoulders. I sat down on the bed and pulled my legs into my chest and rested my head on my knees.

We stood at the door of the small ground-floor flat, an emergency home given to Ben, Jasper and me until we were able to get ourselves back on our feet. It was comfortable and there was a small private garden. The spring air had begun to turn warm and I imagined us three sitting on the grass enjoying a picnic and the warm summer sun healing us.

Ben was on crutches and leant against the wall. I moved out to the pathway to greet the four people as they tentatively approached.

She arrived in front of the other three, striding ahead as she got closer. Her arms were already open. She looked at me briefly and placed a hand on my shoulder. She looked at Jasper in my arms then her eyes were on Ben. She pulled him in to her and they clung on to each other, never wanting to let go. Finally, Ben was released and I was embraced with the same furious intensity by the woman who introduced herself to me as Jenny, and who I would know as my mother-in-law. Ben's real mother.

Ben had an older sister and brother and a younger brother. I was introduced to Emma, Sean and Conner.

Jenny had a strong Irish accent and kept calling him Mikee before stopping herself. But Ben said it was okay, we'd work something out.

She apologised over and over again for letting him go. For turning away for long enough for him to slip away.

Ben told her he didn't blame her. And that he always knew.

She hadn't stopped searching for him for over twenty years.

Because the bond between a mother and son is a special one.

It remains unchanged by time or distance.

It is the purest love – unconditional and true.

It is understanding of any situation.

And forgiving of any mistake.

# ACKNOWLEDGMENTS

Thank you, Amanda Preston, for being the first person to read a very different version of *The Daughter In Law*. You encouraged me to use my knowledge of psychology and write the book the way it should have been written.

Thank you, Hannah Richell, for your advice on writing with babies and prologues and for your blogs on grief and loss. Your words and strength continue to inspire me.

Sarah, Geraldine and Sue, you are all as obsessed with books as I am, so thank you for finding me and never leaving! Thanks for the fantastic chats, all the reading weekends and delicious grub. Thanks, Sue, for reading a very rough first version of the book and still saying it was good!

Darling Kat, you are my sister from another mister, thanks for giving me the best reaction when I told you I was being published. Lend me some sugar, I am your neighbour!

Massive thanks to Kate Nash and Lina Langlee, my wonderful agents, for believing in my writing, supporting me throughout and working so quickly and efficiently to find me the best publishing deal.

Thank you to Amanda and all the team at Boldwood for seeing potential in me and having me as part of the team. I'm so thrilled and excited for what's to come. Thank you, Nia, for being my first editor, for setting the bar so high and encouraging me to dig deeper.

I would like to give special thanks to my parents. To my dad for being a grafter and showing me how to work hard in life and for his inspirational sense of wonderment. I know he would be proud of my achievements. Thanks, Mum, for supporting me on my journey, holding the fort and for always taking us to the library as kids. I still get the same thrill now as an adult whenever I walk into a room full of books that I can take home and read for free!

Chris, thanks for always listening, championing me and being my number one fan. Also for the packets of munchies in the final editing stages.

Savannah, Bodhi and Huxley, my beautiful babies who teach me how to be a better person every day. At such tender ages you have shown so much interest and respect for my writing. Thank you for being brilliant kids and letting me read to you and do all the silly voices.

Finally, thank you to all you readers who have picked up this, my first book and supported me on my writing journey. I hope I can continue to write more books that you will enjoy.

# BOOK CLUB QUESTIONS

1. Although Annie wanted a child badly, her own traumatic childhood meant she displayed signs of covert narcissistic abuse towards Ben. How did she manipulate him as a child and as an adult?

2. Some themes in the book are the mother and son relationship, anxiety and depression, friendships and love. Did you recognise these or any other themes within the book and where did you see them featuring in the novel?

3. The Daughter-in-Law is written in the style of the unreliable narrator. At what point did you decide that Annie was hiding more than Daisy?

4. Daisy's flashbacks to her childhood show that she was neglected emotionally by her parents. What implications did this have on her relationship with Callum and what were the repercussions of that relationship?

5. Annie talks about how Jenny and Daisy were very

similar in the way they looked and presented themselves. It is thought that we often unconsciously seek out a partner who bears a resemblance in some way to a parent. Discuss.

6. Did you feel sorry for Annie in the end?

# MORE FROM NINA MANNING

We hope you enjoyed reading *The Daughter In Law*. If you did, please leave a review.

If you'd like to gift a copy, this book is also available as a ebook, digital audio download and audiobook CD.

Sign up to Nina Manning's mailing list for news, competitions and updates on future books.

http://bit.ly/NinaManningNewsletter

# ABOUT THE AUTHOR

**Nina Manning** studied psychology and was a restaurant-owner and private chef (including to members of the royal family). She is the founder and co-host of Sniffing The Pages, a book review podcast. She lives in Dorset.

Visit Nina's website: https://www.ninamanningauthor.com/

Follow Nina on social media:

 twitter.com/ninamanning78

instagram.com/ninamanning_author

facebook.com/ninamanningauthor1

# ABOUT BOLDWOOD BOOKS

Boldwood Books is a fiction publishing company seeking out the best stories from around the world.

Find out more at www.boldwoodbooks.com

Sign up to the Book and Tonic newsletter for news, offers and competitions from Boldwood Books!

http://www.bit.ly/bookandtonic

We'd love to hear from you, follow us on social media:

 facebook.com/BookandTonic

twitter.com/BoldwoodBooks

 instagram.com/BookandTonic